THE FIRES OF AUTUMN

ROBERT FUNDERBURK

Books by Robert Funderburk

THE INNOCENT YEARS

Love and Glory
These Golden Days
Heart and Soul
Old Familiar Places

DYLAN ST. JOHN NOVEL

The Fires of Autumn

9607

THE FIRES OF AUTUMN

ROBERT FUNDERBURK

BETHANY HOUSE PUBLISHERS
MINNEAPOLIS, MINNESOTA 55438

The Fires of Autumn
Copyright © 1996
Robert W. Funderburk

Published by Bethany House Publishers
A Ministry of Bethany Fellowship, Inc.
11300 Hampshire Avenue South
Minneapolis, Minnesota 55438

Printed in the United States of America.

Library of Congress Cataloging-in-Publication Data

Funderburk, Robert, 1942–
    The fires of autumn / Robert W. Funderburk.
      p.   cm. — (A Dylan St. John novel ; 1)
    ISBN 1–55661–614–7
    I. Title. II. Series: Funderburk, Robert, 1942–
Dylan St. John novel ; 1.
PS3556.U59F57   1996
813'.54—dc20

96–25284
CIP

To the Americans who fought WWII

World War II separated us geographically, but it was the last time America was truly united as a nation. Men and women believed that their country was worth the ultimate sacrifice, that the price of liberty was too dear *not* to be paid. We looked to God for victory, patriotism was a quality worthy of praise, and prayer was accepted as an essential part of our public and private lives. Husbands and wives treasured each other, their children and their homes.

America needs the message and the spirit of this simple and trusting time.

ROBERT FUNDERBURK is the author of THE INNOCENT YEARS series with Bethany House Publishers. Much of the research for this series was gained through working as a Louisiana state probation and parole officer for twenty years. He and his wife have one daughter and live in Louisiana.

CONTENTS

PART FOUR
Man of Sorrows

PROLOGUE

"Don't let them take me, Mama! They'll kill me down in that place!"

The sound of the judge's gavel still rang in the gloom of the almost-abandoned courtroom.

"Hush now, baby," Rachel Batiste, her thin face suffused with this latest and most unexpected sorrow, tried to comfort her son. She glanced down at the high-topped Converse tennis shoes. He had saved every penny for six months in order to buy them. "You're only eleven years old. They'll take good care of you."

Russel, short and chunky with dark curly hair, watched from his place at the table as the judge disappeared through the door to his chambers, putting an end to the day's legal proceedings with a final flourish of his black robe. The boy turned pleading eyes back to his mother. "I'm scared, Mama."

"You'll be all right, Russel." Remy, at fourteen trying to be the man of the family, brushed his brown hair back from his face and placed a hand on his brother's shoulder. "And we'll be coming down to see you anyway."

Wiping his eyes with the tail of his Roadrunner T-shirt, Russel spoke in a quavering voice. "I . . . I won't make it, Remy. I just know I won't."

Remy reached into the pocket of his khaki shirt and handed his little brother a stick of Doublemint chewing gum. "You got to straighten up now, Russ. I know a boy who stayed down there six months and he got along okay."

"Yeah, but he had a daddy to look out for him." Russel couldn't keep the tremor from his voice.

Rachel put her arms around him as the rose-colored afterglow slowly faded outside the high windows of the courtroom. A siren wailed off in the distance.

"Time to go now, son." The short, stocky man in the Maurepas Parish sheriff's uniform opened the gate in the wooden railing that separated the judge's bench, jury box, and heavy oak tables from the rest of the courtroom. The pearl handle of his .357 slanted at a rakish angle from his heavy black holster. With a quick nod of his head, he ordered Russel to follow him.

Russel's eyes grew wide with fear, then he took a deep breath, pushed the chair back from the long table, and stood up. As he passed through the gate, the deputy slipped his hand through the boy's belt at the back. This was not the first time he had transported a terrified juvenile to a state correctional facility.

Rachel and Remy followed them toward the enormous carved oak doors that led to the upstairs foyer, then down the curved marble staircase. The deputy's boot heels rang on the stairs, echoing with a hollow sound from the high vaulted ceiling. Hanging on the hand-hewn cypress wall, black-and-white photographs of judges long dead stared with indifference across the deserted lobby.

Outside on the portico, the four of them stopped, glancing at each other uneasily like actors who had forgotten their lines.

A sudden breeze swept out of the night sky, rustling through the live oaks. Large solitary raindrops began ticking on the leaves and hitting with a flat sound on the hard-packed ground and the stone steps.

With a quick glance at Rachel, the deputy released Russel and hurried down to unlock his white Ford, its front door bearing the gold Maurepas sheriff's decal.

A bolt of lightning splintered the sky as the rain began to fall in earnest, sweeping in from the river, blowing in torrents across the courthouse square and against the plate glass windows of the stores on the opposite side of the street.

Rachel shivered slightly and pulled her black sweater closer about her. She took a red scarf from her pocket, tied it over her long dark hair, then stepped close to her son, taking his round face in both hands. "You'll be all right, baby."

"Mama, why did that man do this to me?" Russel almost wailed against the sound of the rain. "I never took nothin' before. I was just hungry."

Rachel put both arms around her son, pulling him close to her, unable to summon up any more words of comfort. She thought of the times she had rocked him to sleep as a child when he had awakened crying in the night.

"Let's go, son!" the deputy called out from the front seat of the Ford, its engine idling, gray smoke spilling out of the tailpipe into the night.

Russel stepped back from his mother's arms, and with the look of a man being led off to the gallows, thrust his hands deep into his pockets. Seemingly unaware of the cold, pelting rain that soaked him almost immediately, he trudged down the steps and climbed into the car.

The deputy reached over, pulled the door shut, and slid back under the wheel.

Framed by the rain-streaked window, Russel's face looked frozen in gloom, his large dark eyes holding a vacant stare. Its tires making a hissing sound on the wet pavement, the heavy sedan bumped down the curb, turned left, and headed toward the river road.

Rachel's strength suddenly left her. She leaned against one of the huge white columns, sliding down it until she sat on the stone floor of the lofty portico. Her eyes held the same stare she had seen in her youngest son's eyes as he had gazed out at her through the car window.

Remy quickly knelt beside his mother. "Mama, are you all right?"

Taking his hand, Rachel nodded, then whispered hoarsely, "You're all I've got now, Remy. If anything happened to you I just couldn't bear it."

"Nothing's going to happen to me, Mama." Remy's voice broke as he tried to console his mother. "And stop worrying. I'll take care of you."

A black-and-gray terrier, bedraggled from the storm, trotted along close to the white stucco walls of the courthouse. Seeing the woman and the boy, he stopped, stared at them for a moment,

11

then continued on his way, strolling across the street and disappearing down a dark alley.

The rain slackened to a slow drizzle. Beyond the dripping trees, the wet empty streets glistened in the lights from the storefronts.

"We've got to go home now, Mama." Remy took his mother by the arm and helped her up from the damp stone.

Rachel felt she no longer had the energy or the will to speak as she got to her feet. She sensed the reassuring strength of her son's arm around her waist, supporting her. As they walked along the portico in the shadows of the towering white columns, the bell in a church steeple two blocks away began to knell the hour in its slow, unalterable cadence.

PART ONE

JUST A FROG, AFTER ALL

1

SUSAN

Susan St. John, her slender form adding an air of elegance to the simple jade green dress, stood at the cypress railing outside the Cajun Cabin Restaurant, her back to the man climbing the steps from street level. Beyond her, the willows on the far shore of the great river swayed almost imperceptibly in the breeze, the levee rising behind them. Forming their amorphous ranks along the horizon downstream, clouds rolled slowly in from the Gulf of Mexico. Above her, all was shining.

Dylan St. John, uncomfortable in navy blazer and tie, moved quietly across the wooden terrace to Susan. Placing his left hand on her arm, his right hand moved aside the mass of her hair as he kissed her neck where it flowed into her shoulder.

A small shiver rippled across Susan's back. "Hello, Dylan. Say something soft and sweet to me."

Placing his lips against her earlobe, he whispered, barely audibly, "Marshmallows."

"You idiot!" She turned and smacked him on the chest with her small fist.

"Softest, sweetest thing I could think of at such short notice," Dylan joked, gazing at Susan's lips, red and moist, curving in a half-smile. The fine lines of her face, its gentle swirls and slopes and risings coming together in an appealing and lovely oval, never failed to catch at his heart. "Well, almost."

"I think we'd better get something to eat," Susan suggested, a slight flush coloring her cheeks. "Shrimp creole's the special today. You always liked that before——"

"I can take it or leave it," Dylan shrugged, walking abruptly toward the heavy oak-and-glass door of the restaurant.

"Looks to me like you've been *leaving* it most of the time," Susan remarked.

"Eating's a waste of time." He glanced down at the way his coat hung loosely on his lean frame.

Susan turned away. "Well, I *certainly* wouldn't want to waste any of your time."

"I said, *eating* is." Taking her by the arm, Dylan opened the door. "Being with you has never been anything but gain."

Relenting as usual to Dylan's convoluted logic, Susan shrugged and walked past him.

Wide planks, beveled and held in place by wooden pegs, stretched the length of the long, narrow restaurant. Plate glass formed the wall along the river. Waitresses attended to a few other latecomers while college students, black as well as white, cleaned off the round wooden tables covered with red-and-white checked cloths. The clattering of dishes and utensils dropped into plastic tubs punctuated the muted drone of conversations.

Dylan pointed to a table next to the river. As soon as they were seated, a waitress with a red bow that held her peroxide-blond ponytail in place appeared as if from nowhere, obviously peeved that someone would come to lunch at this late hour. "What'll it be, folks?"

"How 'bout if I borrow your copy of *Emily Post*?" Dylan asked dryly.

He was about to follow up on his opening jab when Susan diverted him, "Two specials with iced tea, please."

"You made my day, lady," the red-bowed and black-uniformed waitress grinned, taking a pad out of her skirt pocket and a yellow pencil from behind her ear. "I was afraid for a minute there ya'll were gonna order something like 'Crawfish Henri.' Ol' Henry Bates from Greensburg is one of the cooks, and he thinks that name sounds kinda Frenchy. It's real good, but he takes forever to make the stuff."

"Don't they *pay* you to do this?" Dylan tried to control his irritation.

The waitress glanced at the big schoolhouse clock behind the bar at the other end of the room. "Not after two o'clock, they don't—but if I get home late I gotta pay the baby-sitter extra. She *knows* I can't get nobody else."

Susan glared quickly at Dylan. "How many children do you have?" she asked, her voice gentle.

"Jist one." She tapped her temple with the eraser. "He ain't right though, and most folks won't keep him—includin' my husband. He took off last year. Jist up and left me flat!"

Dylan gave Susan a sheepish look. "The specials will be just fine. And could you bring some coffee?" His tone matched Susan's.

"Sure thang." She hurried off toward a serve-through counter next to the swinging doors that led into the kitchen.

"I know," Dylan muttered as soon as she was out of earshot. "Patience is a virtue."

Small talk filled the two minutes until the harried waitress returned with their food and drinks on a large tray.

Dylan handed her a ten-dollar bill, folded tightly. "You hurry on home now."

"Are you sure?" She stuffed the money deep into her pocket. "Ya'll ain't finished yet."

"We'll be fine," Susan assured her. "You run on along to your baby."

The waitress merely nodded, her face a mixture of surprise and joy as she turned and walked through the swinging doors.

"How much did you give her?"

Dylan shrugged, poking at his food with a fork.

"Don't you think it'd be cheaper just to act civil to people instead of having to do penance?"

They ate in silence, Dylan mostly pushing his rice from one side of his plate to the other.

As they had coffee, Susan asked, "Didn't you enjoy the creole? I thought it was as good as I've eaten."

Dylan stared at the red sauce congealing on the shrimp and rice. "I had a big breakfast."

"You don't eat breakfast."

"This coffee's just right, isn't it? I can't figure out how they

17

keep it smooth when it's this strong." Dylan sipped the rich black coffee, avoiding Susan's eyes. "I never could manage to do that. Neither could you, as I remember. Even growing up in New Orleans didn't seem to help."

"Don't play word games with me, Dylan. If you don't want to eat, now it's your business." Susan shook her head in an almost maternal fashion.

"I hate eating alone." Dylan saw a fleeting image of Susan, cooking a big pot of New Orleans–style red beans and rice in the kitchen of their first apartment. Through the window a red sun blazed through the superstructure of the bridge crossing over the river to the west bank.

"But I have to admit you're right about the coffee," Susan agreed. "It never was one of my strong points, was it?"

"How're your folks doing?"

"So-so," Susan answered noncommittally. "You think you'll go down to see them any time soon?"

"I doubt your mother'd let me in the house." Dylan poked one of the jumbo shrimp onto his fork, holding it up in a tinted shaft of light. He could almost hear the creaking of the boom and the rush of water from the net as fishermen harvested the rich waters of the Gulf. "I expect she still thinks I'm an ignorant redneck. Especially now."

"Not exactly."

"What do you mean?"

"Well, I finally convinced her to read some of your stories," Susan replied almost reluctantly.

"And . . ."

"Now she says you only *look* like an ignorant redneck," Susan admitted, "and act like one." Her wry smile took some of the bite out of the words.

Dylan straightened his necktie against the unbuttoned collar of his white shirt. "That's a distinction I'll certainly cherish. I believe it's the nicest thing she's ever said about me."

"Dylan. . . ." It was a mild plea from Susan, her brow creasing slightly.

"Don't worry, I won't bring it up," Dylan promised, raising his right hand, "that is, if I ever see her again."

"Well, Daddy's looking forward to seeing you again anyway. He says he hasn't had much competition on the court since the last time you came down."

Dylan swallowed the last of his coffee. "I don't imagine he'd get much of a match out of me now. I don't think I've played more than once in the last six months."

"You do look kind of peaked. Don't you exercise anymore at all?" Susan's brown eyes, filled now with a troubled light, appeared as large as a fawn's in her pale face.

"You haven't told your parents about us, have you?" Dylan asked, abruptly realizing that her concern was not only for the state of his health.

A shadow crossed Susan's face as she turned away from Dylan. She put her cup on the table and gazed through the dark glass of the window. In the distance a deep-water tanker plowed slowly downriver. The silence around them grew like the heavy pull of the river when you've almost made it to shore.

Dylan decided to leave it alone. "How're your brother and sisters doing?"

Susan glanced over at him. "Things have gotten kind of complicated, I'm afraid."

"Well. . . ." Dylan continued in a voice not quite free of impatience.

Susan's gaze left the window, lingered briefly on Dylan's face, then dropped to the gold rim of the cup she was tracing carefully with the tip of her little finger. "Mark left the priesthood, Marlene left the convent, and Sarah left her husband"—she glanced up—"all in the same month."

"Not exactly the Holy Trinity, are they," Dylan blurted out before thinking. "I'll bet *that* took your mother's mind off my lack of social graces."

"This is serious, Dylan!" Susan chided, but the corners of her mouth had already begun turning up in spite of her obvious efforts to stop them.

"How's the Catholic Mother of the Year handling all this apostasy?"

"She's lighting a lot of candles," Susan managed to say before the laughter spilled out.

Dylan felt good being able to make her laugh again, to be a part of it, to see the child in her reborn. He had come to believe that this had kept them together during the times when love had worn thin. In these last few months as he fought his way toward sleep on his narrow bed in those hard hours past midnight, he could still hear the soft innocence of her laughter.

Watching Susan regain her composure, dabbing at her eyes with a tiny lace-trimmed handkerchief, Dylan enclosed her hand in his as she reached across the table. He could almost hear an audible crash as the barrier between them fell, the moment piercing him with a fleeting joy.

On the other side of the restaurant the jukebox began to play "San Francisco," Scott McKenzie's anthem of the Haight-Ashbury district's flower children.

Susan's voice reflected the fondness of her memory. "That song always reminds me of the time we went to that 'love-in' at Audubon Park. It was a lot of fun. Remember?"

"Yeah. All those bands under the live oaks and people handing out flowers and smoking pot—jumping in the lake with their clothes on."

"At least no one was violent," Susan replied, as a shadow abruptly crossed her eyes.

"Except for me." Noticing Susan's expression change, the shadow in her eyes, Dylan mentally filled in the part she had left out.

"Except for you," Susan muttered, dropping her fork on the plate and bringing her napkin up to her mouth.

"Well, what did you expect me to do? Just stand there and let that hippie, beatnik, yellow-belly—let him call our soldiers baby-killers while he stays over here writing letters and making speeches to drugged-out sixteen-year-olds who wouldn't know a Communist from a crawfish?"

"You think throwing him in the lake brought him around to your way of thinking?" Remembered anger sparked in Susan's voice. "You've got about as much tact as a charging rhino!"

Dylan leaned forward in his chair, on the verge of shouting now. "He had the same chance I did and he outweighed me forty pounds—thirty of it was mouth, though!"

Susan placed her napkin carefully back on her lap and picked up her fork. "We've been through all this before, Dylan. Let's try to enjoy our lunch."

"Sure. Why not let that bunch of pseudo-intellectual Socialists take over the whole country?"

Susan, cool as an early frost, sipped her coffee, staring across the top of her cup at Dylan.

Well, I did it again. Let her get me into a babbling rage. Dylan forced himself to calm down. Through the bank of windows facing the city, he could see parole officers Mack Snowden and Larry Jenkins walking across the eastern terrace. As they came in the north entrance, Dylan saw Snowden point to a table that would put him and Susan directly in their path. *This pair oughta finish off our meal with a real flourish.*

Watching the two men—Snowden red-faced, bony and neatly dressed, and Jenkins, his wrinkled sportcoat draped over a body as bulky and hard as an oak cask—Dylan already knew the effect they intended with their greetings. Only the words were hidden from him as they approached.

"Hello, Susan. You look lovely this afternoon." Snowden's voice and manner would have done British nobility proud.

Dylan almost grimaced as Snowden turned toward him.

The smirk on Snowden's face hidden from Susan, Snowden continued in his contrived and polished manner. "Dylan . . . Nice to see you *sober* this late in the day."

Thanks a lot! That's just what Susan needed to hear. "How are you, Mack?" Dylan had tried to be on his best behavior, but the next words came out before he could stop them. "I do believe your *mange* is getting better. Vet change your medicine?"

Gripping the back of Dylan's chair with his beefy left hand, Jenkins leaned over until his face was much too close. His lips curled back like a dog about to snarl. "That's not *funny*, St. John!" he muttered under his breath in defense of his mentor and closest friend. His eyes had become as expressionless as a shark's.

"Let him have his little jokes, Larry." Snowden took Jenkins by the arm. "We've got better things to do. We'll have our day soon enough."

Jenkins muttered an obscenity under his breath and straightened up. The two men, strangely reminiscent of Brer Fox and Brer Bear, walked away together toward their table against the far wall.

Susan's face expressed the discontent of a mother with a truant son. "Such *delightful* friends you have, Dylan! You really know how to cheer people up."

Dylan shrugged, gazing out the glass at the afternoon light winking on the yellow-brown surface of the river.

"And that was so *ugly* of you, making fun of Mack's skin condition! He can't help that," Susan scolded. "You never used to talk that way to people."

"Just our way of exchanging pleasantries," Dylan responded in an effort to excuse his loss of control in front of his wife. "Maybe it's the work we do. Speaking of which, I have to get to court down in Evangeline."

"And why do you have to antagonize them?" Susan continued over Dylan's attempt to change the subject. "That Jenkins looks awfully mean to me."

"Just *looks*—that's all it is," Dylan grinned. "He's really just a big teddy bear."

Susan gave him a look of reproof, knowing that her suggestions meant no more to him now than they ever had. "I thought you were working a Baton Rouge caseload."

"I am."

"Why are you going down to Evangeline, then?"

"We're short of men, so I have to work some out in the other parishes," Dylan explained.

"How *is* Emile? It's been *ages* since I've seen him." Susan's smile had returned. Dylan knew she had always approved of his friendship with Emile.

"Planning to run for sheriff in November. He's been chief deputy so long I doubt he'll have any opposition." Dylan found himself almost cheerful at the thought of seeing his old friend in less than an hour.

"I really miss him. The three of us used to have so much fun together."

"Yeah," Dylan mumbled, his face clouding over briefly. He turned questioning eyes on Susan. "Why don't I come over to your place tonight? Maybe we could stir around in the ashes and find a spark or two."

Susan paused a moment, her eyes full of regret, then she said, "No—I don't think so. Not yet."

The muscles at the back of Dylan's jawline moved slowly under the taut skin. "Well, I've got to get to work, then. Maybe some other time." He got up, stepping around the table to pull her chair back.

"I think I'll stay here for a while longer," Susan said, glancing up at him.

"Suit yourself," Dylan replied with a puzzled frown. He leaned over and kissed her softly on the cheek.

"I'm sorry," Susan whispered.

Dylan had expected the reply Susan gave to his invitation. The darkness now clouding his eyes belonged to some other sorrow. "You have no reason to be."

———

Susan watched him leave the restaurant. She had always loved the way he walked, but was never able to decide whether his effortless gait reminded her of a predator or its prey.

The restaurant was almost empty now. A dozen tables away, Snowden ate sparingly as Jenkins hunched over his plate shoveling the food in like a troglodyte. Susan thought of the fury in the big man's dark eyes as he stood over Dylan and wished again that her husband could learn some semblance of restraint. Susan felt a stabbing regret as she thought of the solitary suppers that awaited her, reading in the big chair after her bath and going to bed alone. She longed for the times they had shared, but was still unable to cut the memories of their troubles adrift.

———

"You have any big plans for the summer, Susan?" Maggie Sanders, her short dark hair shot with streaks of gray, sipped her coffee from a heavy white mug as she glanced through the sports section of the *Morning Advocate*. The brown dress draped over her thin shoulders looked only slightly different than it did on its hanger in her closet. She had started teaching the year Susan was born and loved her first graders almost as much as she did the Fighting Tigers of LSU.

Susan poured her own cup of coffee from the pot resting on the scarred gray table in one corner of the teacher's lounge. "I'll probably go on a trip with my folks in August. Maybe take a course toward my master's degree first."

Maggie folded the newspaper, placed it on the table among the ashtrays and scattered magazines, and let her reading glasses drop around her neck on their thin silver chain. "That sounds like an awfully boring prospect to me."

Heels clicking on the wooden floor, Susan walked over and sat down across from Maggie, merely shrugging in reply.

"Why don't you get on with your life, little girl?" Maggie suggested. "You can't pine it away waiting for Dylan St. John to grow up."

"I'm not pining, Maggie." Susan's green eyes flashed as she came to her husband's defense. "Dylan's just going through a rough time now."

"Still whining about his year in Vietnam?" Maggie had no patience with men who drank. "My Harry fought from Normandy all the way to Berlin, and he never used the war to excuse his shortcomings."

Susan put her coffee down abruptly, spilling it over the edge of the cup. Staring into Maggie's eyes, she said in a controlled voice, "Dylan's never *once* spoken about the war. In fact, he'd probably be better off if he did. The only way I found out anything at *all* about what he'd gone through was by writing to his company commander."

"I'm sorry, sugar." Maggie's face softened as she reached across the table, patting Susan on the hand. "Maybe you shouldn't have married him as soon as he got home." She paused a moment, then said, "I know you're still crazy about that man, and I just hate to see what it's doing to you. Guess I'm taking it out on him, huh?"

"I know, Maggie," Susan nodded. "I know. Dylan *is* like a little lost boy in some ways."

"Well, it's a shame we can't pick the men we fall in love with," Maggie sighed. "I guess most little girls grow up dreaming about falling in love with a handsome prince, but when the honeymoon's over they find out he's just a *frog,* after all."

Susan smiled, put her hand over her mouth, then began laughing. She caught her breath, trying to stop, but couldn't seem to control it.

Maggie stared at her, an expression of mild disbelief on her face.

After a few moments, Susan, hands across her stomach and gasping for breath, quieted down.

"It wasn't *that* funny, Susan," Maggie said, conscious of the undertone of hysteria in Susan's laughter. "I think the stress of this separation is getting to be too much for you. Maybe you'd better see a doctor."

Susan shook her head, wiping the tears from her eyes with the back of her hand. "No—no, really! I'm fine. I think I just needed a good laugh."

"I wish I were a comedian with a whole *roomful* of people like *you*," Maggie continued, a look of concern still flickering in her eyes. "I'd make a million bucks."

Susan took a deep breath. "Now—I feel a lot better. Instead of seeing a doctor, I'll just come over to your house when I'm feeling blue, Maggie."

Maggie gave Susan a thoughtful look, still pondering the near loss of control that Susan had experienced. "Why don't you ask Dylan to get out of the law enforcement business? Maybe that's causing some of his troubles."

"He won't listen to me any more than he did to his mother when she tried to talk him out of joining the marines," Susan continued reflectively. "Sometimes I think he thrives on challenges—not as a means of accomplishing anything, but as an end in themselves."

Maggie sipped her coffee in silence, sensing that Susan needed to put her thoughts into words—some of them maybe for the first time.

Susan glanced at Maggie, then continued her soliloquy. "Dylan believes that America has no business at *all* in Vietnam—and what did he do? Joined the marines."

Maggie nodded her unsolicited approval for Susan to continue her speech.

"So he guaranteed himself he'd risk his life in a war he considers unjust for a cause he doesn't believe in. What kind of sense does *that* make?"

"None at all," Maggie answered, giving the reply she knew Susan expected to hear.

"Exactly."

Then Maggie reconsidered. "Unless there was something he didn't want to tell you—or something he really didn't understand about himself."

"What are you talking about?"

Maggie shook her head. "I guess I don't know for sure. It's just that all of us—especially when we're young—do things we simply can't account for. Things with no rhyme or reason—absolutely no logic to them."

Susan listened intently.

"But when we grow up—those of us who do—we begin to think more about the consequences, especially how they might affect the people close to us. . . . Wives, for instance."

"Dylan thinks about me all the time."

"Dylan needs to grow up."

2

SHEPHERD IN THE RAIN

Pushing off with his left leg, shoulders turning, Dylan lunged to the left and planted his right foot, returning the serve with a short backswing, the racquet head moving forward to block it. But the reply was weak and the ball floated lazily across the net, landing just inside the service line.

Dave Blair, sandy-haired, two inches taller than Dylan and built more like a tight end than a tennis player, fastened his pale gray eyes on his opponent, seeking a chink in Dylan's defense. Moving in to the net behind his serve, he chipped a backhand approach to the opposite corner.

Dylan sprinted along the base line, taking the racquet back, his left hand on the throat, the right turning counterclockwise on the grip. Dave was nothing more than a white blur in his right periphery. Head down, knees bent, back toward the net, Dylan swung the racquet in a smooth arc forward and through the ball, catching it in the center of the strings. With his shoulders turning into the shot, the follow-through was high and relaxed.

A stunned look crossed Dave's face as the ball whipped past him ten inches above the net, landing two feet inside the base line. *Forty-thirty.*

"I only hit those when I really need to." Dylan felt the grin spreading on his face.

Dave shrugged and returned to the base line to serve for match point.

As the ball, tossed from Dave's extended arm, reached its apex,

Dylan bounced lightly on his toes preparing for the return, but the serve cracked cleanly down the center stripe for an ace and the final point.

"I only hit *those* on match point," Dave beamed across the net as he walked toward the bench to pack up.

"Good match," Dylan nodded, acknowledging Blair's powerful game.

"Good match?" Blair's grin slipped off his face. "You haven't played in a year and you took me to seven-five in the third. I should have whupped you love-love."

"You did all right for an ultraliberal, bleeding-heart social worker."

"Parole officer," Dave corrected.

"In name only. A whole year since I got you this job and you're still that same bright-eyed, right-out-of-school, gonna-make-a-difference-for-mankind Socialist," Dylan joked, slipping his Dunlop Maxply Fort tennis racket into its cover.

Dave filled a paper cup with ice water from the keg next to the bench, turned it up, and drained it. "Not anymore. I'm finding out that most people on the public dole don't want help; they want a free ride."

"That the reason you left the welfare department?" Dylan plopped down on the bench, mopping his face and drying his hair with a thick white towel.

"Part of it," Dave admitted. "They also smothered me in paper and paid me like a Chinese coolie. Barbara seems to think there's more status in being a parole officer too. You know, dealing with judges and DA's."

Dylan leaned back on the bench, watching two overweight, balding men on the next court huff and puff their way through a rally. Exertion and the merciless July sun had turned their faces the color of boiled crawfish. "Yes sir, if there's one thing we parole officers got, it's status. Why, I was just telling the governor's wife at brunch the other day, 'Ms. Guv'ner,' I said—"

"Okay, that's enough. Come on, let me buy you something cold. It's the least I can do after the thrashing you just took," Dave cut him off abruptly.

Dave's interruption had been in a good-natured fashion, but

Dylan noticed that his face had reddened slightly anyway. *Maybe he actually believes in this status business too.*

"You thirsty or not?"

"Yes sir, Mr. Dave. I'd give a purty for a Co' Coler right now," Dylan responded in his best redneck drawl, walking hunched over and pigeon-toed along the hedge-lined flagstone path leading to the clubhouse.

Glancing at the white-clad players sitting on benches or walking the paths through the landscaped grounds, Dave scowled quickly at Dylan.

Dylan straightened up and dropped the cornpone. *He does believe it!*

Inside the lounge area of the club, they found a table next to a window looking out on the courts. Dave walked over to the bar for the drinks while the mellow voice emanating from the jukebox implored anyone within earshot to help him make it through the night.

Dylan glanced around the room at the healthy, tanned, and stylishly dressed men and women, most of whom were seated along the bar. They seemed imbued with that wet-haired, flush-faced high that animated their conversations and always appeared to increase the decibels of their voices a level or two.

Beyond the heavy glass on the court nearest Dylan, two women were rallying smoothly and effortlessly with that particular roll of hip and turn of shoulder so alien in men. The dark-haired one on the far end of the court, her hair gleaming in the slanting light and swirling about her neck and shoulders, made the game more dance than tennis. Dylan found himself lost in its pleasing choreography.

"You back on the court or walking around in your woods, Dylan?" Dave stood across the table, two thick mugs of Coke in his hands.

"Nowhere in particular. Just thinking."

Dave slumped in his chair. "Did you notice the TV?"

Dylan glanced at the television on a shelf behind the bar. "It's in black and white."

"That's 'cause it's coming from the moon."

"This is the day they land!" Dylan thought briefly how absorbed with himself he must be not to have remembered. "I completely forgot about it."

The bartender, dark-haired and slim, cupped his hands to his mouth. "Okay, everybody—this is it."

The few people who weren't already crowded around the bar got up and ambled over, Dylan and Dave included.

Dylan stared at the blurry picture of the lunar module with a man in a bulky white spacesuit hanging from its side on a ladder. It reminded him of the serials he used to watch at the movies on Saturday mornings.

The bulky figure touched one boot down on the powdery surface of the moon, then the other. With the transmission breaking up, astronaut Neil Armstrong spoke slow, deliberate words that guaranteed his place in the history books: "One small step for man—one giant leap for mankind."

"I wonder who wrote that for him?" Dylan remarked absently, staring at the picture transmitted from a quarter-million miles out in space.

"Don't be so cynical," Dave protested. "Maybe he actually thought it up himself."

"Maybe."

After watching Armstrong's slow-motion antics on the moon for a while, Dylan turned, went back to their table, and stared out at the tennis players.

Dave followed, glancing back at the television one last time before he sat down. "When's the last time you saw your wife?"

"Funny you'd ask. We had lunch together last Friday," Dylan replied, taking his eyes from the court. "You haven't said anything about her in a while."

"Don't want to be a pest." Dylan nodded.

"Well, how'd it go?"

"Not too bad. Kinda like a first date. You know—keeping your guard up," Dylan admitted, glancing back at the court. "Susan didn't comment on my dissolute lifestyle, and I managed not to blubber any. Real grown-up, huh?"

A hint of a smile on his face, Dave cracked a piece of ice between his molars, waiting for more news.

"Sometimes I don't know what's worse—seeing her or not

seeing her." Dylan's eyes narrowed as he stared through the side of his mug at the light glinting off the dark liquid. "She's going to come by my place around eight tonight. We'll see if we can at least *talk* without things getting out of hand."

"You *know* what the problem is." Dave shrugged, his palms held upward. "*Do* something about it."

Dylan continued to stare at the mug. "Is this a *Coke* I see before me—the handle toward my hand?"

"That's a start," Dave agreed. "Maybe you ought to eat something too. I can just about read a newspaper through you, shirt and all."

"No, this'll do," Dylan replied, sipping his Coke.

"What do you weigh—one-fifty-five, one-sixty? That's about right if you're five-eight, not six-one." Dave flicked his hand toward Dylan. "Look at yourself sometime. Clothes wrinkled, stubble on your face half the time—do you even own a comb?"

"Certainly," Dylan answered, an expression of feigned outrage on his face. "I haven't *seen* it in a month or two, but I'm sure there's one around somewhere."

"Beats me what Susan sees in you, anyway," Dave grunted, shaking his head.

Dylan noticed the slight grin on Dave's face. *At least he's not taking himself so seriously now.* "She's captivated by my wit and intellect, not to mention my genteel southern charm."

"More likely it's pity that's deceived her." Dave entered the game. "Comely Dominican graduate from New Orleans' Garden District rescues white-trash outcast, late of the Feliciana hills, from the clutches of perdition."

Dylan glanced toward the door, his face clouding over. "Speaking of perdition, look who just came in."

Dave turned and looked behind him. "Aw, Ralph's not all *that* bad."

Next to Ralph Rayburn stood Ike Jacobs, a short, stocky man with a modest Afro and skin the color of café au lait. After a word or two, Ike walked over to the bar while Ralph, seeing Dylan and Dave, headed for their table.

Ralph Rayburn was not Dylan's best friend. Long and lean and imperious, he came from old money and the two men barely tolerated each other. In this late afternoon hour, Rayburn, dressed like an ad from *GQ* magazine, was already half-smashed.

"If it isn't the scourge of the public defender's office." Dylan went on the offensive, taking advantage of Ralph's alcohol-deadened reflexes.

Rayburn pulled out a chair and slouched down in it, hooking one bare leg over its arm. An arrogant grin crossed his face as he brushed his yellow hair back from his eyes.

Dylan continued the assault. "Better go home and lock up your family, Dave. Judging by his smile, I expect he put a serial killer back on the streets today."

"Dylan St. John," Rayburn responded casually. "My favorite parole officer. How are things going with you Neanderthals these days, St. John?"

Dave flinched at the words.

Dylan, feeling that he should get up and leave right then, had always suspected that Rayburn's insipid expression belied a quality of unacted-upon violence and knew from experience that the man had a calculating mind. "You think that designer tennis out-fit makes you civilized, Rayburn?"

"More civilized than somebody who lives in a shack in the middle of the woods."

An image flashed through Dylan's mind: *In the midst of towering pines and hundred-year-old oaks stood a cottage made of weathered cypress, a porch with a swing and rockers and straight-backed chairs across the front and along the west side. In summer storms and slow winter rain, its tin roof made the sound of country sleep.*

Noticing the far-off look in Dylan's eyes, Rayburn blurted out, "You going catatonic on me, St. John?"

"What?" The sound of Rayburn's voice jerked Dylan back to the present. He smiled benignly into the man's flushed face. "Didn't you know humble surroundings beget purity of heart, Rayburn? Maybe you should move out of that mansion on Park Boulevard and live in a shack for a while. You could use some purifying."

"Ease off, Dylan," Dave broke in. "After all, ol' Ralph here's our guest."

Ike walked over from the bar with a tray of drinks, setting a beer down in front of Dave. "You still drinking sour mash on the rocks, Dylan?"

Dylan glanced at the heavy glass, the dark amber liquid full of reflected light.

Sitting down next to Rayburn, Ike sipped his club soda. He'd grown up on Poplar Grove Plantation across the river from Baton Rouge, a childhood that instilled an impervious drive for success born of dirt roads and tin-roof shacks. A running back in high school, he was scholarship material in every area but size, so he worked his way through law school bussing tables at the City Club, where the movers and shakers came together.

"Haven't seen you around court much lately, Dylan," Ike said, gazing over his club soda. "They finally run you off?"

"Somebody takes a shot at it now and again, but they never really put their hearts into it. Too many forms to fill out," Dylan responded, a kind of deadness creeping into his voice. "I've been out in the parishes some."

"Ralph here has really missed your expert testimony in the revocation hearings downtown. Not much of a challenge for him without you on the stand." Ike patted Ralph on the back like a teammate at the finish line. "He won three straight today against that new assistant DA."

Dylan studied the relationship between Ike and Ralph. He could see that Ike was taking advantage of Ralph's political connections on his way up, but he still wondered who was being used the most. "Anybody I know?"

"Yep," Ike volunteered quickly. "Your star pupil, T-Boy—charged with two counts of simple rape. You remember him—the one you had to tussle with in Judge Madewood's courtroom about a year ago."

Shaking his head slowly, Dylan glanced over at Dave. "What'd I tell you. Pray for your family, Dave."

"Nah! T-Boy's probably hiding out somewhere down in the French Quarter by now."

Ralph gave Dylan a glassy-eyed stare. The double Scotch he had just knocked back had taken the fight out of him for the time being and had slipped him over into the whiskey-friendly stage where enemies are virtually nonexistent. "Don't get Dylan started on our philosophical differences, Ike," he slowly put the words together. "He's gonna be my buddy tonight. Might even show me that palatial estate he inherited from his granddaddy."

"Somebody told me you aren't living out there anymore." Ike took a swallow of his club soda and leaned forward on his elbows. "I didn't think a team of mules could drag you back to town, the way you loved it out there."

"A team of mules *couldn't*," was all Dylan said.

"I think I'll just let that one alone." Ike grinned, noticing the pained expression on Dylan's face. "Man, I'd like to see that place. I haven't had a breath of clean air since I left the sugar plantation."

Dave glanced down at the drink in front of Dylan, a look of admonition on his face. "Well, gentlemen, I have to get on home to the little woman. Ya'll behave yourselves now."

Dylan stared at the drink, ice melting, the whiskey taking on an anemic appearance. He knew the bite would be gone by now, but the spreading warmth would still be there.

Standing up, Dave waited for Dylan to look up at him. "See you tomorrow, Dylan. Give my love to Susan when you see her tonight."

———

Bands of pearl-colored light slanted through the barely open venetian blinds, reflecting dully on hardwood floors. "A Little Night Music" drifted from the clock radio in a futile attempt to disperse the gloom of the July morning. Mozart misnamed his composition. The piece is perfect for a bright morning, full of sun and promise and life. Nothing of night comes through the music and nothing that the morning offered.

As Dylan sat up in bed, he felt as if someone had driven a spike through his head during the night. Throwing back the covers, he swung his feet to the floor, and saw to his amazement that abrasions, scratches, and dried blood covered his legs and arms. He remembered then.

Glancing about the room, Dylan noticed his Converse tennis shoes, caked with dried mud, along with his shorts and white shirt strewn about the floor. A grimy, damp sweatband still clung feebly to his right wrist. *Aspirin. Where did I put the aspirin?*

34

The sound of water running in the bathroom lavatory startled him. A pipe sang, then stopped with a knock as the faucet was turned off. Heels clicked along the hardwood floor of the short hall, moving closer to the bedroom.

Susan walked through the doorway, holding a clean white cloth and a bottle of peroxide. Black pumps and sheer stockings accentuated her slim ankles and long legs. She was dressed in a black pleated skirt and a white silk blouse. A damp oval stained the sheer fabric three inches below her left collarbone.

Dylan felt for a moment that he had never really awakened, so dreamlike did Susan appear to him. It brought an old sweet ache to his chest just seeing her. He had thought her beautiful since that night when they had first met, and he could never understand why most other people thought her merely "pretty" or "attractive." This morning, from his desert of pain and guilt, she had the appearance of a serene oasis.

Somewhere deep inside him Dylan felt, without any words forming themselves in his mind, that all man would ever know of woman was there at that moment, evanescent and eternal.

Fresh from the shower, Susan's face seemed to have a translucent glow, as though porcelain had become flesh. Her near-black hair was pulled back severely, hanging below her shoulders in a ponytail tied at the base of her neck with a red ribbon.

Susan's expression revealed nothing as she stared at Dylan, his face still draining of sleep. She walked over to him, knelt next to the bed, and began cleaning the blood from his legs.

Dylan felt leaden, unable to move as a sense of unreality drifted down, covering him like a cold fog.

Finished with his legs, Susan sat on the bed next to him and cleaned his arms, then carefully wiped the dried blood away from a cut on his forehead and another on his cheek.

As Susan's face moved close to his, Dylan noticed the small puffiness and the hint of dark circles around her eyes. Their green color seemed suffused with a tint of charcoal.

Dylan welcomed the burning pain of his open cuts as simply another form of penance, but it was only a precursor of what he knew he would feel later. "Susan—I don't remember."

"I know you don't, Dylan."

35

"I'm so sorry about this."

"I know that too." Susan's voice sounded cool and weary and full of indifference.

As Susan leaned close to him, completing her intimate yet somehow remote work, Dylan found himself enfolded by her fragrance—gardenias, the scent of love. He had always thought of roses for innocence; gardenias for love. She finished and returned to the bathroom.

Memory's gradual slide into the present came in dim flashes like distant lightning from a summer storm, flickering on the horizons of Dylan's mind.

Running, harsh breathing, and night air burning deep in his lungs, crashing through dark woods, limbs and brush tearing at him, a bottle gripped tightly in his left hand—then breaking clear onto the bluff. Far below, the surface of the river gleaming like wet slate. Behind him, Ike and Ralph were making their noisy, erratic progress, curses ringing out in the darkness.

Cushioned by pine needles, Dylan lay down beneath wind-driven trees, watching a storm move in from the southwest, pushing clouds before it. Ragged mists like outriders raced in the forefront—the moon visible through lace curtains. And behind them rolled the dark and inexorable wall. For a moment a silver white cloud stood alone and shining in all that vast and windless distance—and in its shining, he saw a face.

Then the light of the moon was gone—and the cloud and the constant stars.

Susan walked out of the bathroom and over to the window, brushing out her hair, staring into the gray morning. "Someone must have brought you home. Your car's gone."

Memory slipped a little closer:

A dome light roused him from the backseat of someone else's car; hands lifted him out.

Susan sat down next to him on the bed and began to apply lipstick, tracing that pure curve down to the tiny scar, a white crescent in the left corner of her mouth. "Dave called here about nine to see if you had made it home. Said you were talking with Ike and Ralph about your place out in the country when he left. He didn't have to say anything else."

Dylan stared at a three-inch cut on top of his left wrist, blood seeping out of it.

Susan capped the lipstick and put it and the compact back into her purse. "A twenty-five-mile drive out there and a quarter of a mile walk through the woods at night—in tennis shorts. Then you come in here at two o'clock this morning and don't even notice that I'm sitting on your couch, waiting since eight o'clock for you."

Susan's voice was passionless, sending a chill into the pit of Dylan's stomach more deadly than if she had been angry. Memory returned.

Fumbling with the lock, entering in dim, murky light from the street-lamp shining through the curtains; Susan's face, lambent in the dark. He wanted terribly to touch her, to lie down next to her, but somehow the distance between them seemed impossibly great.

Dylan suddenly realized the casual trifling ease with which he had treated his marriage. The prospect of losing Susan for good was unbearable. He opened his mouth to tell her just once more, *It'll never happen again*, but she quickly pressed her fingers across his lips and closed her eyes, taking a deep breath.

After a few seconds, Susan turned toward Dylan, taking his face in her slim hands before she spoke.

Dylan felt the warmth flowing like a current with an almost healing quality. He had always considered a woman's hands one of the wonders of creation and felt that nothing compared with the touch of the woman he had married. It had been that way since the first time she touched him.

Susan's voice seemed as insubstantial and remote as a fable when she spoke. "No more, Dylan . . . no more. I don't even care anymore why it happens. I do know this, though . . . if we stay together we're truly lost—both of us."

Dylan gazed steadfastly into Susan's eyes as though trying to remember them in every detail, seeing there a misty sadness, redolent of loss, of light failing, of deep shade. In the innermost part of him something suspired and was gone.

Susan dropped her hands to her lap and turned toward the window, speaking as though to herself in a voice that came from another time. "We had such lovely days—all that sunlight in bed on Saturday mornings and the long walks and coffee down by the river . . . the books and the music." Susan stood up abruptly, her brief soliloquy almost finished. "How did we lose it?"

Dylan wanted to shout at Susan not to do this to them, wanted to beg her not to leave, but it seemed as though his jaw had been set in concrete.

Gathering up her coat and overnight bag, Susan walked quickly to the door. She turned, a whisper of a smile crossing her face. "You know what I remember about you the time we met? The way your eyes smiled—even when you didn't. I remember thinking how blue and happy they looked."

Dylan listened for any hopeful sign, a softening of her voice, a kind word.

Susan's face lost its momentary control. "And there was a gentleness in them then. Now there's something—different."

With Susan's words still weighing on him like a stone, Dylan watched her vanish—no glancing back, no slight hesitation as she crossed the threshold.

———

Dylan slowly climbed out of the shadows. Glancing at the clock radio, he realized he had been sitting in the same position for half an hour. A numbness had settled in, like Novocain taking hold. He opened and closed his hands. Movement and reflexes seemed impaired. Grateful for the numbness, he now dreaded the emptiness that would come later—and the iron-cold ache, dull and heavy in his chest.

Lifting a pair of crumpled jeans and sweat socks from the floor, Dylan slipped them on, followed by a blue flannel shirt he grabbed from the bedpost as he walked over to the window.

The day was awakening to a slow, silvery rain. Down below, the school crossing guard was shepherding her charges across the mirrored street. Her smile—a smile no weather had ever defeated—seemed to brighten the air around her.

Beyond the low chain link fence bordering the school ground, children in glistening coats of blue and yellow and scarlet busied themselves with play. Their cries and laughter rose faintly upward like prayer.

Pulling back the heavy leather chair, Dylan slumped down at his desk. He pushed aside stacks of books and papers until he found the poem, begun months ago.

Dry wind in leaves
Rustles like the sound
Of words in a marriage
Grown dry and brittle
In a final autumn.

Beyond the white sleep
Of a dark winter,
Children, in their timeless
Golden games, no longer
Call us out to play.

Dylan crumpled the sheet of paper and flung it against the wall. *How long has it been since I stuck with anything?*

Then his mind tried to pull him free as he stood on the brink of a sad, nearly encompassing hysteria. *It's not really over. It can't be! I know she says she wants it that way, but she can't end it any more than I can. If she could, she wouldn't have talked about us like she did. When it's really over, there's no talk at all . . . only the leaving. She'll see that—I know she will!*

Gazing about the clutter of his bedroom, Dylan's eyes came to rest on a bottle, half-full; beyond it, beneath the edge of the bed, his pistol gleamed faintly in the tin-colored light falling through the blinds.

Time to get up and resume your journey, Dylan. You've still got the same two choices—local or express. All these stops are getting awfully tiresome, but you're not quite ready for that final rush.

3

THE WHITE CADILLAC

Dylan St. John was born in the rolling hills of Feliciana, but he grew up in Algiers, Louisiana, on the "Point." When he played on the grassy slopes of the levee as a child, he would look across a mile of rolling, muddy water to the twin spires of the oldest cathedral in the country. To its left and closer to the river stood the six-storied bulk of the Jackson Brewing Company, makers of Jax Beer.

Both the church and the brewery provided their individual escape routes from the drudgery of the world. The two were separated by: Jackson Square, with its spiked iron fence and artists and entertainers and tourists; the horse-drawn carriages that clattered along St. Peter Street; and the bright, endless span of eternity.

Dylan's first memories embraced the smell of sweat and grease and Dixie Beer and the raspy feel of his dad's calloused hands as he held him on his knee in the garden behind their house. By the time he was five or six, his mother, Helen, would send him around the corner to C. J.'s Bar to get Noah St. John's daily beer. It was never kept in the house, and he never saw his father have more than one.

The three of them would sit on their brick patio with the palm fronds rattling against the stone wall in the breeze off the Gulf, while the smell of jasmine and gardenia and his mother's roses would move in slow waves on the textured air of evening.

Dylan supposed that their talk ran to the small, unremarkable events of the day. That part was gone from his memory. What remained clear was the quiet joy they shared at the end of each day and the light in the eyes of his mother and dad when they looked at each other. At those times, he felt that nothing of the outside world could ever separate or harm them.

Father Nick stood at the microphone on the school auditorium stage in his black suit and unpolished combat boots. He was five-five and wiry, one hundred and thirty pounds of strength and balance. His hair, also wiry, had a dark and wild appearance like his eyes. Near the end of his talk, his voice rang out through the PA system. "I announced Your justice in the vast assembly; I did not restrain my lips as You, O Lord, know. Your justice I kept . . . Alleluia." He stood relaxed and smiling, and Dylan wondered if he could see the relief on the student's faces when they realized he had finished.

"Rise, children," Sister Theresa said, her face like a full moon beneath the white cap as she lifted her arms in front of her, palms upward, "and make your way quietly to your classes."

Eight-thirty and the morning assembly was over. The children had been cautioned against the temptations of the flesh; exampled by the life of one of the saints. Dylan could almost see an endless file of them stretching back through the centuries, in haloed postures of prayer, shunning even bodily functions.

The students made their scuffling, bumping, murmuring way out of the auditorium toward their classrooms. The lockers stood in the hallway just outside—girls on one side, boys on the other.

Dylan felt a delicate touch on his left arm and turned to see Becky Burke, arms laden with books, making even the navy skirt and white blouse of the school uniform look regal. Her blond hair was long, straight as an Indian's, and her eyes were big and dark and somehow out of place in the brightness of her face.

"Thanks for the cinnamon roll," she said. "I didn't get a chance to eat breakfast this morning."

Dylan glanced from her eyes to her cupid's-bow mouth and felt his throat constrict, his knees going soft. Taking a breath, he folded his arms across his chest and leaned back against the locker, trying to look disinterested. "Anytime. We always go over to Susslin's before school. The apple fritters are my favorite." *Apple fritters. That's impressive, Dylan. She'll swoon any second now.*

"Maybe I'll try one," Becky ventured. "Would you mind if I met you there tomorrow?"

That moment would remain as clear to Dylan decades later as the day it happened—at Holy Name of Mary, in that crowded noisy hallway, with a million dust particles dancing in the brilliant light streaming through the transom, and Becky's smile and the sweet feeling it gave him inside his chest that made him think life was too good to be true.

Dylan took ten minutes to walk home from school, in the way thirteen-year-old boys walk anywhere. Across from Trupiano's Market and Deli, where his mother bought thin-sliced ham and Italian sausage and crispy-chewy French bread, he could hear the jukebox through the screen door of C. J.'s—Sinatra's precise and smooth rendering of a ballad about late hours and lost love. The neighborhood men who frequented the bar usually played a Sinatra record or Glenn Miller or maybe Judy Garland singing "Over the Rainbow," which even Dylan thought wasn't bad for an old song. The smell of hamburgers frying on the grill made his mouth water as he passed the takeout window opening directly onto the street.

Dylan thought of Becky and the fragrance of her that morning when she stepped close and straightened the collar of his shirt.

When he turned the corner onto Pacific, Dylan could see the levee four blocks away, where a 1955 blue-and-white Chevy Bel-Air was speeding along Patterson Street. The September sun held a July warmth on the left side of his face and glinted off a white Cadillac parked on the street. It looked almost as long as the front of his house. The left front tire was turned outward and rested against the curb. Behind the steering wheel sat a burly man with curly black hair, a cigarette dangling from the corner of his mouth. He wore a white short-sleeved shirt and an orange and brown striped tie.

A numbness began in the pit of Dylan's stomach, and he felt it spread to his chest and arms and legs like thousands of tiny deaths beneath his skin.

The man got out of his car and walked over to Dylan. "C'mon, son. Let's go in the house."

The day seemed to suddenly perish. Dylan found himself sitting on the curb, tapping with a stick on a crushed beer can that lay at his feet in the gutter. His books rested on the sidewalk next to him. The long shadow of a telephone pole fell across him from behind, stretching across the street and up beyond the next house, and when he stood up he thought the shadow was his own.

The man with the curly black hair stood in front of him.

"Who are you?" Dylan asked through stiff lips.

The man picked up Dylan's books. "John McCain," he mumbled, putting his arm around Dylan. "I'm with the union. Your daddy was a friend of mine."

The conversation hummed and roared around Dylan as people stood and squatted and sat next to him. Flower-scented women with soft hands took his and spoke gently, and the low growl of the men floated down on their whiskey-smelling breaths. Their words held little meaning as he sat on the soft flowered chair next to his mother in Mothe's Funeral Home on Valette Street, but the collective warmth and nearness of people inserted themselves between him and that protean shape in the dark that waited—the lifeless shape he would face again and again in his dreams.

Helen St. John drank coffee from a thin white cup with a silver rim. Sitting erect, she held the saucer on her lap with her left hand. Dylan thought his mother looked very pretty with her sad dark eyes and her skin like pale marble.

A tall woman with blue hair and a black mole on her wrinkled neck was talking to Helen. Dylan looked from his mother to the coffin—a metallic gray, the color of his father's eyes, draped with an American flag—closed and desolate.

Forcing his mind to return to that awful day, Dylan tried to remember what the man with the curly black hair—*John McCain, that's his name*—had told him in their house.

They walked past McCain's white Cadillac, crossed the porch, and entered the front room. The doctor was coming down the hall from his parents' bedroom with the sunlight behind him glancing off the polished wood floor.

The doctor, a sharp-faced man with a tick in his right eye, sat Dylan down on the sofa, pressing his wrist with hard, bony fingers. He said, "I've just given your mother a sedative. She'll sleep for a while. Mr. McCain will stay with you until Amy gets here from Baton Rouge." The doctor looked into Dylan's eyes closely as if examining him, then let go of his wrist. "Is there anything I can do for you now?"

"No sir. Thank you."

After the doctor left, McCain sat next to him on the sofa. Dylan felt the springs give, then rise under him.

"I want you to call me John. And don't worry, I'm taking care of everything," McCain said while unbuttoning his collar and loosening his tie. "You just see to your mother."

"Where's my daddy?" Dylan mustered all the strength in him to ask the question. "How come I never saw you on the dock before?"

McCain took a pack of Camels from his shirt pocket and a silver lighter from his pants, lit a cigarette, and took a long pull. Letting his breath out slowly, he said, "I spend most of my time traveling or in the office. Worked the docks eight years, though." His eyes wandered about the room and rested on a picture of Dylan's parents. Noah St. John had on his army dress uniform. "We lost your dad this morning, Dylan. These things happen. It can be a dangerous job."

The words had little effect on Dylan. The sight of the white Cadillac had already told him. The only thing McCain could tell him was how.

"We were breaking in a new winchman this morning, and the whip caught your dad in the back." The smoke from McCain's cigarette lifted in slim strands, disappearing into the dark air above his head. "He fell between the dock and the ship. We looked for him until about an hour ago. Then I came to tell your mother."

John McCain said he would stay with Dylan the rest of the day, until his sister came in on the bus from LSU. They sat in the garden, John in Noah's chair, with the first fallen sweet gum leaves rustling on the bricks and the banana trees moving heavily in the slow wind.

"Your daddy and me started on the docks the same day, Dylan." McCain coughed and lit a fresh cigarette from the one he had just finished smoking. "I couldn't wait 'til the day I could get away from that bone-grinding work and into that air-conditioned office. Your daddy didn't *want nothin' of it. Said union politics or any other kind would ruin a man sooner or later."*

Dylan remembered very little of what he had said that day, but he remembered everything McCain said. The day faded into dusk and the shadows of the tall, slate-roofed houses lengthened and covered the last scattered pools of sunlight in the garden while John talked.

"When I first got promoted I made less money, but I could wear one of these," McCain said and flipped his tie with his left hand. "I was so proud of my new clothes. Sometimes I'd stand in that cool, clean office, just watching your daddy through the window. He'd spot one boom on the dock and the other on the weather deck in perfect position for the winchman . . . never any wasted effort. And when he was 'greaser,' then made 'gang boss,' he was always pitchin' in wherever the work went slack."

McCain stood up and walked to the back porch. Picking up one of Noah's scuffed work shoes, he stared at it for a long time. "Your dad took care of his men. He never had a 'silent winch' in his crews, so when layoff time came, his men were always the last to go.

"I'd see him out there with that freezin' wind blowin' off the water and wonder why he didn't take this job." McCain placed the shoe back as gently as a supplicant at the altar. "They offered it to him first. He was always smarter than me."

"I don't remember Daddy ever talkin' about you," Dylan said, surprised at his own words.

"Noah didn't have much to do with me after I took the union job. I did some things he didn't approve of," John confessed through the veil of smoke before his face. "He was always loyal to the union, though. I never could figure it out."

"Anyway, when your daddy made 'walkin' foreman'—meant he was in charge of work over the whole ship—that was as far as he'd go. All the big shippin' outfits wanted him to come to work for 'em 'cause he knew the work from the 'skin' to the loadin' ramp better'n anybody, and the men would bust a gut for him. But he didn't want no part of bein' a 'company man.'"

Dylan watched McCain's face fall into shade as the sun dropped behind a rooftop. McCain looked directly into his eyes, then over at Noah's shoes on the porch. "The world can't afford to lose a man like Noah St. John."

Later, in the white glare of the cemetery, people dressed in black and dark shades of blue and brown and gray crowded between the headstones. The priest read from a thin black volume. "May the angels take you into paradise: may the martyrs come to welcome you on your way, and lead you into the holy city, Jerusalem."

Light glinted from the coffin . . . empty. In Dylan's waking dream of his father, Noah St. John still swam with the catfish and the giant alligator gar, breathing water. Sleek as a porpoise, he glided beneath the keels of the ships in the rich depths of the river, his bright hair nimbused in the dark, like cold white flames about his head.

"Let us pray. O God, by whose mercy rest is given to the souls of the faithful, in Your kindness bless this grave. Entrust it to the care of Your holy angel, and . . ."

Dylan's mind left the river, fastening on his last memory of Becky. He wondered if she knew, if she had gone to the bakery the last two mornings looking for him. He wanted to feel her warmth and life, to have her reach up and pull away the cold shroud that smothered, that deadened.

"May his soul, and the souls of all the faithful departed, through the mercy of God, rest in peace."

"Amen," all said in unison.

The priest closed the book, stepped next to Helen, and placed his right hand on her shoulder. "You'd best be going on home now, Helen. Get some rest. There's nothing more to do."

"I will, Father. Thank you so much. It was a beautiful service." Helen took Dylan's and Amy's hands as they walked slowly along behind the people leaving the cemetery.

"Dylan, I know I'm going to expect a lot of you now that Noah's gone, but I'll try not to interfere in your life." Helen's voice echoed a deep sense of grief and detachment. "You let me know if I'm causing too much trouble."

Dylan glanced over at his sister, her auburn hair gleaming in the sunlight. He wished he could tell her to take care of everything for their mother, to just let him be a boy again. But she

47

would be going back to school, and he would stay.

For the first time, Dylan saw Helen St. John as someone other than his mother, the woman who cooked his meals and washed his clothes and was always there to rub Vick's VapoRub on his chest when he had a cold, or bring freshly baked chocolate-chip cookies to his room when he had the blues. He realized she was much more than just his mother. "Don't worry about that, Mama. We're gonna do just fine, and we're gonna have good times again too."

On the way home, Helen sat in the middle seat of the limousine with Amy.

Dylan stretched out on the rear seat. *I'm just beginning to know my daddy. It's too late, and I'm just beginning to know.*

They were passing antebellum and Victorian-style houses whose deep red or gray or green roofs were baking in the September heat. The old homes had second-story verandas and widow's walks, white lattice work and Greek columns and long porches with gray-painted floors, iron fences that were never quite plumb and live oaks with tangled roots that tilted the sidewalks at odd angles. Dylan had always liked to walk these old streets, on sidewalks that were broken and lovely and still held to their purpose.

That autumn was more like a long, wandering dream than reality. Helen stayed in the house much of the time and seemed to sleep more and more. After school, Dylan would go to the river and walk the levee for miles. Day after day the thin white light of summer turned golden as the sun slipped farther south.

The massive steel pylons that supported the bridge from Algiers over to New Orleans marked the halfway point of Dylan's journey, and he would sit under them and rest and listen to the roar of traffic high above and to the lapping of the waves at the river's edge.

Just north of the Jackson Street Ferry, an abandoned wharf hidden by willows reached forty feet out into the river. The boards had turned shades of gray and charcoal and brown and, where nails and bolts had given way, Dylan could look down to the muddy swirling of the current. At its end, the wharf formed a T and was covered by a rusted ocher-colored tin roof. Someone had built a crude bench from a two-by-twelve nailed between the roof supports.

Dylan sat there after school and on weekends, gazing out at the skyline of New Orleans beyond the bridge and at the ships from ports all over the world. Directly across the river he could clearly see the Robin Street Wharf, where his father had taken him on those Saturday mornings in another life. He would imagine himself perched high on a stack of wooden crates or on bales of cotton while Noah moved among the men seeing to the loading and unloading of ships.

That was in the daytime. But at night Noah would come to him in that murky watery world, his hair blazing with light and Dylan's sorrow dying in the radiance of his father's smile. Dylan would move toward him, toward the light and the burning away of sorrow, toward his father, who vanished in a bright vapor when he touched him.

Each time the dream came Dylan would awaken, startled by the pain of death, with the weight of the night heavy on his chest and the slow, stale blood coursing in his veins—then he would remember that Saturday morning two weeks before his father's death. . . .

Dylan had gotten up at 5:30 A.M. to go to work with him, knowing that his father would already be with his coffee and newspaper in the kitchen, as always, or out on their patio if the weather was good, even on Sunday.

As Dylan walked down the hall, he noticed a glow coming out of the kitchen. Quietly approaching the door, he peered in. Noah sat at the table with a Bible open before him. His hands lay on it, and his head was bowed.

Watching his father sitting there with the light from the stove all around him, Dylan felt a soothing warmth begin to flow inside him. Then he saw his father start to smile—not as though something was funny, but the way he always did when he told Helen how much he loved her.

When his father turned toward him, Dylan saw that his face had taken on an appearance that he had never seen before. He thought the expression on his father's face resembled one he'd glimpsed in an old painting once, but then realized that it was far different than that; realized that something had happened to his father that he might never fully understand.

Noah stood up and did something he seldom did. He gave his son a big hug. Then he stepped back, his hands on Dylan's shoulders. "Let's take your mama out to Commander's Palace to eat tonight. A little celebration. How'd you like that?"

Dylan stared at the new smile—could actually feel a kind of peace radiating through the room. And for the first time in his life he knew his father's love had become a part of his own being.

———

On Dylan's first day back at school after the funeral, he walked into Susslin's Bakery at seven-thirty. He heard a few "Sorry to hear's," and "How you doin's?" from his friends, but their conversations were strained and he knew it would take some time before they felt comfortable around him once again. After a minute or two they drifted off, and he was left at the counter staring at the display case.

Mr. Susslin saw him through the swinging doors and walked out from the kitchen. He had skin like kneaded dough and his waistline spoke of years of sampling his products. A white apron covered his T-shirt and baggy khakis, and his graying brown hair was as heavy and greasy as his pastries were light and fluffy.

"Sorry about your dad, Dylan. You doin' okay? You *look* fine," he assured Dylan as he put two apple fritters in a bag and drew a cup of coffee from the large silver urn. "Here's what you need, son. Make you feel like a new man."

Through the plate glass window, Dylan could see Becky making her way across the street toward the bakery. "Excuse me, Mr. Susslin—I'll be right back."

"Sure, son. I was young once myself."

Dylan met Becky out front on the sidewalk, took her books and opened the door for her. She glanced at him once, then kept her head turned away.

Not another one. Not just a "Sorry, Dylan," and back to the company of the fathered masses—the untainted two-parent kids. Dylan put her books on a table next to the window and, as she sat down, returned to the counter.

"She's a real pretty girl," Susslin grinned, placing a half-pint carton of milk and a short, heavy glass on the counter next to the coffee. "You be nice to this one, Dylan."

He laid a dollar on the counter, but Susslin waved him off and walked back through the swinging doors.

Becky poured milk into the glass while Dylan stirred sugar into his coffee. The morning light, shadowing the right side of her face, made her hair shine as though it had been polished.

Becky looked away from the khaki-and-navy-and-white-clothed throng crossing the streets and milling about on the school ground and gazed directly into Dylan's eyes. "Dylan, I'm so sorry about your daddy."

Here it comes, the "I'll-be-too-busy-this-year—see-you-around-sometime story."

"I know you'll be busy this year, but maybe we could spend some time together; you know—just the two of us." Becky's bright face reflected the sincerity of her words.

Dylan's heart rolled over in his chest like a playful puppy. "I think that's a great idea, Becky. Who ever said girls aren't smart?"

4

A Bright, Soft Flow

Dylan sat at the desk in his unkempt apartment trying to come to grips with Susan's leaving. Suddenly the words leapt at him like a 3-D movie. *Self-pity!* He had always despised indulgence in such a destructive and egotistical pastime. *This was nothing but early-morning melodrama. Even the TV soaps wouldn't touch a scene like we just had!*

Standing up abruptly from his chair, wincing at the pain from the scratches on his legs, he spoke the words out loud, "All right, Dylan, you did it again. Now quit your sniveling, you maudlin crybaby, and go to work."

A quick rapping on the door startled him. It opened slowly and Ike's face appeared, full of intent.

Dylan took a deep breath, letting it out in a heavy sigh. "Come on in and get it over with."

"I hope you don't think I'm here to make fun of you," Ike announced, suppressed laughter lurking just behind his lips. "Would a friend do that?"

"Never."

Ike walked over and sat down on the rumpled bed, lapsing purposely into his plantation drawl. "You sho' beat me to dat river last night, white boy. You is a night runner if I ever seed one—sho' is."

Dylan sat back down in his chair, letting Ike's routine run its course.

Glancing at Dylan's network of scratches, Ike managed one

more jibe before the chuckling began. "I think you'd have to agree the briar patch won this time."

Staring blankly at Ike, Dylan waited for him to stop laughing. "How did *you* get through the woods so unscathed?"

"Put my warm-ups on and took my time." Ike's chuckling had wound down to a smile. "Caution and moderation. You ought to try it some time."

"I'd probably die of boredom."

"Boredom's better than blood poisoning," Ike grinned.

"What about Ralph?"

"He's in worse shape than you are—if that's possible," Ike explained. "His wife called this morning and asked me to put him on sick leave today."

Dylan groaned as he stood up. "I kinda figured that might happen. You taking me back to my car?"

"That's why I'm here," Ike offered, then glanced at Dylan, a dubious expression replacing his grin. "Maybe you shouldn't go in today yourself. You look like last week's garbage."

Dylan headed toward the bathroom and a hot shower. "Nothing wrong with me that a cup of coffee and a quick lobotomy wouldn't cure."

———————

Dylan glanced over at the speedometer. "Afraid somebody might be gaining on you?"

Ike was handling his Corvette on the rain-slick interstate with the same intensity he put into every part of his life—accelerating, downshifting, twenty miles above the speed limit, weaving smoothly in and out of the rush-hour traffic.

With a quick shake of his head, Ike replied, "Not me, Chump. I'm always running after—not from." His face revealed an obscure pleasure in driving at the edge of danger.

"Chump?" Dylan repeated impassively, enjoying the verbal sparring. "Is that any way to talk about the only *white* friend you have in the world?"

"I've got more white friends than you do," Ike continued. "Take for instance—Ralph."

"I'd rather not—you keep him." Dylan stared at a Mahatma

rice advertisement on the side of an eighteen wheeler speeding by four feet from his face.

"What's wrong with Ralph?"

"For one thing, I used the word *friend*," Dylan answered. "Not an *acquaintance* who treats you like some kind of displaced tribal chieftain."

"You just might be onto something there, white boy," Ike mumbled.

"No *might* about it. Now, slow this rolling coffin down," Dylan said flatly, then continued with contempt creeping into the tone of his voice. "How can you stand to be around Ralph and those other champagne brunch and afternoon tea sweethearts?"

"You never learn, do you?" Ike shook his head slowly. "Having the right contacts is *everything* if you're ever going to amount to *anything*. You got no ambition or you'd understand that."

"Oh, I understand the process," Dylan objected. "I just don't understand why you think it's so important—getting to be like Ralph's bunch."

Ike eased back on the accelerator and turned off the radio. "When I was a little boy my granddaddy used to read Bible stories to me. One of them was about a beggar and a rich man."

"I already know it," Dylan mumbled, staring at the traffic whizzing by. "My granddaddy was a preacher, remember?"

"The way you been actin' lately, it won't hurt you to hear it again," Ike shot back. "Anyhow, the part of it I remember is there was this big gulf between them and nobody could cross it."

Dylan groaned, leaning his head back on the seat.

"One time I went to the veteran's hospital in New Orleans with Granddaddy, and he took me out to the lakefront. We stood there on the seawall, and I thought that big gulf in the Bible must look just like Lake Ponchartrain. He told me that way over on the other side was Mandeville."

"A geography lesson too," Dylan muttered. "This story has *everything*."

Ike continued, "*Mandeville*. It sounded like heaven to me. That lake was so big though, I figured nobody could ever cross it."

"Your granddaddy should have told you about Jonah and the

whale. Then you woulda known what a boat was."

"You oughta leave the comedy to Bill Cosby," Ike advised, staring through the rain-streaked windshield. "Well, *now* a causeway runs all the way from New Orleans to Mandeville. That's kinda what I'm doing, Dylan—building my *own* causeway over to where the rich folks are."

Dylan glanced at Ike, wondering if he realized the irony of his story.

"And you better believe," Ike went on, "if it takes using this 'some of my best friends are black' fad that seems to be the 'in' thing with rich liberals like Ralph, now—I'll do it!"

As they turned into the parking lot of the club, the morning rain cast a sheen over the tennis courts, abandoned as though behind a cool gray curtain. The tires made a sibilant sound on the wet blacktop as Ike wheeled his sleek Corvette up next to Dylan's faded blue Volkswagen.

"Ike, you mind if I suggest something?" Dylan asked, his hand on the door latch.

"You can *suggest* anything."

"Get hold of a Bible and read that story for yourself. You might want to cancel your causeway project."

"What's goin' on here?" B. J. Ball, his curly hair shining with oil, pranced into the parole office lobby like a thoroughbred behind the starting gate. Rumpled khakis stretched across his ample stomach. "I've got places to go and people to see."

"Donice called a meeting," Roger Lemley offered, wiping the film of sweat from his bald head with a clean white handkerchief. Roger always knew what was going on.

Ball spat a stream of tobacco juice into a metal trash can near the office entrance. "Why do they always do something like that on *my* field days?"

"What's the matter, B. J.?" Dave asked, walking out of his office. "You afraid they'll quit biting before you get there?"

Ball glanced around nervously, stepping close to Dave. "Will you shut up? Donice's already threatened to give me permanent court duty. You know I can't handle that."

"Maybe you shouldn't wear those fishing pants the same day every week. It's getting pretty obvious, B. J." Dave grinned. "Make some night runs with us, and you can be legal while you drown worms the next day."

Snorting and clearing his throat, Ball quickly changed the subject. "What's this meeting about, anyway?"

"Must be some pretty heavy stuff," Dave replied, winking at Dylan. "Martin's coming down from Oz to rub elbows with the hired help."

"I wish you wouldn't call State Headquarters *Oz*," Lemley observed, in an obvious attempt to correct Dave.

"Dylan started it. The rest of us just follow his shining example," Dave replied.

"You think he'll have on his serious face and wear his official adult costume," Dylan added, feeling he had little to lose since Dave had already dragged him into the fray.

Lemley shook his head disdainfully. "It wouldn't hurt *you* to act like an adult occasionally, Dylan. You might win the academy award if you could pull *that* off."

Snowden, Jenkins, and some others drifted into the makeshift lobby of the once-condemned warehouse that the state in its benevolence—and to some political crony's profit—had rescued from the wrecking crew.

Ball, looking relieved that the heat was now off him, giggled loudly, snorted, and spat in the wastebasket.

Noticing the crease denting Ball's hair just above ear level, Dylan stared directly at his head. "I certainly admire your contempt of authority, B. J."

Ball stopped laughing, a glint of suspicion in his eyes. "What are you talking about?"

Dylan nodded at Ball's head. "Wearing that hat with the fishing lures on it to Donice's meeting."

Grabbing the top of his head, Ball realized too late what had happened. He threw a few curses back at the men who laughed at him. Even Lemley smiled a second before he caught himself, clearing his throat self-consciously. Some still throwing a few barbs at a red-faced Ball, the men began hauling a motley assortment of chairs into Donice's office.

Carrying a battered gray chair with stuffing spilling out one corner of its seat, Dylan contemplated Lemley's remarks. *Maybe he's right about my attitude. Sometimes I feel like I'm slipping in and out of high school with the in's gaining on the out's. Martin's not all that bad. He started at the bottom right where I am and learned how to play the game. All he did was keep his mouth shut except to agree with anyone who made more money than he did, and now he's made it to headquarters. An original thought would probably put a large crack in his skull, but so what. I'll just keep my mouth shut and do better.*

As Dylan walked into Donice's office with the others, he saw that Dale Martin had taken Donice's chair and moved it around to the front of the desk as if Martin was still "just one of the boys" in strict adherence to the current issue of the civil service booklet *Mid-Level Management Techniques.* He reared back in the chair, fingertips pressed together in front of his chin, the glossy toes of his shoes barely touching the floor, dark tie knotted perfectly on a starched white shirt, no jacket—everything straight from the book. After Martin's next promotion, Dylan fully expected him to put the jacket back on and return to the other side of the desk.

Martin gave the men an avuncular smile as they filed into the office past him. "Dylan, your hair's a little too long on your neck there. We do have certain rules to comply with."

Still aching from the confrontation with Susan that morning, Dylan retaliated before he could stop himself. "That's easy for you to say, Martin. You don't *have* a neck."

Martin's face was glowing, his lips tight.

Well, so much for the "I'll-do-better routine." Dylan kicked himself mentally as he looked at the anger burning in Martin's eyes. *He won't forget this one.*

———————

The quick violent midsummer thunderstorm hit without warning. Lightning streaked the dark sky, and heavy drops of rain chased people underneath awnings and into doorways. Ten minutes later steam rose from the streets under the white heat of the afternoon sun.

On his way back from lunch, Dylan had ducked into a parish library, located across a landscaped boulevard from the statue of a

Confederate soldier. Browsing through the poetry section on the second floor, he heard a voice rising above the muted sound of a crowd. Stepping over and raising the tall wooden window, he gazed down through the screen at a white Cadillac parked crosswise in the street.

On the roof of the car, a tall black man in a dark suit spoke to a crowd of about two hundred blacks spilling out from the sidewalks into the street. "We are no longer chattel! The white devils have oppressed us for too many years."

Cheers and shouts of encouragement rang out from various parts of the crowd.

The man continued in a stentorian voice, clipped and precise in its accent. "The hour of our deliverance is at hand."

A black-and-white police unit arrived at the edge of the crowd, its siren winding down to a low growl. A lone uniformed officer stepped out, slipping his nightstick into the ring at his belt. "You people are going to have to disperse."

The man on the car roof glared down at the officer. "Are you the representative for the Caucasian race?"

"I'll do 'til one gets here."

Other black-and-whites as well as unmarked units began arriving on the boulevard and side streets. Several ambulances pulled in behind their ranks. City police, sheriff's deputies, and a few state police began assembling under a live oak near the Confederate soldier surveying the scene below him impassionately. They put on their helmets with plastic face shields and took out their nightsticks. A few jammed shells into riot guns. Overhead, a state police helicopter circled with an ominous clatter.

Twelve black men in their dark suits and bow ties formed a line across the street in front of the Cadillac. The crowd milled around behind them, some holding bricks, bottles, and assorted boards and sticks.

A short, stocky man in a helmet and gray business suit stepped forward between the opposing armies. "This is your last chance to disperse!"

The tall man atop the Cadillac was unimpressed. "You white devil, one of us is going to die today!"

Forty or so officers formed a line and marched forward, several more on their flanks. Bottles and bricks began arcing toward them from the crowd as they charged, nightsticks and shotguns at the ready.

The two lines plowed together and became a mass of twisting bodies and flailing gun butts, nightsticks, and bare fists. Contorted faces spouted blood to the dull cracking sound of heavy wood splintering bone.

From the safety of his window, Dylan gazed down in grief and horror, an image of Goya's *The Third of May* forming at the back of his mind.

The man on the Cadillac leaped down, sprinted the few yards to the man in the gray suit, and wrestled him to the street. Struggling to take the pistol, he pulled it free and brought it to bear on the officer's chest, a guttural scream of rage escaping from his throat. As he pulled the trigger, a shotgun barrel appeared inches from his head—then it vanished in a flash of fire and thunder.

A black man in a white shirt climbed atop the Cadillac. Holding a heavy revolver with both hands, he emptied it at two uniformed officers dragging an unconscious man toward the line of ambulances. Both crumpled to the street. As he reloaded, the sharp crack of automatic rifle fire sounded from above. Three red blotches stitched across his chest, hurling him backward into the crowd.

As the helicopter clattered away into the distance, stertorous breathing, groans, and open weeping punctuated the disquietude of silence that descended upon the boulevard. The crowd had vanished but for the dead and injured. Smoke hung in the air along with the smell of cordite. Steam still rose from the pavement where blood and sweat mingled with the grime of the city.

Thirty seconds had passed since the lines met.

Ambulance attendants worked in the aftermath with a calm efficiency. From behind the Cadillac, a boy of no more than twelve moved on numbed legs, both hands clutching his stomach, a bright soft flow between his fingers. His eyes were glazed with disbelief and shock. A terrible keening rose from within his frail, shirtless chest, "Mama . . . Mama . . . Mama . . ."

" . . . said you saw the whole thing."

Dylan glanced up. A man in his mid-twenties with wheat-colored hair almost to his shoulders stood across the table from him. Wearing a white button-down oxford shirt and navy tie loosened at the collar, he held an open steno pad with a yellow pencil poised above it.

Coming slowly out of a foglike trance, Dylan mumbled, "I'm sorry?"

"The librarian." Using his pencil, the young man pointed to a plump woman in a flowered dress, pounding a stack of papers one at a time with a rubber stamp. "She told me you saw the whole thing from that window over there."

The clock at the far end of the room over the desk showed ten minutes after two. Dylan realized that more than an hour had passed since the last ambulance had wailed off toward a waiting emergency room. The grisly tableau down in the street had kept playing over and over again in his mind. He stood up, walking with a wooden gait toward the door to the right of the clock.

"Wait a minute!" The reporter with the poised pencil hurried after him. "I need to talk to you. Don't leave yet. Just give me five minutes."

Dylan stepped into the afternoon sunlight, glanced at the stained pavement still cluttered with empty shell casings and makeshift clubs, then walked a block and a half down toward the river before he crossed the boulevard at Lafayette Street and headed back to his office.

———

Two Muslims, three officers, and one child died. Thirty-seven people were injured. Newspapers attributed the incident to "out-of-state agitators." Elijah Muhammed in Chicago, as well as local black leaders, disavowed any connection with them. The black preachers and politicians swore their fealty to the powers that be, and the mayor praised the black community.

What virulent strain in our land precipitates such violence—that twelve strangers would go to a distant city, unarmed, and face strangers armed with pistols and shotguns? How did they come to have so little regard for their own lives? What ethos is being spawned in the back alleys and closed rooms of forgotten neighborhoods?

———————

Built in 1841, the parish courthouse in Clinton was the oldest in Louisiana still in active use. Massive white columns on all four sides formed a peristyle for the Classic Greek Revival architecture and a domed cupola was set into the leaded plate roof. The grounds were dominated by ancient live oaks, omnipresent guardians of southern tradition.

As Dylan parked near the low stone steps leading up to a brick walkway, the crowns of the oaks, stirred by a summer breeze, were flashing green-gold in the late afternoon light. Staring at the setting, right out of the vanished Antebellum South, he could see why such films as *Desire in the Dust* and *The Long Hot Summer* had been filmed there, but the drama playing out today didn't stop with a director yelling "cut."

"Dylan St. John! Where in the world have you been keeping yourself?" Billie Ashford, bubbly as always, wore her usual court outfit, charcoal-colored tailored suit and white silk blouse. Her brown hair was shiny-clean, touching her shoulders. She wore straight bangs and a bright Colgate smile. "I haven't seen you in ages! What are you doing up here?"

"Handling a revocation hearing. They keep me on the move a lot these days."

Billie put her arm around a black child about four-and-a-half feet tall and weighing maybe fifty pounds, who began sniffling and rubbing his eyes with both hands. "I guess they figure you're less likely to stir things up if you don't stay in one place very long."

"You know I don't do that anymore!" Dylan protested, then changed the subject. "Who's your buddy here?"

"This is Anthony White," Billie smiled. "Anthony, this is Mr. St. John. He used to work with me at the welfare department."

Dylan squatted down, his face on a level with the boy's. "What's the matter, partner? It can't be as bad as all *that*, now—can it?"

The child put his arms around Billie's waist, staring up at her. "Miss Billie, what dat judge see in my eyes?"

"Come on, Anthony. It'll be all right," Billie answered reassuringly, opening the door of her red Falcon. Shaking her head sadly, she glanced at Dylan.

Anthony climbed into the car, looking like a toy figure sitting on the front seat.

"What's this all about?" Dylan asked, standing up and turning away from the face of the child.

"The judge committed him to the Department of Corrections," Billie explained, digging through her purse for her keys. "He's only eight years old."

"What're you doing handling it, then?" Dylan knew this particular judge was known to bend the law until it resembled a legal pretzel. "Someone from Juvenile Services should be here, not Foster Care."

"No one had any idea he was going to do this!" Billie's face glowed with anger. "I had already found foster parents who were ready to take Anthony, but the judge wouldn't even listen—just kept saying, 'He stole that stuff. Just look at him—you can see it in his eyes!' "

"This is an eight-year-old kid getting locked up with sixteen- and seventeen-year-old thugs, Billie." Dylan glanced toward the courthouse as though it were to blame for the injustice. "What'd he steal—a bottle out of the judge's private stock?"

Billie rattled it off like her grocery list. "Vienna sausage, bread, and a jar of mayonnaise. *That's* why I was taking him out of the home. The poor thing was *starving!*"

Dylan glanced at Anthony, his eyes wide with fear and bewilderment.

"But he took it from a hunting camp that belonged to the judge's son-in-law," Billie finished, wiping her eyes with a Kleenex she had taken from her purse.

A battered pickup roared past them and turned left, heading up the Liberty Highway toward Mississippi.

"It's always the little ones who get the raw deals," Billie continued. "Did you hear about the riot down in Baton Rouge just a couple of hours ago? Somebody told me a twelve-year-old boy got killed."

"Yeah—I heard." Dylan saw again the terrible despair and terror in the eyes of the dying boy.

"And Jerome, Anthony's brother, is another prime example," Billie continued, on a roll against injustice now. "Eleven years old and he's spent three years in a foster home. His mother asked me to check on him, and I can't even *find* him—and I *work* for the department."

"How could the state just lose him?"

"Who knows," Billie shrugged. "Maybe he's with another family, and it just didn't get recorded in the files. Everything's so confusing these days. So many changes."

"Well, he'll turn up sooner or later. Kids don't just *disappear*," Dylan tried to assure Billie. "Can you do anything at all for Anthony?"

"See if they'll keep him in isolation 'til I can get him out somehow. I'd better be going." She seemed to take some comfort in her own words.

Dylan had always known Billie to be prone to sudden mood swings, but the downside was usually short-lived.

"How are you and Susan getting along these days?" Billie's eyes held a hopeful look as she stepped close to Dylan.

"Could be better."

Billie leaned forward on tiptoe, kissing Dylan on the cheek. "Come by the house for coffee sometime."

Dylan watched Billie get into her car and drive off with Anthony, sitting rigid as a toy soldier on the front seat. Another Confederate soldier gazed down on them from the monument on the courthouse grounds.

After a two-minute visit with the judge upstairs in the courtroom, Dylan's business was finished, the hearing canceled as the man on probation had been knifed to death in a local juke joint the night before.

Walking along next to the huge white columns on his way back to his car, Dylan noticed Billie's Falcon stopped at the Exxon station on the far corner of the courthouse square. Anthony was helping her put gas in the car. Even from that distance, Dylan could see the smile on the boy's face. He hoped it would last.

Taking a back way home, Dylan followed a narrow road that

wound down out of the Feliciana hills toward the city. Gravel spanged off the underside of the little Volkswagen, humming along in the shadows of the big pines.

A few miles south of Clinton, the road crossed Lost Creek. A dirt lane led down through the sweet gum and briar patches to white sand beaches, free of swimmers and fishermen at the moment. Dylan pulled off the road, parking the car under an ancient magnolia where the leaf-covered floor of the forest gave way to the packed dirt and gravel and sand of the creek bank.

Dylan walked toward the creek with the sand scrunch-scrunching under his shoes. He sat on the trunk of a poplar that had been deposited by the last high water. Its root system still carried soil and the leaves were just beginning to turn brown.

A breeze rustled through the trees behind Dylan and set the creek's surface rippling with light. The sun on his back felt somehow warm and cool at the same time, as though it had difficulty discerning the seasons. He could smell the clear green water, the damp sand at its edge and the pungent odor of creosote from the pilings of the bridge.

Lately, or so Dylan felt, his past had declared war on the present. Skirmishes between past and present erupted without warning. He could find no way to think his way out of them or run away from them. So as the past came flowing in, he allowed himself to be carried away once more on its current. . . .

The river was so wide, Dylan felt as though he and his father were traveling to the other side of the world when they crossed the bridge spanning it. As the sun's first rays glinted on the superstructure of the bridge far above him, night mist still hung languidly over the water's surface. Staring down through the window of the pickup from a hundred and fifty feet above the river, he thought it looked like an upside-down sky just before the rain began.

They took the Camp Street exit, turned right on Calliope to Annunciation, which took them back under the ramp of the bridge and continued on through the Irish Channel. At the corner of Annunciation and Felicity, Patrick Dolan ran his doughnut stand. "Dolan's Doughnuts" in yellow letters curved around a green shamrock. He served coffee as well as café au lait, which is what Dylan always ordered.

Dylan loved to watch the little man blend the hot coffee and hot milk from shining metal pitchers, forming the rich tan mixture that seemed to warm his stomach for hours. The doughnuts weren't the square-shaped beignets of the French Market, but they were soft and sweet and always fresh.

Dylan and his father sat at wooden stools along the sidewalk under a canopy that was attached to the tiny green-and-white building and supported by iron pipes. Noah St. John, his hair combed straight back without a part and so blond it seemed to give off its own light, read the *Times Picayune* while Pat kept the doughnuts frying and served his other customers.

Noah's and Pat's conversations usually started with, "How's business, Pat?" Noah would say, leafing through the paper to the sports section.

Pat would begin wiping the formica-covered counter, his freckled arms corded with muscle, and reply, "Awful—just awful. This president we got don't care one red cent about the workin' man."

"You got no problem then, Pat, since you don't work"— Noah would grin behind his paper—"unless you call jawing at customers all day work."

Pat would give Noah a quick frown and continue his diatribe against the failings of the current president, his cabinet, and their families. "Things keep going this way, I'll be out of business inside of six months."

Pat had been going out of business for thirteen years, according to Noah's count.

The two men touched on sports, politics, married life versus being single, and most of the time an old army buddy or two— usual barbershop fare.

And then Pat refilled Dylan's cup and said, "You may be as tall as your daddy one day, boy, but you'll always be on the lean side like your mama. Them bones ain't made to carry much weight. If it wudn't for that and that dark hair though, you'd be a dead ringer for him. Just hope when you get your full growth"—he'd glance to see Noah buried in the RBI's or pass completions or zone defense—"that you'll be half the man he is."

And so it went when Noah would bring Dylan along with him on those Saturday mornings when he had only three or four hours to work.

"Keep your grease hot, Pat," Noah said as he drained his cup, folded the newspaper, and unfolded his long legs from under the counter.

"You 'grease the work' like I taught you to, Noah."

For the rest of the ten-minute drive to the wharf, Noah told some story of how he and Pat worked together as longshoremen and when Pat had been the "greaser," the man who ran the work on his side of the hold. That was before a cable snapped one foggy December morning, dropping a crate of machine parts on his leg, which now needed a heavy brace to keep him ambulatory.

The sudden dopplered whining of a heavy truck, echoing from the underside of the bridge, jolted Dylan, and he found himself caught somewhere in time, suspended between a New Orleans wharf and a Feliciana creek bank.

5

THE GREEN DRAGON

"Sit down, B. J.!" Dale Martin had come down from *Oz* for an unscheduled meeting, and Donice was nervous, taking it out on anyone in hearing range. It just happened to be Ball. "And shut up for a change, will you?"

Ball, his frayed khakis still smelling of fish and worms and spilled beer from the previous week's outing, slouched down in a battered wooden chair, sliding it as far from Donice's desk as he could get it.

"The rest of you too!" Donice sat on the edge of his desk, wanting badly to get the whole thing over with.

"Could be a Halloween party, Donice." Jenkins, who put one in mind of a short, overweight Frankenstein, seemed to have gotten the wrong brain, just like the character out of Mary Shelley's novel—it apparently did little more for him than maintain his vital functions. "Maybe he's got some candy."

Donice stared at Jenkins in disbelief. "Larry, why don't you at least *act* like you've got some sense!"

At that moment, Martin, in the proper attire for middle-management, strolled in, smiling at everyone as they dragged their chairs in from the lobby, placing them in a ragged semicircle around Donice.

The word was out on Donice. He was afraid that Martin had come down as headquarters' hatchet man to make an example of him for sleeping on his office couch during the day after doing private investigative work all night. Always a terrible judge of people, he confided this to his secretary, who let it slip to Ball, who promptly told the entire office—and several people who just happened to be passing through on their way to another department.

"Fellow probation officers," Martin began, endearing himself to everyone in the room.

Ball spat a stream of tobacco juice noisily into a cut-off milk carton.

Martin squirmed and continued, "Headquarters has sent me here because of something extraordinary that your office administrator has done."

Donice's wrinkles deepened into cracks, and his eyes and mouth began to sag as though his face was breaking apart and about to slide away from his slicked-back gray hair, down into his lap.

"He's been around long enough to know that it wouldn't escape our attention," Martin continued.

Donice's face slipped another half-inch.

"Today marks his twenty-fifth year of service to the department," Martin beamed. "I know you don't like the limelight, Donice, but we couldn't let you get by without a little something to commemorate it."

Donice tried to stifle a sigh of relief.

"Congratulations, old timer." Martin stood up, handing Donice a small gold pin attached to a white card.

Donice's face began to reform as he slowly returned from the brink of shock. "Thanks."

Martin, as bureaucrats all do at such auspicious occasions, began the mandatory trip down memory lane. "When Donice and I were in the field together we handled some rough characters, didn't we, Donice? I remember . . ."

Donice had been out of the field years before Martin came to work for the department, and you could count the number of arrests Martin had made on one hand, with change. Somehow he always managed to get the cops to do it for him, but he had told and embellished the stories so many times that they had become a necessary part of his life.

Donice had climbed almost back to his normal state again and interrupted Martin, "Those were the good ol' days, weren't they, Martin?"

"Sure were, Donice." Martin smiled broadly. Usually his talks were interrupted only by yawns and groans.

"Yeah, Martin, I keep telling these young fellas that nostalgia just ain't what it used to be."

Martin stared at Donice with the expression of a chicken trying to do an algebra problem. "Come on, Donice—I know you're getting old and forgetful, but let's try to stick to the subject."

Dylan heard a few raindrops splat on the air conditioner outside the window next to where he was sitting. In a few moments the drumming sound of autumn rain worked on him like a sedative, and he slipped away from Martin's soporific voice into a dreamlike state, picturing himself tied upright to a heavy wooden chair in a darkened room. On the wall in front of him, Eleanor Roosevelt, circa 1930s black-and-white footage, went about doing charity work in the slums of New York, while from behind him the narration of the film boomed in a dead, endless monotone.

". . . boring you, Dylan?"

"Huh?" Dylan sat suddenly upright, opening his eyes wide, blinking the fog away. "Sorry, Martin. I had a kinda rough night." He regretted the words before he finished speaking them—too late.

"Looks to me like you've had a rough *year*," Martin beamed in retaliation for Dylan's sarcastic remarks back in July, getting a few chuckles from his captive audience. "And if I'm not mistaken, jeans are banned for office wear by the dress code."

"I believe you're right, Dylan," Eddie Gill chimed in. He had become a solid company man in three months' time. "Looks to me like you slept in somebody's alley."

A Martin look-alike in dress and white sidewall haircut, but his physical antithesis—tall and gangly with a prominent Adam's apple, Eddie could have ridden out of the pages of *Sleepy Hollow*, pursued by the headless horseman. He showed a certain tenacity his first day on the job, though, when he came to work in a white suit and the other men lined up in front of his desk, ordering Fudgesicles and Eskimo Pies. After enduring that, it became obvious he was there for the duration.

Martin opened his mouth to continue his monologue when Wes Kinchen spoke up, "Martin, I know this meeting is important, but I got a call just before we came in."

"And?"

Wes ran his hand through his thick red hair. At six-five and two hundred and forty pounds of bone and whipcord muscle, proportioned like a sprinter, Wes had let his hair grow down over his ears and shirt collar. This, however, failed to bring a reprimand from Martin. Wes's faded jeans and LSU letter jacket apparently looked like a business suit to Martin also, for all the notice he took of them. "And it was about a feller I've been trying to find for months. Donice can brief me on the meeting later."

"And?"

"And this guy needs to be in jail."

"Oh."

Snowden was rolling his eyes at the ceiling, and Dave was barely hiding a grin.

Martin seemed awestruck that someone would ask permission to go out and work in the rain. He turned to Donice. "What do you think? Can he make it up?"

"Let him go. I don't want my little ceremony to interfere with the job."

"This guy's got rabbit blood in him, Donice." Wes was pushing his luck. "How 'bout letting Dylan go with me?"

"Take him!" Donice snorted, shaking his head. "Maybe the rain'll wake him up."

Wes and Dylan left the office quickly, walking down the hall formed by eight-foot partitions that broke up the expanse of warehouse into numerous ceilingless offices. Twenty feet above them, a sheen of moisture had accumulated on the underside of the corrugated iron panels that formed the roof of the old building.

Wes moved with controlled power, favoring the right knee, which had been destroyed by a blindside block in his third year as middle linebacker at LSU. With his strength and speed, he received a dozen offers from the pros his first and second years, but he had wanted to get his degree first.

When Wes lost his ability to play football, it left a hole in his life bigger than the ones he used to punch in the offensive lines. The things he was trying to fill it with were only making more holes, in different and more vital areas.

"I have to hand it to you, Wes." Dylan felt ecstatic at being rescued from Martin's meeting. "I think you even had Pete believing you about that phone call."

"Why wouldn't he? It's the truth."

"What? You mean to tell me we're *actually* going after somebody?" Dylan became quickly incensed at the thought of having to chase someone down on such a dreary day, in the even drearier places he knew they would have to go.

"Yep."

Dylan's face lost all humor. "Wes, this isn't one of those days when you have to show the world that you're immortal, is it? 'Cause I'd just as soon stay here and let Martin bludgeon me to death with his fantasies, if it is."

"Nah. It ain't," Wes remarked absently. "I just want to find Odell before he snatches all the purses in town."

"All this for a purse snatcher."

Wes stepped into his office and began raking papers around on his desk. "He broke some old lady's arm this last time."

Dylan knew there was no way out now.

"I just wrote that address down twenty minutes ago. How could I lose it already?" Wes dug deep into his file drawer. "I've got the mind of a seventy-year-old man."

Dylan glanced about Wes's eight-by-ten office, furnished with a beat-up gray metal desk, a matching four-drawer filing cabinet, and the scarred wooden chair that he sat in. Above the desk, tacked to the thin paneling hung a picture of a Zane Grey-type cowboy with the caption, *There's a lot of things they didn't tell me when I signed on with this outfit.* Memos and scraps of paper had been taped at random on the two walls nearest the desk and on one corner sat an eight-by-ten color print of Wes's wife and five-year-old son.

"I don't hear you talking about Vicki and Chet much anymore, Wes." Dylan gazed at the thin redheaded boy leaning close to the blond woman with her sad, lovely smile. A seascape formed the backdrop. "They doing all right?"

"Great. Let's get outta here."

The gray cloud cover held a rumor of brightness, and the rain had become a gusty drizzle as Dylan and Wes made the four-block walk to the parking garage. As soon as they got into Wes's Volkswagen van, he reached beneath the seat for a small glass bottle. Shaking out several white pills, he swallowed them dry.

"Vitamins, Wes?"

"Blood pressure," Wes replied, trying to sound casual. "Doc says the job's getting to me."

Dylan glanced down at the bottle, lying on the floorboard at Wes's feet. "Strange."

"What's strange?"

"The druggist forgot to put a label on that bottle. You'd think that would be illegal."

"Knock it off, Dylan! You ain't exactly the mental health poster boy of the year," Wes growled.

Listening to Wes grinding the starter, Dylan almost got out of the van. Then he thought about the times Wes had given him backup, as well as the alternative of sitting in Donice's office, listening to Martin for another hour or two.

"Guess you think I oughta get drunk like the good Lord intended all us southern boys to do, huh?" The engine caught and Wes revved it loudly.

"Let's just get the job done, Wes."

"Good. I got you out of that meeting 'cause I can depend on you in a tight spot, not for a counseling session." Wes threw a balled-up scrap of paper at Dylan. "Navigate."

As Dylan tried to read the faded address, Wes flicked the knob on the radio. Backed by Big Brother and the Holding Company, the raspy voice of Janis Joplin shrieked out indecipherable lyrics to something that impersonated a song.

Dylan directed Wes to the address on the paper. It turned out to be a ramshackle concrete building called the *Green Dragon*. Flattened beer cans and bottle tops littered its rutted gravel parking lot.

Dylan discovered that the music inside the bar was even louder than that in Wes's van. They shouldered their way over to the bar through the crowd, through smoke and fumes and the smell of two dozen brands of aftershave and cologne. Barely discernable by the light of a Pabst Blue Ribbon clock, the barmaid, her earrings the size of barrel hoops, glared sullenly at them while she wiped shot glasses clean with her apron.

Leaning across the bar, Dylan shouted, "Is Odell Jackson working today?"

"Huh?"

"Odell Jackson! You know who I mean," Dylan persisted. "They call him 'Wolf Man.' "

"Sorry. Can't hear you," the barmaid smiled, turning to put a glass on the shelf behind her.

Just as Dylan cupped his hands to his mouth to try again, the bar suddenly brightened and the music ground to a halt. He turned around quickly.

Wes had jerked the heavy curtain rod down from the only window in the place and stood next to the jukebox, its cord in one hand and his Colt Commander in the other.

The scene had the appearance of an image frozen in a searchlight. Forty people, mostly large black males, stood motionless in whatever position they were in when Wes pulled the plug. Dylan fought an urge to curl up and suck his thumb—or break for the door.

Wes stared at the barmaid a full five seconds while she fidgeted behind the bar, staring at the floor. "He's off today," she finally whined.

More silence and another three seconds of the stare followed as she looked up. Then she grabbed a pencil stub from a glass on the shelf, wrote something on a torn envelope, and handed it to Dylan. "That's where he stays."

"Thank ya'll very much for your patience and hospitality," Wes boomed, jamming his Colt into the shoulder holster beneath his jacket.

All eyes were on Wes as Dylan made his way gingerly through the crowd, following him outside.

Walking over to the van, Wes turned around, took a deep

breath, and blew it out of his mouth. "That was *great!* Bet the ol' adreneline's really humming now, ain't it?"

Dylan stood directly in front of Wes, his nose ten inches from the big man's face. "I've known some redheaded men who were relatively sane, Wes, but everyone who had freckles was a little nuts—and you've got the most freckles of any of them. Get me back to the office!"

"Slow down there, partner." Wes took a step backward, holding his palms outward.

Dylan's words continued to pour forth in a torrent. "I'd rather Martin bore me to death than die on some concrete floor full of cigarette butts and dried vomit. You're certifiable! You'd need a year of psychotherapy before they'd even *admit* you to the insane asylum!"

"Settle down, boy. I think you're startin' to lose it," Wes urged, reaching for the envelope Dylan had forgotten he still held clutched in his hand.

Dylan gave him the envelope as he leaned against the side of the van, waiting for the watery feeling in his knees to subside.

Wes held the envelope out to the light, squinting as he tried to decipher the scratching on it. "Looks to me like it says 147 Redbone Alley."

Running his hand through his hair, Dylan mumbled, "Probably on the National Registry of Historic Homes."

Wes grinned over at him. "Glad to see you got your sense of humor back. You looked a little pale around the gills for a minute or two there."

Dylan stared at Wes, already appearing bored and distracted. "Can I ask you a personal question, Wes?"

"Let 'er rip."

"Are you familiar with the term *death wish?*"

The rain had ended as they took College Drive to I–10 and headed west, crossing over City Park Lake. To their right, beyond the lake, golf carts glided up and down the gently rolling slopes of the course.

As the gray ceiling of clouds began peeling away, showing cracks of blue, a cool breeze from the north sent the temperature on a downward ride.

Dylan rolled up the window of the van. *Just once I'd like to remember to bring a coat along when one of these fronts comes through.*

———————

Redbone Alley was not at its best in the daytime. The double row of shotgun houses—decorated in an assortment of imitation brick siding with slabs peeling off, tar paper, and bare wood—ran straight back from the wooden railroad trestle to the trees. Bicycle parts, scrap iron, broken toys, worn-out tires, as well as worn-out people were sharply lighted and shadowed under the strengthening sun. A few chickens pecked about on the bare ground.

After Wes parked his van on the street, he and Dylan walked underneath the trestle and into Redbone. On the first porch they came to, a school-bus seat groaned under the weight of a pink housecoated, yellow-slippered black woman who occupied it from end to end. A white plastic radio, its cord running through the window, gave off a tinny stream of the blues.

"You boys got to be up to no good coming in here. Ya'll don't look like de type to be handin' out no food stamps," the woman muttered, sizing them up immediately as she stared straight at Dylan. "Yo' name St. John, ain't it?"

"Yeah," Dylan admitted, not at all surprised that a total stranger knew him. On the streets, the names of anyone carrying a badge got around quickly. Dylan turned toward Wes. "This is—"

"Ever'body know who he is," the woman interrupted, never once looking directly at Wes while she continued to spoon buttered grits into her mouth from a dented aluminum pot.

Wes took two steps toward the porch, making a quick bow. "At your service, madam."

The woman rolled her eyes at Wes, then turned them back on Dylan.

"We're looking for—"

"I know who you lookin' for," she broke in again, pointing with her spoon. "Das his daddy on de poach right over yondah."

"Thanks," Dylan shot back before the woman could cut him off again.

Three houses down, on the opposite side of the alley, a man

somewhere between fifty and eighty years old sat on the top step of his porch in a glare of sunlight. As Wes and Dylan walked toward him, he took off his Stetson, wiping his face and the top of his head with a white handkerchief. His white dress shirt was neatly pressed, and you could shave with the crease in his khaki trousers.

"Doggone if we haven't run across somebody skinnier than you, Dylan."

The man merely stared at the bottom step.

Wes squatted down next to him. "Mr. Jackson, we're looking for your boy. You seen him today?"

"You know how he got dat nickname, *Wuff Mane?*" Jackson raised his head toward Wes, something enigmatic in his faded brown eyes. "When he was a little bitty boy I took him to see dat pitcher show. He howled like a wuff for weeks. Das when I give it to him."

"Mr. Jackson, is Odell here?"

A screen door slammed hard at the back of the house, the sound close enough to the sharp crack of pistol fire to send Dylan and Wes diving for cover.

Flat out on the ground, Dylan peered around a block pier at the corner of the house. He saw Odell running toward the street through an overgrown vacant lot. Dylan scrambled up and after him. When he reached the trestle, he felt himself soaked to the waist from running through the chest-high, rain-drenched weeds.

Odell already stood on the last crossbar of a heavy piling twenty feet above Dylan. He reached up and pulled himself over the top just as Dylan started his climb.

Somehow Dylan, trying to catch his breath, found himself standing on the crossties on top of the trestle. He stared down between the beams to the street that curved up and out of Redbone in the direction Odell was running, taking the crossties three at a time. Dylan followed at a careful two.

In the distance, Wes's van screeched to a stop on the tracks at the spot where they intersected with the street at the top of the slope. Odell stopped, staring at Wes, already out of the van and walking deliberately toward him. He glanced back at Dylan, again at Wes, then took two quick steps on a crosstie and a third on air.

A sound like a dry limb cracking rose from below, followed by a scream rising in pitch like a siren.

———————

Next to Dylan in one of the orange plastic chairs arranged in broken rows throughout the crowded lobby sat a woman of about eighteen. She wore faded jeans and an army fatigue shirt with a black screaming-eagle emblem on the sleeve. Her dark blond hair hung limp, stringy, and unwashed on her shoulders. A smell of cigarette smoke and two-day-old deodorant drifted in the air around her.

A fifteen-year-younger version of the woman lay curled in the next chair, her head on her mother's lap. The child's left arm bore a bandage made from a torn sheet. Blood oozed slowly from beneath the filthy sheet and onto the chair, then dripped down into a puddle on the floor.

Dylan gazed at the woman's face. Her expression held little more than nerves and agony. "Has a doctor seen your baby yet?"

"A nurse seen her when we first got here," the woman replied with a smile that was short two teeth. She seemed glad that someone—anyone—was interested. "She said it wasn't too serious. They'll get to us soon as they can."

"What happened?"

"Her daddy shot her." The woman spoke with an aimless, disaffected quality in her voice. "He didn't mean to. He was trying to shoot *me* and the bullet went through the wall into the room where she was."

Dylan glanced down at the child, wondering what other horrors she had grown up with.

"When he heard her holler," the woman continued, "I reckon he thought he'd kilt her 'cause he took off like a scalded dog. Hope he don't come back this time."

"You know the police have to be notified about this. It's the law."

"Oh, we done did that!" the woman explained, nodding her head. "Filled out a whole bunch of papers and everything when they come out here."

"Good."

On Dylan's left, Odell began moaning again, holding his lower leg and rocking slowly back and forth, his foot wobbling loosely with the movement.

Wes returned from the reception window and sat down next to Odell. "Hang on, convict—somebody'll be out to get you before too long. I just made a reservation for you in the prison ward 'til they can get you fixed up. The doc that looked at your leg said it's gonna take some surgery."

Odell continued to rock back and forth, groaning, not even bothering to look up.

"One little piece of advice, Odell."

Odell stopped rocking, squinting up at Wes with liquid, pain-filled eyes.

"Next time you get the urge to fly—take an airplane."

The double doors of the emergency room banged open, but it was apparent that the emergency no longer existed. A white-suited attendant pushed a gurney steadily and almost silently across the lobby toward the *No Admittance* sign. An arm had fallen from underneath the sheet, swaying slightly with that unrestrained freedom that only death can give. The arm was smoothly and gracefully muscled, without the bulk that would have come later with manhood. Tattooed on the outside of the bicep, the words *Born to Raise Hell* eulogized a brief and violent life.

The man in white pushed the body of the boy on through the door and down a dim hall toward the light at the far end.

PART TWO

—

THE SUBSTANCE OF NIGHT

6

THE MEN IN DARK SUITS

A white-haired deputy in a too-tight uniform waved Dylan past the *Official Vehicles Only* sign into the parking lot at the back of the courthouse. Pulling his Volkswagen into a spot next to a city police unit, Dylan, wearing faded jeans and tennis shoes, killed the engine and got out, pulling the seat rest forward. "Here's your new home, Odell. After a month in the hospital, I guess you're about ready for a change."

Odell, garbed in his prison-issue orange jumpsuit, looked sullen and dark in the backseat. Lifting his walking-cast out with both hands, he climbed clumsily out of the car. "This place ain't fit for a dog to live in."

"Ease off, convict." Wes leaned on the car's roof, grinning across at Odell. In his scuffed cowboy boots and denim jacket, he looked like he had just climbed off a horse. "You just had it too easy out there. All them pretty nurses waiting on you."

Odell merely grunted, hobbling across the parking lot after Dylan.

The three of them walked down the long concrete ramp, past a deputy armed with a shotgun, and into the cellarlike gloom of the courthouse basement to the glassed-in cage of the radio room. The communications boys were having a busy day, their radios popping and crackling with incoming messages. The elevator, accessing the fourth-floor jail, stood directly across from them.

"You don't have to hang around here," Wes offered, placing his .45 into one of the half-lockers on the wall next to the elevator. "The regular paperwork plus this medical business is gonna take a while to finish. You can go on back to the office if you want to. I'll walk to my van."

Dylan gazed at Wes's face, slack-looking now that he had touched down from one more brief chemical flight. He would probably make it all right until dark.

"I've got to run on down to Evangeline when I leave here—to handle a trial and get the judge to sign some warrants. Emile wanted to talk to me about something too." The doors of the elevator slid open, and Dylan ushered Odell inside before him. "Besides, I want to see what all this extra security's for."

"How *is* ol' Emile what's-his-name doing down there?" Wes, his face pale and beaded with perspiration, leaned against the wall as the elevator whined slowly upward.

"Emile DeJean?"

"Yeah. That's him."

"Okay, I guess. He doesn't talk about it, but losing his son has really aged him."

"What happened to him?" Wes mumbled, wiping his face with the palms of his hands.

Dylan remembered the time the three of them had gone fishing shortly before Robert had left for Vietnam and how he had questioned Dylan about what it was like being in combat. "He got killed in the Tet Offensive."

"That's rough. I always did like ol' Emile even if he does call me *cher*." Remarkably, Wes pronounced the word the way the Cajuns do—*sha*, as in "shack", not *sher*, as in "sheriff." "I haven't been around them French people much, but I don't think I could ever catch on to their ways."

"That's all right, Wes; they probably wouldn't understand yours either."

Dylan stepped out of the elevator into the booking area of the jail. *Something heavy's going down here, all right.*

Distinguished-looking men carrying leather briefcases and wearing tailor-made suits spoke with each other in hushed tones, ignoring everyone else. The deputies were going about their duties in a robotlike fashion. A hushed tension had settled down over the room.

Walking over to the long counter after seating Odell with several other prisoners, Dylan whispered, "What's going on, Jerry? For a minute there, I thought I'd walked into a Senate committee meeting by mistake."

A burly man in his late twenties limped over. He wore a John Deere baseball cap, in defiance of the dress code for deputies. "Hey, Dylan, how you doin'? Come on back here. It'a gonna be a few minutes before I can get to you."

Dylan walked around behind the counter to the coffee service. Glancing at Wes, who was already seated at a table filling out forms, he poured two cups of coffee and sat one next to Wes. Then he took a spoon from a glass of water the color of swamp mud and tried to scrape sugar off the inside of a quart Mason jar.

Jerry eased over from the counter. "Them men ain't politicians, Dylan," he explained in a hushed tone. "Almost as bad, though. They're them hotshot Yankee lawyers the Black Muslims hired. The sheriff thought if he let the lawyers walk 'em down to the courtroom, they'd be less likely to cause trouble."

Dylan knew now the reason for the armed deputy at the ramp entrance. "I forgot all about that riot trial starting this week. How long you think it'll last?"

Jerry shrugged and turned to his stacks of paper.

Dylan sat down on the table where Wes was doing his paperwork. "You ought to give out antibiotics with this coffee, Jerry. I think I change the oil in my car more than ya'll do the water in that spoon glass."

Speaking in a flat voice, Jerry didn't bother looking up, "If you parole officers would ever drop something in the kitty we might be able to afford some clean water."

"You hear what happened out in San Francisco at the Rolling Stones' concert?" Dylan preferred conversational boredom over silent boredom.

"I don't *care* what happened to that bunch of dopeheads."

"They hired the Hell's Angels as their bodyguards." Dylan noticed a line of men in dark suits standing just beyond the final electric door leading out of the main jail unit.

"Figures."

"And one of them stabbed a guy to death at the concert. He was trying to get to the stage."

Jerry glanced up. "What'd they expect that bunch of thugs to do—social-work him, ask him how long it took his mama to potty train him?"

"The Stones were playing 'Sympathy for the Devil' when it happened. Ironic, huh?"

"If you say so." Jerry had obviously lost interest.

At the harsh buzzing noise of an electric lock, Dylan glanced around. The first man in the line, who looked like an ad out of *Ebony* magazine, stepped through the door at a signal from a deputy. Nine others marched out behind him, exactly three feet apart; all more than six feet tall, wearing neat dark suits, large bow ties, close-cropped hair, they had the builds of wide receivers. Each carried a small black volume of the Koran in his right hand, held close to the body. Their faces portrayed no hostility, no love, no fear, no compassion. Dylan felt as though he was looking into clear water in a glass bowl on a white surface—nothing showed through.

Another deputy opened an iron door next to the elevator and the ten men, followed by their attorneys, filed down the narrow spiral staircase to the courtroom.

"I'm glad that's over for today. I'll be off duty when they come back." Jerry dropped a stack of forms in a shallow wooden box on a shelf below the counter. "Them fellers give me the heebie-jeebies. They ain't normal."

Wes straightened his sheaf of papers and walked over to the counter. "Here you go, Jerry. Odell's gonna make a fine addition to your little finishing school here. You might want to keep your hand on your wallet when you check him in, though."

"I remember him." Jerry glanced over at Odell, who was proclaiming his innocence to another prisoner. "We got our own special rehab class for his kind."

"I'm gonna go over and see Judge Graves about setting up a revocation hearing. He'll want me to bring him up to date on Odell, and that's gonna take a while." Wes's hand shook slightly as he rubbed the stubble on his chin.

"You going tonight?"

"Probably, if I get this business over with. The DA's office is gonna want to know about this one too." Wes wiped the beaded perspiration on his forehead with the back of his hand. "If I don't make it back to the office today, I'll see you at the garage about midnight."

"I think there'll be six of us," Dylan grinned. "You get to ride with the Fudgesicle man."

"Splendid." Wes surveyed Dylan's clothes. "You *are* going home to change before you go see the judge?"

"Certainly. What do think I am—a kid?" Dylan didn't even consider telling Wes that he had planned on going directly to the courthouse in Evangeline, having taken little notice of what he was wearing. He had done something like that only once before, rushing to court in Clinton, barely making it in time after finishing an all-night arrest run. The judge had come within an inch of jailing him on a contempt charge.

———

A shudder shot through the ferry as the heavy diesels churned it free of the landing and out into the current toward the Evangeline shore. At the bow, having changed into his usual navy jacket and tan slacks, Dylan leaned on the rail, watching the river slide rapidly beneath him. The water was so muddy and thick it looked more solid than liquid, as though it could be walked upon.

The rounded bow barely missed a water-dark log, one bare limb lifted toward the sky as it wallowed on the swells left by the ferry. Dylan thought of the journey it would take, drifting slowly down to the Gulf through the south Louisiana landscape: past Acadian cottages and stately mansions—Greek Revival, Victorian, and Gothic—and the ghosts of those long-vanished—gray-white and high-columned among the moss-silvered oaks; past the century- and two-century-old churches with their graveyards full of men and women who worked and loved the land; past the lakes and the primeval Atchafalaya swamp, home to deer, black bear, muskrat, alligator, heron, the lethal cottonmouth, and crawfish; and then under that final bridge to the final city, ending at the great southern littoral of marsh and barrier island.

Dylan conjured up memories of that final great city on the

Mississippi—New Orleans, more European than American, that lovely, sinister, sensual city where he found his wife.

Beneath the huge open-sided circus tent on the parade ground of the Algiers Naval Station, a dance was being held to benefit victims of the latest hurricane to come roaring up out of the Gulf. On a small, hastily built platform, a local band enthusiastically assaulted the melody of a top-ten hit. People danced on the clipped grass, sat on folding chairs, or stood talking in small groups. They drank soft drinks out of ice-cold bottles or beer poured into paper cups.

Discharged that morning from the Marine Corps, Dylan had flown in from Parris Island. Finding his house empty, he had downed a few with the regulars at C. J.'s Bar, then strolled the old neighborhood, attracted by the music and laughter coming from the naval station.

Dylan lost his heart at the first sight of Susan. It scared him to death. He thought he had never seen anyone so pretty—or so unapproachable. Feeling weak in the knees, he sat down in a chair and stared at her through the throng of dancing, drinking, noisy people for a full ten minutes.

Finally, he saw her date, a crew-cut defensive-lineman type, get up and walk off across the parade ground. Unable to stand it any longer, Dylan stepped to the makeshift bar, downed a double whiskey and threaded his way through the crowd toward the far side of the tent where Susan sat—solitary, remote, achingly lovely.

The band had begun a discordant version of "Wooly Bully" when Dylan leaned over close to Susan and brayed above the din, "Would you like to dance?"

Susan, wearing jeans, tennis shoes, and a white cotton blouse, stared up into Dylan's slightly glassy blue eyes, noticed his deep tan and the marine uniform. "To that?" She made a face at the band. "I only slow dance."

Squatting next to her chair, Dylan would not be put off so easily. "We could wait for a minuet. That might be slow enough for you."

Susan edged back in her chair.

"Of course, my powdered wig's at the cleaners and my silk stockings are in absolute ruin after that nasty business at the palace," Dylan continued straight-faced.

Her clear green eyes wide in disbelief, Susan murmured, "Pardon me?"

"I just got discharged from the marines this morning." Dylan tried an appeal to her patriotism. "Surely you wouldn't deny a veteran one little dance."

Susan glanced over her shoulder, obviously looking for her date to return and rescue her.

"Look, I'm harmless. I grew up right here on the 'Point,' graduated from Berman, and went to LSU."

A hint of recognition flickered in Susan's eyes. "Did you play on the tennis team at LSU?"

"Hey, you were in school, then?" Dylan felt overjoyed that they had something in common. "How come I never saw you?"

"It's a big school." Susan began to relax. "I only saw you play one season. Did you graduate?"

"Nah. I still have one more year."

Susan glanced at the uniform. "You dropped out and joined the marines?"

"Yep."

"Whatever for?"

A grin flickered across Dylan's face. "I keep asking myself that same question."

Behind Dylan, the band began playing "Blue Moon," amazingly soft and on key.

Dylan stood up. "How about that dance, now that we're old friends?"

"Why not?" Susan smiled. "One dance couldn't hurt."

Pulling himself out of the past, Dylan gazed at the huge pile of white shells used to repair the ferry landing on the west bank of the river. They provided a beacon for the Cajun culture that lay beyond the levee. North of the city, on the redneck side of the river, gravel served the same purpose.

After the ferry had been moored and the ramp lowered, Dylan pulled into the line of cars moving up and over the levee. As he drove toward Evangeline, through the Cajun realm of fast tempers and slow-moving bayous, the blood seemed to warm and slow in his veins in time with the flow of the land.

———

Emile leaned against one of the massive square pillars of the Evangeline Courthouse. With his black hair, gray-flecked and touching his collar, he looked more like Jean Lafitte in time-warp than the Chief Deputy for Maurepas Parish. A cutlass would have looked more at home in his hand than the slim leather briefcase, and the gray pinstripe suit coat seemed stilted on his broad chest and shoulders.

"Dylan, my fran', con mon sah vah." Emile shook Dylan's hand, then clapped him on the shoulder.

"Sah vah bien, Emile. Now if it's all right with you, let's speak the mother tongue."

"French *is* my mother's tongue," Emile grinned, his teeth white against his tan face. "Daddy's too. You said that real good. We'll make a Cajun out of you yet."

"I don't know about that. I don't think my mouth was made for this language."

"That's because you don't know how to take things easy. You relax the mouth when you talk, and the rest of the body follows along," Emile explained patiently. "Then you ready to pass a good time."

"That sounds like fun," Dylan agreed, glancing at the courthouse, "but right now I got to pass a not-so-good time in Judge LeBlanc's courtroom."

"No you don't. I just left there," Emile explained. "The lawyer got a continuance."

"That figures. These things are always decided on the courthouse steps," Dylan grumbled. "Well, I've got some warrants for him to sign anyway."

"C'mon, I'll go with you. Then we'll take a ride."

"If I have time."

"You got time."

A scattering of people walked across the courthouse grounds and up the wide stone steps, returning from lunch for the two o'clock trials. They wore overalls and business suits, dresses and jeans and khakis. The Cajun dialect ran through their midst as strongly as a genetic trait, binding them all together as family. The present seemed little more than a thin and transparent facade, leaning heavily on the past.

Dylan felt as if he stood at the threshold of another time, in another country as he crossed the portico, up three steps into the main lobby. Twin marble staircases curved upward onto the main floor landing outside the courtroom.

A mural painted by a local artist in the early part of the century covered most of the left wall. The painter achieved national recognition some years later, but his genius was evident in the early work—a gray-haired fisherman paddling a pirogue down a dark bayou; a family crawfish boil in front of an Acadian cabin; trappers, shrimpers, and loggers; and a white church in bright sunshine with horses and buggies in the shade of the tupelo gum.

On the right wall, a dozen black-and-white prints of past judges hung as an afterthought. Even in this bastion of the law, the voice of the people still rang clear.

Dylan felt that he could almost walk into the mural. "Is the artist still alive?"

"Uh-huh. Moved to New York not long after he finished this," Emile explained. "He knew the old ways were about finished. I think he probably figured he couldn't keep them alive in his work if he stayed 'til the end. Guess he just wanted to keep his memories clean."

Dylan, fascinated by the strange and unique way of life, continued to stare at the mural as he listened to Emile.

"He really did a good job with the way people lived back then. I wasn't around for much of it, but Daddy said that's the way it used to be." Emile gazed at the scenes as though he had known the people in them for a long time. "The two big wars and the oil drilling hurt us some, but we're a pretty tough bunch. Some parts way back in the swamp haven't changed too much."

"I'd like to see that."

"You're about to."

Dylan gave him a puzzled frown.

"Ol' J. T. Fontenot from Bayou Ramah and his wife, Andreé, had a knock-down-drag-out after thirty-five years of marriage. She had him charged with aggravated battery."

Filing into the courtroom with the crowd, Dylan and Emile

took chairs at the long mahogany table to the left of the judge's high bench and inside the carved rail that separated the legal arena from the spectators. A few parish deputies and local attorneys with nothing better to do were already seated to watch the afternoon contest.

Light slanted in harshly from the high windows as though a giant Diogenes stood outside, seeking his one honest man. *Looking over a courtroom would be certain to prolong his search*, Dylan mused.

The man being sworn in on the witness stand was short, round, and bald, with a smiling red face. Wearing khakis, a plaid shirt, and scuffed lace-up work boots, he could have passed for a hairless Santa on the way to his summer garden.

" . . . So help you God."

"I gah-roan-tee, cher."

"The correct response is, 'I do.' "

"Das what I said when I got married." J. T. grinned at the white-haired lady holding the Bible. "I don't hardly say dat no more. One time was too much, yeah."

Dylan settled back, unable to dislike the pleasant man, no matter the charge against him. "That must be J. T."

"Yep."

"He looks like an old cherub."

Emile pointed to a sharp-faced young man in a three-piece suit. "And that's Fox, the assistant DA, fresh from the city. This might prove mildly interesting."

"Why would J. T.'s lawyer let him take the stand on a charge like this?"

"Look at him; would you convict him?"

Dylan gazed at "Jolly J. T.," as he had already begun to think of him. He wanted to go play in his backyard, ask J. T. to tell him a story, go fishing with him. Dylan also wanted his lawyer if he ever got arrested.

After J. T.'s last remark, Fox walked back to his table and shuffled some papers around while the giggles died down in the courtroom. Then he pranced back and forth in front of the jury box as a show of confidence, before he turned to J. T. "Mr. Fontenot, I understand that you and your wife have had a somewhat stormy marriage. Am I right?"

The defense attorney raised no objection.

"Das put it mildly, cher. *Hurricane* is more like it. I did ever'-thing you could taut about to get along wid dat woman, me." J. T. glanced at his wife, his eyes twinkling. "I don't know what else I could did."

"Could you elaborate?"

J. T. glanced at the jury, then at the judge, and then shrugged his shoulders.

Judge LeBlanc motioned Fox over to the bench, speaking in a hushed voice. "Could you simplify the questioning? Mister Fontenot's education is limited."

Shaking his head, Fox stepped over directly in front of the witness stand and with a slight condescending edge to his voice, spoke slowly and distinctly, "Tell us about your problems."

"Das what I'm gonna did. But before I talk I wanna say so-met'ing." J. T. turned his palms upward in front of his body. "De whole t'ing got off to a bad start."

"Go on."

Fontenot looked at the jury, shaking his head as though he had been interrupted by a rude child. "My bes' fran, Sady Thi-bodeaux, he tole me I got to be boss wid my marriage. He say I ain't got to use plenty words, jes tell her dat."

Fox rolled his eyes upward in a show for the jury. "I don't see the point in this."

"If you jes' hush, you gonna see plenty," J. T. admonished. "Anyhow, I got home from work and I holler at her, 'Got youself in de kitchen.' " J. T. gazed over at the jury and shrugged, "So she brought herself in de kitchen."

Dylan had begun to enjoy the show.

" 'Sit yourself down,' " J. T. continued. "She sit herself down. Den I look her straight in dem two eye and tell her, 'Me, I'm gonna be boss wid dis house.' Dis really surprise her."

"Well, what did she do?" In spite of himself, Fox found him-self caught up in the story.

"It surprise her so much I don't see her for tree days."

"She left you?"

93

J. T. shook his head slowly back and forth. "Den I could see her jes' a little bit out de corner of dis right eye here," he explained, pointing to his eye.

Suppressed laughter and fits of coughing moved in sporadic waves over the audience. Judge LeBlanc rapped loudly on the bench with his gavel, calling the courtroom to order.

Fox, obviously unprepared for this turn of events, glanced over at Andreé Fontenot seated on the front row, her head swathed in bandages, her left arm in a cast. Rather than presenting a picture of the abused wife as Fox had hoped she would, with her angular features and dark hollow eyes, she bore an amazing resemblance to Boris Karloff in *The Mummy*.

"Did your wife strike you?" Fox had lost control of the questioning now.

"Strike? Das what you do wid matches. Dat woman buss my head open wid an iron skillet."

Fox took one look at the jury box and knew he was in big trouble.

"Sady, das my fran I tole you about, he got to drive me to the hospital. Dey took dem ashtray picture of my head, but nuttin' was broke inside dere."

After bringing the courtroom to order again, the judge called Fox and J. T.'s lawyer over to the bench for a conference.

Emile grabbed Dylan's folder, walked over to the bench, and laid it in front of the judge. He began signing the documents without reading them or interrupting his conference.

Returning to the table and dropping the folder in front of Dylan, Emile picked up his briefcase and motioned for Dylan to follow him. "Let's go. This could take hours."

As they left the courtroom, the trial continued.

"After dat, t'ings was kinda rough for a lotta years. . . ."

Small clouds, high and white, were scattered across the sky like ethereal sheep grazing in a blue pasture. An errant wind from the north breathed across Dylan's face, bringing a damp message from the approaching rain, like the ache of an old wound.

"Is this Fontenot character for real?" Dylan found himself becoming more and more intrigued with the Cajun people as they walked down the steps of the courthouse.

"J. T.?" Emile grinned. "He lays that accent on a little thick when he wants to, but basically he's just being J. T."

"What happened to his wife?"

"I saw this coming years ago," Emile explained, "even tried to get Andreé to ease off a little, but she told me she knew how to handle her husband."

"J. T. always worked hard and did whatever it took to put food on the table—fished, trapped, farmed, did odd jobs. He loved his family, but he also loved his Saturday night boureé games and the beer drinking that always went along with them. Never got sloppy, though—always home by midnight and never missed 6:00 A.M. mass."

Emile sat on a concrete bench under an ancient magnolia tree and leaned back, watching the play of sunlight through its leaves. "Andreé couldn't stand it, grated on her nerves like a squeaky gate. Said it wasn't proper. I think she just hated to see him have a good time. She always looked as if somebody just told her a real sad story. You never saw two people so opposite."

"Anyway, their youngest daughter got married a couple of months ago, so there was just the two of them. That first Saturday night, Andreé waited up for him as usual."

"Will you hurry up and get to the good part?"

"I'm gonna did dat, cher, if you jes' hush you mouth. Andreé always punctuated her temperance lectures with a broom handle, cooking pot, lamp—whatever was handy. The priest probably wouldn't have recognized J. T. without the Sunday-morning knot on his head. But even a man as easygoing as J. T. can get pushed too far, and that was the too-far time for him."

"From the look of her in the courtroom, he made up for a lot of years that night," Dylan observed.

"Nah, J. T.'s got too good a heart to hurt anybody that bad— even Andreé."

"Well, she sure didn't do it to herself."

"Almost," Emile grinned. "She waited for J. T. on the back porch and went after him with a piece of stovewood. He didn't know who it was coming out of the shadows, so he decked her with a right."

"One punch did all that?"

"Falling down the steps did most of it," Emile explained. "Their porch is six feet off the ground."

Dylan sat down on the bench next to Emile. "All those years of fighting like that and nobody called your office or welfare for the children?"

"People back in the bayous like to keep things in the family; they handle their own problems." Emile shrugged. "There's a stigma about getting mixed up with the government."

"They're probably better off in the long run."

Emile stared at Dylan as though he were a baby saying his first words. "Sometimes you surprise me with your good sense. Especially coming from somebody who gets *paid* for meddling in other people's business."

Dylan laughed, thinking how Emile was able to see right through all the labels that the bureaucrats were so enamored of sticking on everything and everybody. "What's going to happen to our friend J. T.?"

"*Not guilty*—no doubt about it," Emile answered with no hesitation. "Fox is just trying to make a name for himself with this aggravated battery charge. If he'd let Andreé cool down a little, the whole thing would have blown over, but now he's determined to go all the way."

"Fox's questions were more like the defense than the prosecution," Dylan observed. "That didn't make a bit of sense to me."

"First time out of the chute for him," Emile remarked absently. Having already guessed what the outcome would be, he had apparently lost interest in the trial. "And Fox's got the kind of confidence that comes entirely from two special parts of his makeup."

Dylan gave Emile a puzzled frown.

"Ego and ignorance." Emile stood up, stretching lazily. "J. T. looks like such an easy mark, too. Like my old Uncle Laurant used to say, 'You got to look out for dem extinguishing circumstances.'"

7

GUARDIAN ANGELS

"Guess I'll head on back to the city." Dylan walked along with Emile on the hard-packed ground beneath the trees. "Thanks for getting those papers signed."

Some dark problem had clouded Emile's face. He was slowly gazing around as though the solution might be somewhere on the courthouse square. When Emile's eyes returned to Dylan, Dylan knew he wouldn't be going back to the city just yet.

"I need a favor."

Dylan tried with little success to imitate the Cajun accent. "Whatever I could did, you jes' axe me, cher." He knew now that the problem was more serious than he had imagined. Emile almost never asked favors. He was far more likely to dispense them liberally.

Ignoring Dylan's laughable accent, Emile held to his course. "There's a fifteen-year-old boy, Remy Batiste, in the downtown jail over in Baton Rouge. They say he's too violent for detention—I know better. I think you had his daddy, Buck, on probation a year or two ago."

Dylan remembered the man and his wife, Rachel, whose dark beauty was rapidly vanishing, swallowed up by the life her husband had drawn her into. He had moved his family to the city to get a better job, at least that was what he told her. "He headed for parts unknown after a few months. Dumped his wife and two boys."

"That sounds like Buck."

Back then, Remy was a chunky thirteen-year-old whose hair hung in his eyes most of the time. Dylan would throw the football around with him or shoot a few baskets when he went to check on Buck. He remembered once taking the boy to the zoo. "I'll do what I can, but the Juvenile Department's gonna handle his case. What'd he do anyway?"

"Simple battery," Emile grunted, "on the Director of the Juvenile Department—decked him."

Dylan thought it was another of Emile's jokes. "C'mon, what'd he *really* do?"

Emile continued in a level voice. "His mother's living back here now so I'm trying to get jurisdiction, but I get stonewalled everywhere I turn."

"He really punched out Jim Donaldson, huh?" Dylan wanted to laugh, but the concern on Emile's face stopped him. "I always knew he wasn't the John Wayne type, but I didn't think a kid like Remy could take him. Why?"

Stopping under a live oak, Emile watched the slow traffic moving around the courthouse square. "Don't know, really. Rachel told me he was upset about his little brother being locked up at LTI in New Orleans."

Dylan wondered how Remy knew that Donaldson was connected with LTI. "Maybe he just saw Donaldson's name on a letterhead."

"Maybe."

"What's Russel in for?"

"Shoplifting—first offense," Emile muttered with disgust. "We had an ad hoc judge who thought he was Roy Bean that day. Kid should've gotten a good chewing out and sent back home."

"Has Rachel seen Remy yet?"

"Once. He wouldn't tell her a thing." Emile glanced both ways, then walked quickly across the street. "Think you can get in to see him?"

Dylan followed, dodging a chubby boy in a khaki uniform speeding by on his bicycle. "Nothing to it. Once I get past the front desk, nobody cares *who* I see."

Turning right, Emile headed along the sidewalk. "*One* more

question. What do you know about this fellow Donaldson and his lackeys?"

Emile never threw labels around casually. Dylan knew there must be substance in his words. "Not much. They pretty well kept to themselves up there in Oz."

"In what?"

"Oz—state headquarters."

"That sounds like something *you'd* come up with," Emile reproved mildly.

"Everybody seemed to like it," Dylan shrugged. "Well, not *quite* everybody. I think the subtlety of it was lost on the headquarters people."

"You want to answer my question?"

Dylan felt the sting in Emile's tone. "Donaldson—moved from the West Coast ten years ago, close to the governor; the people around him are a real tight-knit bunch—like cops."

"They may be tight-knit, but they're nothing like cops," Emile frowned. "Can you see if Madewood will transfer jurisdiction back here?"

"That's *two* questions, Emile." Dylan suddenly felt cut adrift from his surroundings, his mind clouded. Hardly aware of what he was saying, he focused on Susan to regain his grip on reality. "You said you only had one more."

"Very good, you can count!" Emile had reached his white Blazer with the green Maurepas Parish Sheriff's insignia on the doors. Unlocking it, he turned back toward Dylan. "We had almost ten minutes of sensible conversation before that last remark. Puberty must be just around the corner."

"Sorry." Dylan felt a quick stab of guilt, knowing how concerned Emile was about Remy. "Sure, I'll talk to the judge. Madewood always liked me . . . for some reason."

"Thanks, Dylan, and don't be sorry. If you lose your sense of humor in this business we're in, you're finished." Opening the door, Emile leaned on it with his elbows. The full weight of his forty-five years seemed to press down heavily on him. "Maybe I'm just getting old."

"No, it's always rough when kids get a raw deal."

Emile slid in behind the wheel of the Blazer. "Hop in. I want to show you something."

"I better get on back."

Emile didn't reply; he merely gave Dylan that stare that he had never been able to refuse.

Whatever it is, it's important to him. Dylan walked around to the passenger's side and got in.

———————

Emile drove in silence through the child-loud, shady streets of Evangeline. School was out, and children walking and on bicycles made their way home, shouting to one another, giggling, playing out their innocence in the spendthrift fashion of the very young. Mothers and dogs waited for them at front gates and on porches like the next shift of guardian angels taking over once the school bell rang.

Dylan thought of Remy and his brother, imprisoned by the insensate power of the law. Who would watch over them? And then there was Rachel, alone in her grief. He began to see behind the smile that Judge Madewood had put on each time they had left his chambers for the courtroom and, almost as though the judge spoke from the backseat of the truck, his words rang out through time, "Onward, clothed in the awesome majesty of the law."

Leaving the town behind, they barreled down a two-lane blacktop heading for the swamp. Emile's lips were tight, his eyes shadowed with thought.

Dylan felt the silence almost like a veil between them. He ripped through it. "You gonna throw me to the gators for my smart mouth, Emile, or is this a secret mission?"

Emile shelved his thoughts and glanced at Dylan. "I don't think our gators would have you, and I've shut down all the missions for today. Relax and enjoy the scenery."

As they slowed down in front of Anthony Fama's Mercantile, the gray-haired regulars on the wide front porch interrupted their "spittin' and whittlin' " long enough to wave at them. A black-and-tan feist rose from his nap on the steps, barking twice as they turned right on the shell road that intersected the blacktop.

Emile took off his tie and threw it into the backseat. When he turned on the radio, strains of fiddle and accordion filled the truck, accompanied by a soulful voice singing about his lost love "Jolé Blond."

The Blazer wound along next to the cane fields paralleling the bayou. Its dark surface glinted in the diluted afternoon light. In a flash of white, a snowy egret sailed from the top of a tall tree on the opposite bank, leveling out over the water. Dylan watched the dual flight of the bird in air and water, tracking them on the left. As they outdistanced it, it arced smoothly across the bayou and settled in the shallows of the far shoreline, standing like a watchful spirit at the swamp's perimeter.

Five minutes later, Emile parked under a tin-roofed shed on a narrow strip of land between road and water. It joined a board-and-batten cypress cabin with a gallery facing the bayou. A homemade pirogue and a ten-foot aluminum bateau floated next to a small, weathered dock.

Emile got out, walked over to a battered row of school lockers standing in a corner of the shed, and began changing into khakis and a blue chambray shirt. Reaching into another locker, he tossed Dylan a rumpled sheriff's uniform and a pair of muddy cowboy boots, a size too large.

Dylan picked the boots up, beating them together to knock the mud off. "Have these things ever been cleaned, Emile?"

"They'll do for where you're going—unless you want to look pretty for the cottonmouths."

"Cottonmouths—this late in the year?"

"We haven't had a good cold snap yet." Emile hung his suit in a locker. "This front coming through now might send 'em inside for the winter."

Dylan surveyed the building. Another bateau hung from the rafters on nylon straps, and a ten-horse Mercury was screwed down tight to a two-by-four nailed to the wall. Hunting and fishing gear hung from nails and cluttered the shelves and floor. "Don't you ever have any of this stuff stolen?"

"Nobody gets up this way much but the locals." Emile headed for the dock. "The oil companies really opened up the basin though, with the canals they dug to get their drilling rigs in."

101

Dylan clomped along behind Emile in his muddy, too-big cowboy boots.

Emile knelt down on the dock next to the pirogue. "We're getting more and more of those big bass boats and houseboats every year."

"Signs and portents, Emile. Some people might call it progress." Dylan stared with misgiving at the fragile craft Emile had begun to untie from the dock. "I hate to ruin your fun, Emile, but I'd just as soon step into a floating syrup bucket as that thing. You sure it'll hold both of us?"

"If you can't trust the local fuzz, who can you trust?"

Dylan gave the bateau a longing glance.

"Maybe you're right," Emile shrugged, retying the pirogue and climbing down into the bateau. "C'mon. We've only got a couple of hours of daylight left."

As Dylan stepped into the bateau, the oversized boots threw him. The bateau thrashed back and forth in the water, forcing him to do a balancing act until Emile grabbed the side of the dock, steadying the boat.

Emile stared at Dylan, shaking his head back and forth slowly. "Forty years traveling these swamps and I'll end up drowned by a redneck in baggy pants."

"Sorry."

"You just sit still and straight," Emile instructed, "and I'll try to keep us dry."

Emile paddled directly across the dark, glassy-smooth bayou toward a black willow, its fall-dry leaves hanging down to the water's surface. As they got closer, Dylan noticed a narrow opening in the leafy wall. They passed through it into a ten-foot wide channel and the premature twilight of the towering tupelo gums, cypress, and sycamores. The silence, immediate and overwhelming, fell upon them. Striated light of a pale gold color reached downward from the crowns of the trees. Only the gurgle of Emile's paddle and Dylan's suppressed breathing marked their passage.

Time seemed to have lost its way among the arboreal pathways of the ancient place. Dylan felt that it must have changed little since the Acadians first came here more than two hundred years before.

A sudden brightness brought them into the lake.

Emile rested his paddle across the gunwales, letting the bateau glide toward the afternoon sun. "Can you see why we love this country?"

Awed by the beauty of the lake, Dylan took a few moments to reply. "I didn't even know a place like this existed! Look at the size of those cypress!"

"This place has been in my family for a *long* time." Emile sounded like a father talking about his firstborn son. "You've only seen the parts of the basin that the federal government has 'improved.' This is the way all of it used to be."

Dylan saw that the lake was an irregular oval of about a hundred yards across and three hundred yards running north and south. Lily pads fringed the entire perimeter like a living green necklace. Cypress crowded the shoreline, august and gray-bearded, "stoic old men" of the deep and ancient swamp.

Emile paddled toward a houseboat made of weathered cypress with a wooden deck built on a steel barge, anchored twenty-five yards from shore. He backpaddled, stopping the bateau inches from an opening in the low railing bordering the houseboat.

"You sit still, 'Big Boots.' I didn't come this far to have you capsize us now."

"Hey, you're talking to an officer of the court! How about a little respect?"

Emile grunted, pulling the stern of the boat around.

Dylan glanced down at his borrowed boots, afraid they'd cause him to stumble into the lake. "Where did these things come from, anyway?"

Tying off the stern, Emile motioned for Dylan to do the same with the bowline. "Who knows? They might have belonged to a prisoner."

"Great! He probably had toe-rot."

Emile gripped the side of the houseboat with one hand and the bateau with the other, holding it steady. "Let's see if you can climb aboard, cowboy."

Adjusting for the size of his boots, Dylan swung smoothly onto the houseboat.

"Just like a real swamp rat," Emile admitted, following Dylan.

From the modest height of the houseboat, the lake's dark surface became transformed into a huge mirror as the sun continued to fall from the narrow slice of sky above the swamp. Streamers of Spanish moss hanging from the cypress were backlit, bright around the edges, dark gray in the center.

Emile fetched a couple of cane-backed chairs from inside and the two of them sat facing the shadowed western shore. Cicadas droned in the trees.

"This is where I come alive, Dylan." Emile's voice sounded almost drowsy, as though sleep lingered on the edge of it. "Robert and I spent a lot of weekends out here."

Dylan couldn't remember Emile's speaking of his son even once since he got the news that Robert had been killed in the Tet Offensive. *He's finally coming to terms with it. Maybe that's why he wanted me to come out here.*

"You get to see the grandkids much?"

"Not a lot." Emile ran his hands through his hair, leaning forward on his elbows. "Mary's living in Dallas now. I think the memories here were too much for her."

Dylan watched a blue heron lift out of the shallows at the south end of lake, climb the darkening air, and disappear beyond the towering line of cypress.

"Anne gets home every month or so." Emile spoke of his other child as though cloaking himself with family against the pain and the loss.

"Where is she?"

"New Orleans. She's doing commercial artwork now," Emile replied, rubbing his chin between thumb and forefinger. "Says she's doing some serious painting on her own time, but it doesn't pay the bills."

"Sounds like a sensible girl."

"She is," Emile agreed. "You'd like her. Maybe you'll get to meet her sometime when she comes home."

"You're not spoiling them grandbabies, are you?"

"Certainly not!" Emile stood up, walking over to the rail.

"Mary says I am, but then what does she know? She's never been a granddaddy."

"I think that's when seeing so many kids getting their lives messed up really started bothering me—since I had grandchildren." Emile walked slowly along next to the railing as he talked. " 'Course, we never used to have much crime down here either; hardly ever had a divorce, no drugs at all. No use thinking that way though. Like old Thomas Wolfe said, 'You can't go home again.' "

Dylan was slightly surprised at the literary reference.

Emile stopped, staring at the tea-colored water. "Speaking of kids, don't forget about that Batiste boy."

"I won't."

"That's a real puzzle. In the last twenty-five years I've dealt with every parish in this state I guess, but I've never had this kind of problem getting cooperation."

"Don't worry about it. We'll get it straightened out."

"You want a shot of coffee?"

"Might as well."

Emile opened the door leading into the houseboat. "Just be a minute."

Muffled kitchen sounds wafted from inside the houseboat, which rocked slightly as Emile moved about. When Dylan looked out across the lake again, a yearling whitetail had materialized on the far shore. Caught by the last sunlight slanting through the trees, the animal glowed a warm brown.

Flanked by two thick cypress knees, the deer glanced about, testing the breeze, pawed the surface clear of vegetation, and bent down for a drink. At that moment, a swirling of water disturbed the vegetation forty yards to the left. The deer jerked his head up, but, seeing nothing, continued to drink. As he turned to leave, the still, dark surface exploded in geysers of white water and tumbling lily pads.

The steel-trap jaws of the alligator raked across the back and side of the bewildered fawn, severing the spine. Then he vanished.

Lying in the shallows, eyes glazed with shock, the yearling kicked feebly, trying to get to his feet. Just out from the shore, hooded eyes like black walnut shells, along with a length of dark ridges appeared on the surface. The silence was complete except for the faint splashing of the yearling.

With a flick of its massive tail, the alligator moved forward, slowly and deliberately grasped the yearling's hindquarters and slid backward into the depths of the lake. A reddish-brown froth slowly began dissipating in the opening where the covering of vegetation had been torn apart.

Emile stood just outside the door, lowering the .30–.30 from his shoulder. "Let's go inside."

Dylan got up and followed him into the houseboat.

The kitchen counter held a two-burner stove and a stainless steel sink. Above it a length of window looked out across the lake. Emile stood in front of the stove, dipping boiling water from a pot with a demitasse. Pouring it slowly into the top of a scratched, dented coffeepot, he waited for it to drip through, then added more. A rich aroma filled the kitchen.

Sitting down at a metal table with a white enameled top, Dylan watched Emile pour the two cups of rich, dark coffee. Stirring in a spoon of sugar, he stared at a patch of purple sky through the span of glass.

Emile sat down heavily. "Why don't you leave that rat race up the river, Dylan?"

"And do what?"

"Come work for me."

Dylan took a sip of the sweet, hot coffee. "All the probation and parole is handled by the state."

"I want you to be my chief deputy when I get elected sheriff," Emile said earnestly, staring across the table. "We've got a good bunch of boys now—loyal, honest, hardworking—but they don't have much education and times are changing fast. You know criminal law *and* the juvenile laws—even attorneys don't know much about the juvenile system."

Surprised by the offer, Dylan didn't know what to say. He was more accustomed to people wanting to get rid of him.

Emile leaned forward, elbows on the table. "You don't belong in all those tall buildings and traffic jams; people from all over the country up there—talking funny. It just ain't a civilized way to live, Dylan."

Dylan smiled. "It's mighty tempting after seeing how pretty this place is down here."

Emile felt Dylan coming over to his side.

"But I'm trying to put my marriage back together." Dylan leaned back in the chair, his face growing cloudy. "If I moved down here that would finish it. Susan barely lasted six months on my place out in the Felicianas."

Giving Dylan a level stare, Emile declared bluntly, "And when you moved back to town with her, the two of you *still* couldn't make it together."

"You just might be onto something there."

"Susan's a fine girl from what I know of her. Comes from a good family, but you two are about as different as two people can be."

"They say opposites attract."

"Maybe, but with you two it's like pairing a butterfly with a billy goat."

Dylan downed the rest of his coffee. "Don't think you can flatter me into taking that job, Emile."

"Let's go back outside," Emile grinned. "It's pretty enough this time of day to make *you* pay *me* to work down here."

"Maybe so," Dylan agreed, "but I'd have to have something to pay you *with* first."

Standing up, Emile collected their cups and washed them in the tiny sink. Then he paused before going out the door. "Think about my offer, Dylan. I think you'd like living down here with us Cajuns and our watery ways."

Sitting back on the deck, Dylan gazed out across the lake as individual trees on the far shore crowded together to form a solid wall against the coming night. The absent sun had brushed the air above them with streaks of gold and rose and violet. Three early stars appeared in the sky and in the lake.

Standing next to his car parked on the courthouse square, Dylan waved at Emile as he made a U-turn and headed home.

The night marshall, his cap resting down on his ears and his khakis bagging in the seat, strolled by making his early rounds.

Across the street, the neon-bright window of Paw-Paw's Café framed a man and a woman and two ice cream sundaes on the table between them. She reached across the table with her good arm, taking the hand of the bald man with the smiling red face. They leaned forward and kissed.

Dylan leaned back against his car, a flicker of hope rising in his spirit. He believed that he would never understand what brought a man and a woman together—and what kept them together. *Maybe there's hope for us yet.*

Dylan got into the car and turned the key in the ignition. His heart sank as he heard only a dull clicking sound. With a groan of disgust, he put the gearshift into neutral, got out, and began pushing, his left hand on the doorframe, his right on the steering wheel. When he got the car up to a slow crawl he jumped in, jammed it into first, and popped the clutch. With a cough and a sputter, the engine caught, and, with a sigh of relief, he revved it up.

The streets of Evangeline were quiet as Dylan drove past the old turn-of-the-century houses heading out of town. An occasional porch light and the blue-white glare of television sets through windows broke the darkness.

Crossing the old turnstile bridge over the bayou, Dylan headed north toward the city on Highway 1 along the west bank of the Mississippi. Soon he hit the frenzy of grinding season, passing through Cinclare Plantation. Tractors towed buggies piled high with cane from the local fields while flatbed trucks roared along the highway from the more distant ones, all drawn to the sugar mill like bees to their hive. Stalks of cane lay scattered along the blacktop and the dirt side roads, casualties in the race to beat the first hard freeze of the year.

Rising out of the fields, the mill itself stood between the highway and the levee in faint silhouette against the distant glow of city lights. Clouds of smoke rose into the night air from fires burning the leaves off of the stalks of cane.

The scene reminded Dylan of the Celtic celebration of

Samhain. He could almost see hooded Druid priests making their grisly rounds in the countryside, collecting offerings for their celebration of all things cold and dead on their night of fire and the powers of darkness.

8

BLUE-LIGHT SPECIAL

Through a series of electric buzzers and metallic clangs, Dylan made his way to a long corridor at the rear section of the downtown jail. On his left, the dayroom was sparsely fitted with benches on three walls and a single metal table with built-in seats sunk into the center of the concrete floor. Fifteen or twenty men wearing orange jumpsuits sat in small groups or stood about, smoking, playing cards, talking; two of them were merely staring into space with the empty, hopeless gaze of incarceration.

Several of the prisoners walked over to the bars that lined the corridor side of the dayroom. Some held onto the cold iron; others dangled their arms limply, resting them on the cross braces.

"Hey, Dylan. When am I goin' to court, man? This place is killin' me."

"Tell that Public Defender to git hisself up here. I ain't seed him in a month."

"Mr. St. John, would you please mail dis letter for me? I ain't got no mo' stamps."

Dylan walked over to try and placate some of the men he knew and some that he didn't. They *all* knew there was little or nothing he could do for them, but most had been forgotten, abandoned, and it gave them a thread of hope, a brief glimpse of something outside their barred and barren existence, a touch of a world where despair and boredom and fear came in much smaller portions.

"Come on, St. John, that bunch'll keep you all day if you let

111

'em." The burly deputy, using a blunt key in a ring of about twenty hanging on a heavy belt draped below his belly, opened a gray metal door across from the dayroom.

Dylan stepped into a narrow hall, lined on each side by three solid iron doors. All were closed except the last one on the left. A high window at the far end filtered sunlight in through years of dust and old spider webs.

"What a nice place!" Dylan turned back to the deputy. "Ya'll have family rates on the weekends?"

The deputy's mouth twitched, but seemed unable to form a smile. "Only place we got to keep the juveniles separate from the adult population. That's the law, you know."

"Yeah, I heard that somewhere."

"I'll be back to get you in ten minutes." He slammed the heavy door and locked it.

Walking down the hall, Dylan stopped at the last door, then stepped inside. It took his eyes a while to adjust to the darkened cell. A battered iron cot stood against the wall to the right. On its stained mattress ticking and striped pillow, Remy slept on, undisturbed.

Near the opposite wall a round hole gaped darkly in the floor. Near it a foul liquid was pooled in small hollows of the rough concrete. The air in the cell reeked of urine and years of unwashed bodies.

"You're not much of a housekeeper, Remy." Dylan stared down at the boy, remembering back two years. He had grown considerably, balanced between child and young man.

Remy stirred, stretched, opened his sleep-dulled eyes, and struggled up into the ruin of his youth. His hair still hung down in his eyes. "Hi, Mr. Dylan. You're the *last* person I expected to see in *this* place."

"I didn't know if I'd ever see you again *anywhere*, Remy. I'm sorry it's here." Dylan thought of other boys in their troubled teens whom he had seen in places like this one. He glanced at Remy's standard-issue orange jumpsuit. "Does that space suit come with a helmet?"

Remy smiled as he always had at Dylan's corny jokes. He gazed at Dylan's slightly rumpled pants and jacket. "Looks like you started shopping the blue-light specials at K-Mart. You used to dress pretty good."

Dylan thought of his dirty clothes hamper and closet back at his apartment. Since Susan left he could barely find two socks that matched. "Not anymore. They don't pay me enough for that." Dylan kept a straight face. "I get to the Salvation Army box early though—you know, before all the good stuff's gone."

That got a laugh from Remy. Then he rubbed the sleep from his face.

Dylan surveyed the room again. "They didn't let your mama back here, did they?"

"No sir. They took me to a room up front."

"Good. She's got enough to worry about without knowing you're in a place like this."

"The lawyer came back here though," Remy went on. "When can I get out of here?"

"I'm working on that right now. Emile asked me to get you transferred back home." Dylan held Remy's gaze. "But I need your help. Why did you go after Donaldson?"

Remy looked away, hanging his head, arms resting on his knees, hands clasped in front of him.

"Remy, do you trust me?"

He glanced up, brushing his hair back from his face with his left hand. "Yessir."

"You remember back when Buck was beating your mama up almost every night and you finally told me about it?"

Remy nodded. "You took him out for a cup of coffee one day and he didn't do it anymore after that."

"Well, if you tell me what went on between you and Donaldson, I might be able to straighten this out too."

As he stared into Dylan's eyes, Remy's voice trembled slightly, "You was always straight with me, Mr. Dylan, but I just can't do it."

Dylan decided to pull out all the stops to try to get Remy out of his untenable position. "Your mama's in pretty bad shape now with both her boys locked up."

Remy stared at the floor.

"There's not much chance of getting Russel out right now,"

Dylan continued, playing his trump card, "but you could be home taking care of her."

Remy looked up again, tears flooding his solemn brown eyes and spilling out onto his cheeks. He hung his head again, shaking it slowly back and forth.

"I have to be going, then. If you change your mind, tell the deputy named Jerry you want to see me—nobody else."

Remy nodded.

Dylan knew the boy well enough to realize there was nothing to be gained from continuing. He sat down next to Remy on the cot, placing his hand on the boy's shoulder. "One other thing."

"Yessir."

"Don't tell your lawyer or anyone else I was here—and take care of yourself." Dylan felt helpless, but now even more determined to get the boy out. "Anything I can get you?"

"Get me out of here."

"I'm trying, Remy. I'm trying."

———

"Jerry, what can you tell me about the Batiste kid?" Dylan probed.

"From Maurepas Parish. That's about all I know," Jerry shrugged.

"This is his first offense. How come he's not being sent back to the parish of residence?"

"Beats me," Jerry replied absently, shuffling the bureaucracy's paper lifeline. "They never tell us nothing."

"Well, let me know if you come up with anything." Dylan turned to walk over to the elevator.

"Hold it a minute," Jerry called out. "I forgot the simplest thing." He opened the heavy green-backed blotter, running his finger down the left column. "Here it is. 'Hold for corrections, Juvenile Department.' I thought there was something a little different about this."

Dylan walked back to the counter. A gunmetal glint shone in his eyes as he placed his hand, palm down, on the stack of forms Jerry was sorting through. "This is important. Did anything else unusual happen with Remy?"

Jerry started to protest, noticed the change in Dylan's face, and scratched his head instead. "There was this *one* thing."

Dylan remained patient.

"Donneley . . . no—"

"Donaldson."

"That's it!" Jerry snapped his fingers. "That feller who's top dog in the juvenile office."

"He came to see Remy?"

"Yeah. Surprised me too!" Jerry glanced at his papers. "We don't get the shiny-shoe fellers in here much. Kinda favored them Yankee lawyers."

"Interesting."

"I seen him on television before, but I never expected him to show up in *this* place."

"Thanks, Jerry."

"Anytime, Dylan."

Dylan took the jail elevator down to the basement, then walked up the stairs leading to the front lobby of the courthouse. Beneath a marble arch at the main entrance, three deputies sat at a folding table. Another searched a bearded, bushy-haired man of about thirty, wearing tight jeans, cowboy boots, and an expression of contempt.

Stepping outside, Dylan glanced up at the admonition posted on placards attached to both sides of the wide glass doors, *Everyone entering courthouse is subject to a search of his person.*

"Hey, Dylan. Is that the latest fad?" A grin spread across George Newton's wide face as he glanced at Dylan's ankles. "One black sock and one blue one." Newton sported his new sergeant stripes and commanded the three deputies like Patton did his tanks.

Trying to look like Jimmy Stewart in *It's a Wonderful Life* after he got kicked out of the bar, Dylan leaned over the table, glancing around furtively. "George, maybe you can help me. I need somebody with pull."

Newton stopped laughing, puffed himself up a little, and leaned back in his chair, arms crossed over his barrel chest. "What kinda trouble you in now?"

"City police caught me sleeping in my car."

"So what."

"They arrested me for impersonating a deputy."

Dylan had a full second to get out of Newton's way before he rocked forward, swinging a roundhouse right where Dylan's head had been.

Walking down the wide stone steps beneath the spreading live oaks, Dylan listened to George's fading commentary about his ancestry and personal life. Following St. Phillip Street to North Boulevard, Dylan crossed it at the same spot where the past summer a child had cried out for his mother—and died. He forced the memory from his mind.

Taking Third Street north toward the capitol, Dylan stopped briefly at the Paramount Theatre, looking over the ad for *Easy Rider* with Peter Fonda, Dennis Hopper, and Jack Nicholson. *Somebody said they shot part of that at Blackie's Café over in Morganza. Maybe Susan would go see it with me.*

As he crossed Florida Street, Dylan glanced to his left. The sun had begun sliding down the sky toward the cane fields across the river, but its brightness held little warmth. He continued on into the shadows of the stores and office buildings glancing at the slow afternoon traffic. A few people trickled along the sidewalk in the calm before rush hour.

In front of the State Library a man of about sixty—or maybe forty, it was hard to tell—wearing a pea coat and a week's growth of stubble going to beard, lay asleep on a wooden bench. He clutched a quart of Gallo to his chest, a few ounces of the liquid glowing redly near his heart. Asleep, there was something inviolate about him, his face serene as a child's—but night was closing in. Dylan wondered what demons would circle his bench as he slipped back into the netherworld?

Staring down at the man, Dylan took out his wallet and peered inside—not a shekel, not a sou. He wrote, "IOU five dollars," on the back of his business card and tucked it between the man's arm and the bottle. *At least I'm not drinking that stuff, not sleeping on a downtown bench in the daytime.* Even as he thought the words, others came right on their heels, *Not yet, you're not!*

As Dylan continued north he glanced up at the capitol building, towering against the autumn sky, but his mind had already taken another turn. He pictured his grandfather, a Baptist preacher for most of his seventy-four years. With his wild white mane of hair, he had the appearance of an Old Testament prophet. He would not have tolerated the man on the bench, would have awakened him and preached the evils of alcohol to him from the Word. ". . . nor drunkards . . . shall inherit the kingdom of God."

Dylan suddenly longed for the times he would sit and talk with his grandfather in the little book-filled, schoolroom-smelling office in the grove of pine trees behind his house. *All those years I could have gone up there anytime I wanted—now he's dead and buried, and it's too late.*

Neither of Oliver St. John's sons fulfilled his desire for a spiritual heir to follow in his footsteps in the preaching profession, so he looked past them to his first grandson. In the old man's heart, Dylan had become his youngest son and his final hope that the anointing to preach the gospel would continue in his own flesh and blood.

Dylan's birth was announced from the platform of the old tabernacle at the midsummer convention during Oliver St. John's twelve-year reign as State Overseer. He lifted his firstborn grandson in his arms before the entire congregation and anointed him from a horn of oil as Samuel had done with David three thousand years before.

Dylan remembered the last time he had seen his grandfather, shortly before his death. He had spoken of the old times when he was a young preacher pastoring three churches, riding to them on horseback. Not once did he mention his hope for Dylan's life, but in those fiery, gentle eyes the longing remained.

When her husband had died, Dylan's grandmother had returned to the little Mississippi town of her birth to spend her remaining years. Dylan pictured her, slim and neat, her rich brown hair going gray. He thought of the summers they had worked together in her flower gardens when he was a child, sharing lemonade on the porch, cool evening breezes and the plaintive cry of the whippoorwill, and her reading the Bible to him at bedtime.

Whenever Dylan heard the word *Christian*, he thought of his grandmother.

Donaldson took office space in the Pentagon Courts, original site of the state university, and before that, Pentagon Barracks, military headquarters for France, England, Spain, and finally the United States. It was home to Zachary Taylor and birthplace of his son, who became a Confederate general.

In 1861 the Louisiana State Guard overcame the United States troops housed there, taking the garrison and the arsenal. A year later, the Confederate General Breckinridge fought a desperate battle with the Union army and navy under Williams and Farragut.

Grant, Lee, and Sherman walked the grounds, as did Clay, Lincoln, and Jefferson Davis.

In marked contrast to Donaldson's office, Dylan's—where most of the parole officers were sons of the Deep South—was an abandoned warehouse, former site of an auction barn and before that stables and feed sheds.

Dylan mused on the southern attitude toward progress. With the opening of the oil and gas industries and the chemical plants along the river from Baton Rouge to New Orleans, the modern-day carpetbaggers flocked into south Louisiana like immigrants to a foreign land. They climbed for the best plums while the southerners sat around waiting for them to fall off the trees. *Maybe we deserved to lose the war.*

Dylan entered the building to the rich smell of age and floor polish. His footsteps on the heart pine floor echoed flatly as he crossed the lobby toward the men's room under the painted gaze of long-dead governors and generals. Inside he stared at the black-and-white tile and the mirror's unforgiving scrutiny of him in a blaze of neon.

I could be a cross between the winner of a worst-dressed contest and an unsuccessful hit man. Gotta quit working so many nights. My eyes are starting to look kinda nutty.

After a few moments with soap and water, Dylan quit trying to improve the unimprovable, combed his thick dark hair back with his fingers and slowly shook his head. *Donaldson probably won't see me anyway—even if he's in. In the year I worked for his de-*

partment, he only spoke to me once. The distance between upper management and the field, Dylan knew, could be measured in light-years.

Dylan walked over to the receptionist, ensconced behind her desk. She was perfect—not beautiful, not even very pretty, just perfect—hair, nails, dress, the whole works. And she stared at Dylan as if he were something she had just stepped in.

"I'd like to see Mr. Donaldson, please."

"Miss Perfect" wore an expression of superiority laced liberally with pain. Dylan could almost feel her wiping him off her shoe.

"Do you have an appointment?"

"Not yet, but I'm expecting a call from the governor any day now—I hope its something in Administration."

Not a trace of a smile on the rouged and powdered face.

"Sorry, bad joke. No, I do *not* have an appointment."

"Please have a seat." She pointed a perfect finger to a chair in the remotest corner of the room and, after Dylan sat down, picked up the phone.

Ten seconds later, Donaldson walked out of his office at a brisk pace, exuding all the energy of a five-year-old after a meal of Hershey bars. "Dylan, good to see you again."

"Huh?"

Donaldson grabbed his hand, pumping it vigorously, pulling him from the chair as he directed him toward the office. "Come on in. What's on your mind?"

"How do you get your hair to stay in place like that?"

A quick furrow passed over Donaldson's smooth brow, but he passed it off.

What a stupid thing to say! Think before you open your big mouth! He did *ask what was on my mind, though.*

Donaldson's secretary peered wide-eyed over her shoulder. Following Donaldson, Dylan half-turned toward her, blowing on his nails, polishing them on his shirt front. Then it hit him! *Something's wrong here!* The temperature in his chest started to plummet as he entered the inner sanctum.

Donaldson's office, reflecting the man, was all dark wood and polished brass, redolent of an English pub. Incongruously, framed and matted prints of the New Orleans Mardi Gras hung garishly from the heavy paneling.

"What can I do for you, Dylan?"

Dylan swung his gaze around to Donaldson. He was also perfect. Streaked with the exact amount of gray that women call "distinguished," his dark styled hair shone with care. His camel's hair jacket and wool tie combined the casual with command.

Careful, you're in uncharted country here, and you have seldom paid any attention whatsoever to the compass. "Well, uh, Mr. Donaldson, there's a boy in the downtown jail that I'm kinda worried about." Dylan felt like a first-time truant sent to the principal's office.

Donaldson nodded for him to continue.

"His mother lives in Maurepas Parish, and I'm trying to get jurisdiction transferred so he can stay with her 'til he goes to court here."

Donaldson placed his arms on his desk, leaning toward Dylan, the expression on his face sage and concerned. "This kind of deplorable condition that the children of this state are subjected to is precisely what I have resolved to ameliorate and eventually extirpate. We must bring government home to the people in order to forge a better future for our children. Do you agree?"

Trying to remember what "extirpate" meant, Dylan mumbled, "Yessir, I do."

"This business of detaining juveniles in adult facilities like the downtown jail is particularly repugnant to me," Donaldson continued his elegy. "I'm thinking of giving consideration to a number of alternatives to this, one of which might be drafting a list of remedial possibilities."

Mired in the quicksand of Donaldson's grandiose words, Dylan had almost forgotten why he was in the office.

"Substantial progress has been made in this area; however, there are propitious options as yet unexplored. I'd like to hear your ideas on this. By the way, why did you leave us? It always pains me to lose one of our promising young probation officers."

Dylan had the feeling that Donaldson had sharpened his words and dipped them in curare before flinging them in his direction. "I, uh, don't really know. Guess I just haven't decided what I want to do yet."

"Well, no one knows what the future holds, but we would be pleased to have you back with us. Is there anything else I can do for you?"

Anything else! Did he do something for me? "Just a minute. I think it slipped my mind. Oh, yeah, what about the boy in jail, Remy Batiste?"

"Remy Batiste, Remy Batiste—that name sounds familiar. Yes, yes, now I remember. He's the young man who came to my office last week . . . extremely upset over something." Donaldson seemed lost in thought. "One of the Capitol guards had to subdue him. I never was able to determine exactly what the problem was. Seems there was a younger brother in New Orleans."

Donaldson stood up and walked over to the window, hands clasped behind his back. When he turned back toward Dylan, the light, for an instant, caught a face mired in anguish. Then he straightened up and regained his composure. "You know, Dylan, I even saw him briefly in jail, but he was totally recalcitrant."

Dylan remembered what "recalcitrant" meant.

"I see as many of these kids as my schedule permits, but I must admit that some of them are not amendable to any type of rehabilitation." Donaldson gave Dylan a paternal stare. "Some of them even respond to my kindness by trying to besmirch my reputation."

Donaldson paused before continuing, "However, a man in my position must studiously avoid any hint of impropriety and even the suggestion of using his government position for personal gain."

Feeling that he was about to doze off, Dylan abruptly sat up straight.

"This has always been my practice and always will be." Donaldson's voice rose as if building toward a big finish. "There are many issues we wrestle with daily, but always at the forefront must remain our commitment to keeping our promises to the people we represent."

By this time, Dylan could not have repeated one word that Donaldson had spoken. As Donaldson paused to breathe, Dylan blurted out, "Can you let Remy go live with his mother 'til the court date?"

"What?"

"The boy in jail."

"Don't give it another thought."

After the heavy barrage of words thrown out against him, Dylan felt victory coming too easily. "You'll have the hold on him dropped?"

"What hold?"

"At the jail," Dylan explained. "There's a 'Hold for Corrections' on the books."

"Must be some sort of misunderstanding. Don't worry about it." Donaldson dismissed the problem with a flick of his wrist. "Remember, Dylan, what appears to be is not always the truth, and the truth is not always what it appears to be."

What's that got to do with getting Remy out of jail? Dylan stood up.

Donaldson had turned away, staring out the window at a frail and ancient-looking grounds keeper in overalls raking leaves in the courtyard.

Feeling that he had survived the meeting unscathed so far, Dylan walked quietly over to the exit, hoping to leave without Donaldson starting up again. He opened the door quietly, but Donaldson went on from across the room, "Dylan . . ."

What now? "Yessir."

"Keep smiling."

Keep smiling?

Outside in the reception area, "Miss Perfect," her desk cleared away for five o'clock, glanced up from her emery board long enough to glare at him.

Feeling good about his meeting with Donaldson, Dylan blew her a kiss on his way out the door.

9

ANOTHER DREAM

Ten minutes past five and the office was deserted, typewriters asleep under their covers, the heat turned off. Dylan walked down to Wes's office, took his size forty-eight field jacket from the hook on the door, and put it on. Going back to his own office, Dylan sat down at his desk and called Emile. He was on his way home, so Elaine, his secretary, patched the call through.

"That you, Dylan?"

Dylan sensed the urgency in Emile's voice, although it was partially garbled by static. "Yeah. I just left Donaldson's office a few minutes ago."

"He actually saw you?"

"Scary, ain't it? I just went there on a whim." Dylan pulled the jacket around him against the chill of the office.

"What did he say?"

Dylan tried to remember the smoke screen of words that Donaldson had laid down in his office. "I have no idea what most of it meant. I think he's going to let Remy go home with his mother, though."

"You think it'll be that simple?"

"We'll just have to wait and see." Dylan took a switchblade knife with a stag handle out of his desk drawer. He remembered the night he took it from a bearded Vietnam veteran in a smokey barroom after he had put him under arrest for parole violation.

"The wheels of justice grind a little slower up here, Emile."

"Grease 'em a little, then."

123

"I just might do that," Dylan responded, a plan coming to mind. "I'll go see Judge Madewood. In case something goes wrong, *he* can take care of it if *anybody* can."

"Good." The static cut through Emile's voice. ". . . need to cover all the bases."

"One thing bothers me about this, Emile."

"What?"

"Donaldson went to see Remy in jail." Dylan flicked the knife with a snap of his wrist. It sunk deep into the door facing, quivering like a tuning fork. "He talked all around it but never gave me a straight reason."

"Typical reaction for a politician, even an appointed one like Donaldson." Emile's voice held a subdued contempt. "Anything suspicious looking, like Remy busting into his office the way he did, and they go on automatic camouflage whether they did anything wrong or not."

"Maybe you're right."

"Going to see him in jail is strictly out of character, though," Emile conceded. "That's too much like having a *real* job. What did Remy tell you?"

"Nothing at all," Dylan admitted. "I figured he'd say *anything* to get out of that place too."

"Well, keep in touch," Emile suggested. "I'll go out and tell Rachel what's going on with her boy."

"Good idea."

"And, Dylan . . ."

"Yeah."

"I appreciate this."

"Don't be too generous yet. I've got a feeling we're just getting started on this one."

As Dylan hung the phone up, a sudden chill hit him. He pulled the too-large jacket closer around him, staring out into the gloom of the office.

The November wind moaned in the eaves of the old building like a restless autumn spirit, eager for the coming of winter and warm sleep. There would be no heat in the place until the janitor came in at 5:00 A.M.

Dylan began to hurry through his files, getting some names

and addresses for the coming night's arrest run, but his mind was still digging through the trash pile of the past two hours, trying to find some incriminating evidence—some clue as to the real story behind Donaldson's fancy-worded facade.

Donaldson's a real puzzler: welcoming me like the prodigal son returned, actually going into a smelly jail to see Remy—all strictly out of character for management types like him. Then this business about visiting other kids who are locked up when his schedule lets him. Maybe it's part of his game plan to impress people with his hands-on leadership—or maybe it's all a lie. What's he covering up? Child labor? Drugs? Staff incompetence? Must be something that could cost him his job.

Forget it, Dylan! Get Remy back home with his mother, and just forget it!

Writing names and addresses in a steno pad, Dylan leaned back in his chair, sorting through a stack of case files in his lap. He sang a song under his breath, "Makin' a list, Checkin' it twice, Gonna find out who's . . ."

Dylan tied a red bandana across his face in the manner of hold-up men in the old black-and-white western movies of the thirties and forties. His patrol had hit the twelve-foot-tall elephant grass, and the pollen it gave off choked the men on the blistering hot, sultry days in South Vietnam. Four inches wide at the base, the blades of the grass were dull green and deadly, their edges like razors.

Through the forest of grass the men walked single file, strung out at two- and three-yard intervals. Every forty-five minutes a shot rang out a quarter of a mile to the northeast—a Vietcong scout tracking them, giving their location to his comrades.

Dylan trudged along behind Corporal Vince Cannelli, a stocky, curly-haired baker from Queens who hit fifty-nine out of sixty on the rifle range even though he had never picked up a rifle before enlisting in the marines. The two men had become fast friends with a fierce loyalty that only another marine could understand.

At 14:30 hours the elephant grass thinned away and the village appeared, bamboo and straw hooches located near the bank of a sluggish coulee coated with algae. Dylan had smelled the place two minutes ear-

lier—the reek of animal dung, dead fish, and dog boiling in an iron pot over a fire pit.

The men dropped their packs heavily to the ground at the edge of the tree line. Canteens sloshed, lighters clicked open, and cigarette smoke rose in the heavy, breathless air. Over in the village, children played with a mangy dog on the bare ground between the straw-roofed hooches.

"Another day of humping," Cannelli grunted, taking a long pull on his canteen.

"Yeah, but it ain't all bad," Dylan muttered. His fatigues, soaked with sweat, would turn white and crusty with salt when they dried. "We get to set up an ambush tonight. Claymores, flares, the whole works."

Cannelli's bushy eyebrows wriggled like twin caterpillars. "I think you're nuts."

"It beats lying around waiting for them to come after us." Dylan lit a Camel, picked a piece of tobacco from his tongue, and leaned back against a tree.

"What's Carver doing?"

Dylan glanced at the eighteen-year-old Kansas farm boy whose hair was the same color as the wheat he used to harvest. Carver had walked over and squatted down with the children, rubbing one tiny child's head as he offered them candy from his ration pack.

Like a phantom, a woman clad in black pajamas appeared in the shadowed doorway of a nearby hut. She pulled the pin on the grenade held in her right hand, leaped into the sunlight, and sprinted toward Carver.

"Carver! Behind you!" Dylan rolled over, grabbing his M–16 and spinning around with it in one smooth motion, bringing the sight to bear on the woman. A child, his thin frame caked with dirt, wandered aimlessly between Dylan and the woman. Dylan couldn't force his finger to press the trigger. "Carver!"

Carver stood up, turned around, his eyes wide in surprise and disbelief as the woman slammed into him, pressing the grenade between their bodies in a final embrace.

Dylan heard the grenade's muffled thunder, saw a quick red blossoming before he shut his eyes and jerked his head away.

"Uhhh. . . !" Dylan awakened with a sharp intake of breath. Too little sleep had left him with that dead, hollow feeling that he carried during much of his tour of duty in Vietnam.

Rummaging around in his desk drawer, he found a pack of Rolaids and chewed a half-dozen.

The strangers came out of the darkness thirty seconds after Dylan came out of his dream. They both wore felt hats jammed down on the stockings pulled over their heads and faces. The first one slammed a fist into Dylan's stomach as he pushed up from the chair to defend himself.

Dylan felt himself tumbling backward, the chair turning over. His head hit the floor with a sickening thud, sending bright lights spinning around the pain that surged behind his eyes. Half-conscious, he felt heavy shoes slamming into his side and legs as he doubled up, pushing himself against the wall to protect his head and stomach. In seconds it was over.

Lying in the darkness, Dylan heard someone whistling "Bye Bye, Blackbird." It sounded hollow and far away. *The night watchman.*

A few words of the song inserted themselves into Dylan's half-conscious state. *Pack up all my care and woe . . .*

The wind was dying as Dylan stood atop the levee in the first hour of the day. Laid out before him like an ethereal carpet, a white mist floated above the mile-wide expanse of water. Laboring upstream behind a double file of block-long barges piled high with oyster shell, a tug voiced the substance of night on the river with the lonesome moan of its whistle.

To the south, in the glare of the sodium-vapor lamps, steelworkers clambered about on the beams and pilings of the new I–110 bridge. Standing skeletal in the ocher glow of the industrial section three miles to the north, the old Earl Long Bridge blockaded the deep-water vessels.

The muted whine of an eighteen-wheeler followed Dylan as he swallowed the last of his coffee from a paper cup and turned away from the river, toward the levee and back into the city. He walked up the hill to the state parking garage, nursing his bruised ribs and the dull ache in his thigh.

At the moment he sat down on the hood of his car parked in the shadowed ground level, he decided to keep what had happened in the office to himself—at least for the time being. He had gone over his sizeable list of enemies, but had found no suitable candidates for the men who had come at him in the darkness. It had proven to be a frustrating but altogether sobering exercise.

Waiting for the others, Dylan mused on how he had ended up in the cold, damp garage in the middle of the night. For a while the early morning arrest runs had been fun as childhood games had been fun; grown men getting paid for playing cops and robbers. Time had a way of wearing threadbare the fun.

Dave drove up first. He was always first except for the nights Dylan didn't make it home at all. Two years after Dave's divorce, he had married his wife a second time in the universal hope that passion would transcend all differences, conflicts, excesses. It wasn't working out this time either. The evidence of that was on his face as he got out of his Mustang and slammed the door.

"You look like death, Dylan."

"I've always heard if you live with someone long enough, you start to look like 'em."

"Oh no!" Dave moaned, raising his eyes toward the ceiling. "You're not in one of your wounded-poet moods, I hope. I don't think I can handle that tonight."

"You and wifey have a little spat?" Dylan was not in a mood to handle much of anything, either. "Weeds taking over the little vine-covered cottage? Frost on the marriage bed?"

"All of the above!" Dave shot back, anger rising in his voice. "Maybe you can give me some fatherly advice, Ozzie, soon as you and Harriet get back together."

Dylan calmed himself down, knowing it would be a long night with the two of them flinging verbal darts the whole time. "I thought ya'll were getting along better—this last week or two, anyway."

"You know Barbara. She changes like the weather—like the Loooo-siana weather."

Dylan slid off the hood of his car. "You know something—I think I just figured out how we can make enough money to get out of this business."

"I'm ready."

"We've both got investigative experience."

"Yeah. So what."

"Simple. We scour the whole country 'til we find a happily married couple in their twenties—then we sell them to the Smithsonian."

"Capital idea, but too late. The species became extinct on December 16, 1953." Dave sat down, leaning back against one of the massive concrete pillars. "I read all about it in *Newsweek* a couple of months ago."

Dylan squatted down, picking up a few concrete chips and tossing them out into the darkness. "What's the trouble with Barbara this time?"

"She wants to take a trip for Christmas on money we don't have. Says she wants to go somewhere different—someplace she's never been before."

"How'd you get out of it?"

"I told her to try our kitchen—in front of the stove."

"Well, if that didn't make her happy, I don't know what would."

"That's what I thought."

Dylan stood up and shrugged. "Guess you just can't please some women."

A cry of tires on pavement echoed through the cavernous parking garage. Wes's van bumped over the raised entrance, coming to a screeching halt two feet from the concrete pillar Dave was sitting next to.

Dave glanced up at Dylan, an expression of dismay on his face. "Flaps down, landing gear up and locked."

" 'Fraid so," Dylan nodded. "Looks like our boy's off on another chemical flight."

Wes stalked around the van, strapping on his Colt. "Where's the Fudgesicle Man? We need to get this show on the road."

Dave stood up, brushing the grit from his pants. "Eddie'll be here."

"Nice coat you got there, Dylan." Wes stared at his own baggy field jacket hanging on Dylan's lean frame. "You look like a rooster with socks on."

"I didn't make it home to get mine," Dylan replied, rolling up both sleeves. "I'll give it back tomorrow."

Wes waved him off, staring nervously at the entrance to the garage. "No hurry."

Eddie drove in at a sedate five miles an hour in a sedate dark four-door sedan, parking sedately next to Wes's rolling disaster. Wearing a neatly pressed dark suit and tie, he got out and took a tan trench coat from a hanger in back. He folded the coat across his arm and walked toward the other three men.

This was Eddie's first arrest run, and he had marshaled his sartorial defenses.

Dylan glanced at Eddie's get-up. "Sergeant Friday, I presume."

Eddie ignored him, handing a sealed letter to Dave. "Mack called me and said he wanted you and Dylan to meet him at this address in about two hours."

"What do want to do 'til then?" Dylan asked Dave, taking the envelope and tearing it open.

"Hold on there, Dylan! Mack told me this envelope was for Dave."

Dylan glanced up, taking the address out of the envelope. "It's all right, Eddie. I've got Top Secret clearance."

"That's the truth," Wes chimed in. He had been doing side-straddle hops since Eddie drove up. "I was in the office the day President Nixon dropped it off."

Eddie's face had become flushed, and he appeared to be swelling up like a toad.

"By the way, Dylan," Wes continued, breathing a little heavier with the exercise. "I was also in the office when your latest wino friend came by. You owe me five dollars."

"I'll pay you when I sell my dog."

"You ain't got a dog."

"You know I'm good for it on payday, Wes," Dylan assured him. "Don't I always pay off those IOU's?"

"Yeah. Thing I can't figure out is why you do it?" Wes stopped jumping. "All they do is go out and buy more wine."

Dylan pondered the question briefly. "It's all I can think of to do for them."

Dave folded the list he had been looking over and put it in his back pocket. "Henry's overdue. We haven't picked him up in six or eight months now."

"Fine with me." Dylan headed for the car.

"Wait a minute! What about me?" Eddie asked the world at large.

Dylan glanced over at Wes, who had switched to push-ups. "Go with Wes. You'll be safe with him."

"You'd think Henry would learn, sooner or later." Dylan gazed out at the nearly deserted streets. A calico cat, mincing across the dew-wet grass of a front lawn, stopped and stared at him with big yellow eyes as he passed by their car. "If he just pays the restitution, he's home free."

"The man hates to work. Guess he thinks we'll forget about him."

Dylan wondered why Dave hadn't arrested Henry Waller sooner. Sedentary, easy going, and living with his parents, Henry was an easy mark. He could only surmise that his daddy's working for one of the judges for thirty years had to be the reason.

Trying to enforce court orders on men like Henry eventually wears any of us down when so many get turned loose two or three days after you lock 'em up. Politics! It puts a revolving door on the jailhouse.

Five minutes later, Dave pulled over to the curb. The house sat back from the street on a little rise in a cavern of huge cedars and sycamores that blocked most of the light from the street, leaving it near dark and uninviting.

Dylan got out and walked up toward the porch. As he reached the steps, a deep growl rumbled out of the darkness. He took one step backward just before the explosion went off under the house, ending with the clank of a chain snapping taut.

From behind Dylan came the sound of Dave's voice. "First time they've had that monster tied up in months. He never would let me get out of the car."

Turning around, Dylan glared at Dave, leaning against the front fender, his arms folded.

On the front porch, safe from the beast beneath the house, Dylan pounded on the door. In the time-honored tradition of passive resistance, the oldest person in the house answered the door—in this case Henry's daddy. The old man's bald head, fringed with gray, shone dully in the porch light.

"Tell your boy to get his clothes on. He's going downtown with us."

Invited inside, Dylan and Dave waited, listening for any suspicious sounds from down the darkened hall. Ten minutes later Henry shuffled into the living room, shirt unbuttoned, suspenders trailing over the waistband of his shiny trousers, pointy-toed shoes in his hand.

"You ready to go, Henry?"

Squinting in the light from the naked bulb hanging on a cord, Henry gave his answer. "Err-uh. Err-uh. Oh."

"That's profound, Henry. Get your shoes on."

As the three of them walked across the porch, a rumbling of 3.5 on the Richter scale rose from beneath it to greet them. But the worst was still to come—listening to Henry's monologue on the way to the jail.

"Ya'll done messed up another good job I got. Startin' at seb'n o'clock dis morning. How I'm gonna pay back dat money when I can't work? Ya'll ain't treatin' me right. I is a mane jes' like you is a mane."

Dave glanced back over his shoulder. "Henry, why is it your jobs always seem to start the same morning we pick you up?"

"Jes' works out dat way. How you 'spect me to know when you comin' to get me, anyhow?"

"What are you grumbling for? You know your daddy's going to get you out," Dave growled toward the backseat. "Besides, to-day's fried chicken day at the jail."

Henry thought about that, but not for long. "Jes gimme one mo' chance and . . ."

And so it went until they deposited Henry in their no-interest, non-insured bank account.

As Dave drove toward their meeting with Mack and Larry, Dylan felt an undefined sadness somehow seeping into him from the night air.

"Well, that takes care of Henry for another few months," Dave remarked to no one in particular. "Then we'll get one of

Martin's *Court-orders-shall-be-enforced* memos and start the whole
thing all over again."

Dylan flicked on the radio. B. J. Thomas was singing his gentle, bouncy hit, "Raindrops Keep Falling on My Head." "I think
I'm beginning to get a little disenchanted with this work."

"You know what your problem is, Dylan?"

"I think I'm about to find out."

"You're a purist," Dave volunteered. "But only a part-time
purist. You usually mess around just like the rest of us. Then along
comes someone like this Batiste kid and *bingo*—you're suddenly
the Knight-Errant of Camelot."

Dylan couldn't picture himself clad in armor astride a white
charger.

Dave made a sharp turn, leaning into the steering wheel.
"That should make you a hypocrite, except for one thing. You
really *believe* in what you're doing."

"How did you know about Remy?"

"You're serious, aren't you?" Stopping for a red light, Dave
glanced around, then ran it. "Everybody in the system knew
about it a half-hour after you saw that kid in jail. This isn't a Nor-
man Rockwell painting we're living in here, Dylan."

"I think you're making something out of nothing." Dylan
tried to dismiss the whole thing. "Since when do the big money
boys ever pay any attention to some poor kid with no connections
who got himself in a mess?"

"The word's out for some reason."

"I'm just trying to do a favor for Emile—and for the boy's
mother."

Dave took a deep breath, blowing it out heavily. "Something's
different about this one."

"What's wrong with giving the boy a hand?"

"I think you'd better leave this one alone."

"He doesn't have anybody else."

"Leave it alone, Dylan."

PART THREE

THE SECRET

10

TOWER OF BABEL

The rambling old turn-of-the-century home stood on the edge of a decaying business district of secondhand furniture stores, neighborhood bars, and unneighborly pawn shops. In its heyday, it had likely belonged to a moderately wealthy man with a large family. In the chill of the predawn morning it stood stark and unpainted amid the vacant lots, abandoned buildings, and years of litter—a home to one man, maybe.

Dave parked across the street, and he and Dylan walked over to Snowden, in his tan overcoat, and Jenkins, wearing a heavy plaid shirt and work boots.

Dylan noticed Snowden giving him an especially nasty look. "Is he in there, Mack?"

"Don't know," Snowden glowered. "What I *do* know is I'm tired of giving five dollars to every bum that comes in the door with a note from you. That's fifteen bucks you owe me this month, and I want it now."

"Payday for sure."

"We won't forget it," Jenkins growled.

"Throw him a dog biscuit, will you, Mark? Jenkins reaced a massive arm toward Dylan's collar, but Snowden fended him off. "Forget it, Larry."

Dave stepped into the fray. "We gonna stand here all night arguing nickels and dimes?"

"Take the back." Snowden headed for the front door with Jenkins in tow.

Dylan gazed at the front of the house, bathed in pale light from the street. The sides were mostly shadow. He walked with Dave to the back, covering the corner opposite him.

Dylan pulled his Smith and Wesson "Chief Special" from his belt. *Gotta get a holster for this thing one of these days.* Feeling silly after thirty seconds of holding the pistol, he stuffed it inside his waistband at the small of his back, wishing he still had the .45 he carried in Vietnam.

After five minutes, Dylan walked over to Dave's corner of the house. He sat on the back steps, elbows on knees, head down, half asleep. Muted conversation drifted around the corner from the front porch.

"What's going on?"

Dave glanced up. "I believe Mack's trying to rehabilitate our boy inside."

"He always was a little too windy." Dylan peered around the corner toward the front. "I'm going up there."

"Suit yourself."

The scene on the porch was playing to climax. Snowden's patience fund had been depleted and he snatched the screen door open, breaking the latch. He and Jenkins tried to push the wooden door inward, but the man inside was more than a match for them, managing to slam and lock it.

Dylan gave the man a second's thought, then sprinted toward the back of the house.

Dave stood at the back door, holding a broom like a baseball bat.

"What're you doing?"

Dave kept his eyes on the back door. "Heard the commotion! I'm gonna stop him!"

"You gonna tell him, 'Stop or I'll sweep'? Use your gun!"

"Oh yeah!" Dave fumbled in his coat pocket, pulling out an ancient .25 automatic he had taken off a parolee six months earlier.

Dylan frowned at the tiny pistol. "Maybe you'd *better* use the broom."

"No. It works now. I fixed it."

Just then a head, turned toward the front of the house, poked out the bathroom window three feet away. Dave held the .25 level, his arms extended. When the head turned around, the nose on it was six inches from the muzzle.

"Freeze!"

With a choking scream, the man disappeared inside the window in a clattering, banging fall.

Dave remembered there was no round in the chamber, tried to jack one in, and jammed the pistol.

Dylan felt secure for the moment. "I think you scared him with your gun that won't shoot."

"Yeah. I hope *he* doesn't have one in there that *will*." Dave leaned against the house.

"Give me a boost up," Dylan said, pointing to the still-open window. "I'll go in and open the back door for you. I think two of us with one gun can handle him."

Hearing a noise up front, Dave peered around the corner. "Mack's leaving!"

"You're kidding!"

They watched Snowden pull off, leaving Jenkins standing at the curb.

"Here." Handing Dave his pistol, Dylan headed along the side of the house to the street.

In spite of his size, Jenkins shifted from one foot to the other in his uneasiness at being away from Snowden.

Dylan walked up, his face full of disbelief. "We've *got* this guy! What went wrong up here?"

"Mack said there's a legal problem with the warrant. Something about not being able to enter the domicile."

"That's a good word, *domicile*. I guess he took our warrant with him."

"Yeah." Jenkins glanced down the empty street. "He's gone to get some deputies to execute it."

Dylan stepped next to an ancient cedar, putting it between him and the house behind him. "Larry?"

Jenkins sat down on the curb, fumbling with his boot strings. "Whadda you want *now?*"

"How many warrants have we handled—just like this one?"

"I don't know. Maybe this one's different."

"Let me rephrase that." Dylan squatted down, staring into Jenkins' eyes. "How much crazier do you think Mack's gonna get before he gets somebody hurt?"

Silence. Jenkins' neck assumed the appearance of a bloated thermometer, the color rising slowly toward his face.

"What was it *this* time? A period left out, a misspelled name? His compulsive order's getting out of hand."

"He's the supervisor."

Dylan sensed he was getting nowhere, but pressed on. "Larry, the guy in this"—he jerked his thumb back toward the house—" 'domicile' is crazier than Mack—maybe. He might be shootin' a load of courage in his arm right now, and he really likes big guns. We could have gotten him quick. Somebody's got to do something about Mack."

"At least he doesn't drink on the job."

"That's a big help! I feel much better now."

Larry's face glowed in the half-light, his eyes like buckshot in his fleshy face. Dylan remembered Dave telling him that the big man, who outweighed him by eighty pounds, kept automatic weapons and a few hand grenades under his bed. He decided to let the whole thing drop.

"Maybe you better go on back with Dave," Jenkins muttered. "I got it up here."

"Splendid." Dylan turned and walked to the back, keeping an eye on the windows.

"What's the problem?" Dave used a pocketknife, trying to un-jam his pistol.

" 'The hand that signed the paper felled a city.' "

"I hate it when you talk like that."

They sat in the damp weeds on cardboard boxes that Dave had found under the house, their backs against a huge pecan tree, years of dead limbs scattered beneath it.

"He hasn't got a gun," Dave observed. "He would have done something by now."

Dylan's mind strayed again to that rainy July morning four months before when Susan left him. It occurred to him that he was bothered less and less by situations like this one—and that in itself was reason for concern. He had been ready to go through the window after the man inside with no thought for what might happen to him. *What a stupid thing to do!*

"Probably getting stoned."

"What?" Dylan heard Dave's voice, but the words had not registered. He glanced toward the street. A half block down, Larry's bald head shone faintly above the hood of his car, his arms stretched across it, holding his .357 in both hands. "Look at our hero."

"Don't take it out on him. Mack's the legal genius that shut us down."

"You're right. He's just using good sense."

"Maybe we ought to try that sometime," Dave suggested, still staring at Jenkins.

"First thing tomorrow."

"I'm beginning to think I might not make it much longer if I don't."

Dylan merely shrugged, unable to comprehend what was happening inside him. At that moment, he had a much greater fear of returning to his empty apartment alone than he did of going in after the man inside the house.

A loud crack split the night. Dylan dove flat out on the ground just before a clumping sound came from twenty feet behind him. He lifted his head slightly.

"Pecan limb," Dave mumbled.

Lying in the weeds, Dylan felt a warm breath, then a cold nose against the back of his neck. Turning around, he saw a small black-and-gray terrier, his hair hanging in his eyes.

The dog, his tongue out and tail wagging, stared happily back at Dylan. He was in no apparent hurry to continue his nightly patrol of the neighborhood.

"He probably thought you were dead," Dave said, taking his place on the box.

"I'm still not sure *myself.*"

The little dog trotted over to the back door, scratched on it, waited, then scratched on it again. Raising his leg, he made a parting statement before wandering off through the weeds.

Dylan watched him disappear. "I see he shares our opinion of his master."

Dave and Dylan sat like two commuters on their cardboard boxes under the pecan tree. Dylan felt the night gathering strength in those last hours before dawn and the same sadness returned like an owl from the hunt, its talons warmed by flesh.

———

"Wake up."

Dylan felt Dave's hand on his shoulder, shaking him. He forced himself up from the warm darkness of sleep. Blinking his eyes, he stared toward the street and saw two sheriff's units pull in behind Snowden's car.

"You think Mack got the National Guard for backup?" Dave asked.

Dylan grunted, but his mind was on the two deputies carrying riot guns as they ran from their car toward the rear of the house where he and Dave sat in the deep shadows. It was obvious they didn't know anyone else was around.

Suddenly the man in front spotted them and dropped to his knees, jacking a twelve-gauge shell into the chamber—a sound far worse than the clanging shut of a cell door.

Dylan fumbled for his badge as the policeman's partner caught him in the blinding beam of his flashlight. Holding the badge out into the brightness, he shouted, "Parole officers! Don't shoot!"

"It's St. John. I might have known." The deputy pointed the barrel of the heavy shotgun toward the sky. "Everything all right back here?"

"Yeah! He's still in the house." Dylan spat the words out hoarsely.

Both deputies headed toward the front.

"Mack forgot to tell 'em we were back here." Dave slumped back down on the box.

"A trifle. Mack can't be bothered with trifles." Dylan felt a chill at the back of his neck. He knew it didn't come from the night air.

Up front, the lights from the sheriff's unit flashed legal admonitions to the neighborhood. A deputy on a bullhorn promised Armageddon, complete with fire and brimstone, if the man in the house didn't come forth immediately.

Dylan felt like a third-string bench warmer, hanging out in back of the house with Dave.

Dave voiced the feeling for both of them. "I hate being around the pros like this. Makes me feel like a kid."

"Embarrassing, ain't it?"

Walking back to the car, Dylan saw their quarry, wearing nothing but jeans and a leather vest, walk out of the house between two deputies: handcuffs and leg-irons, arms like fence posts, shaved head. Grinning!

The man stared straight at Dylan. *Goat eyes in the face of a man.*

Dylan glanced at Dave who was studiously avoiding the eyes of the man with the shaved head. "Didn't this guy used to have hair down to his shoulders?"

Dave paused, his hand on the door handle. "I think so." He still didn't look at the man.

A simulacrum of memory troubled the back of Dylan's mind. "It bothers me when they shave their heads like that."

Opening the door to Dave's Mustang, Dylan felt something brush against his leg. The terrier bounced past him onto the front seat and over into the back of the car where he sat erect and motionless in the middle, staring directly ahead through the windshield.

Dave glanced back at the dog, then at Dylan. "What do you think?"

"Probably can't afford a cab. Let him ride."

Dave sped along an elevated portion of I–110 north at seventy miles an hour. He called it his driving therapy. They sailed down the long curve that took them due west toward the capitol. It rose across the lake in front of them like an art deco Tower of Babel. Passing the governor's mansion on their right, they skirted the lake in the upward curve that headed south to another raised portion of the interstate.

Spinning along above the city, Dylan seemed to see fragments of the day's events drift like motes in sunlight—then abruptly they transmogrified. He suddenly saw himself as an archaic and risible figure, a ragtag and tattered scarecrow of a man riding a spindly

143

steed in quest of dragons—a specter with a zealot's burning eyes, trailing the sad litter of his years.

Is this what I'm turning into . . . or is it what I already am? Dylan forced himself to stop thinking.

"Well, I'm feeling better," Dave admitted. "You want to try Redbone? We could haul 'em out of there all night and still have plenty for the rest of the year."

"No thanks. I wouldn't care for some. I just had any."

"Any what? Some . . . any. What are you talking about?"

"Redbone. I don't want any more. I went there a couple of days ago. Once a week is enough for me."

"You're punchy, Dylan. Did you get any sleep at all?"

"Slept like a baby." Dylan's mind flashed on the dream he had earlier back at the office. "Like an innocent, milk white, cotton-soft, breast-nuzzling, bouncing baby boy."

"You need the boys in the white coats is what you need," Dave grinned, "with a heavy-duty net. But maybe a shot of coffee'll get you by 'til morning. Mae's all right?"

"Splendid choice. Maybe they'll waive the coat-and-tie requirement."

Mae's Café, an amalgam of ambition and decadence, sat like a weathered crone in a working-class neighborhood that was heading rapidly toward poverty. Stucco and brick combined in a ragged-looking facade, with concrete blocks filling in the damaged areas. Only the metal frame of the awning remained, the cloth rotted away in some previous generation. Iron grates covered the door and the two large plate glass windows. *Jesus' Name Apostolic Temple* stood next door.

Proximity to the governmental complex and down-home cooking purchased a clientele of politicians in the palmy years. One of Mae's more famous patrons, a singing governor, made news when he rode his horse up the steps of the State Capitol. During his previous term, he made movies in Hollywood.

Now the daylight crowd was still spotted with government officials, but the downhill slide of the area had numbered their days as patrons.

Dave parked across the street. Getting out, Dylan left the door open for the dog, who glanced at him, then continued to sit as still and unblinking as a hood ornament.

Assorted kinsmen of the night sat at the counter, tables, and booths inside Mae's. Food smells battled for attention in the heavy air with fried bacon and grilled onions the hands-down favorites. One booth in the far corner near the only bathroom stood vacant.

As they sat down, Dave reached for a plastic-covered menu that looked as though it had been there since opening day. "You gonna eat something?"

"I never eat on an empty stomach."

Dave peered over the menu. "Somebody's gonna stick an IV in you, before long."

Lorraine Guidry, a waitress at Mae's for eight years, waddled over, carrying two heavy white mugs of coffee of the approximate color and consistency of hot tar. "Dylan, you a sight. I'm 'onna brang you home one day and feed you, then arn them clothes."

Dylan motioned Lorraine closer.

With a puzzled frown, she leaned down.

"I'm doing some undercover work right now. This is my wino outfit."

"I be dog." Moderately impressed, Lorraine offered her professional opinion. "You doin' it real good." Then waddled back toward the kitchen.

Dylan stirred sugar into his thin tar, tasted it, and shoved it away.

Cigarette smoke and bits of conversation hovered in the air as the night wore on toward another uneasy dawn.

Sipping his coffee, Dave watched the comings and goings of the café, but his eyes were focused inward on thoughts that were forming, becoming solid. "Dylan, I'm worried about you."

"Don't be."

Dave continued as though Dylan hadn't spoken. "I know you enjoy these little jousts with the system. Maybe in juvenile work you even made things a little better for one or two kids. That's one reason you do it."

"What's the other?"

"You like the challenge," Dave replied, an edge in his voice.

"You've got this sophomoric urge to prove yourself, show 'em you won't back down."

Dylan leaned against the back of the booth, a smile flickering at the corners of his mouth.

"What you're totally oblivious to is that these little waves you've been making are starting to be felt at the top. You're not faceless anymore."

"So."

Dave's voice took on a somber tone. "So that's a dangerous thing when you're at the bottom, like you are, and somebody who won't let well enough alone—like you."

"You expect me to live my life in shadows and shades of gray, Dave? Some things are black or white—whether we want them to be or not."

"I'm asking you as a friend, Dylan. Let this one go. Remy'll be all right."

"I can't do that," Dylan said with assurance. "If you see something wrong, maybe even evil, and you don't do anything about it . . ." Dylan stopped, leaned forward on his elbows, and stared directly into Dave's eyes, ". . . you become part of it—or it becomes a part of you."

Dave merely stared down at his coffee, shaking his head slowly back and forth.

"How do you know so much about all this, anyway?"

"I just do. The signs are all there," Dave answered enigmatically. "But you'll never back off, will you."

Dylan knew that Dave didn't really expect him to answer the question.

The smile left Dave's face, his lips tightened, and the light in his eyes changed.

Staring at his friend, Dylan realized he had never seen an expression like it on Dave's face before—something resembling resignation at war with resolve.

Finally, Dave relaxed, leaning back in the booth as if a burden had somehow been lifted. He stared across the café with an emptiness in his eyes where the light had been.

Dylan had the feeling that a vacuum had been suddenly created in the air around him. Something gave way and he seemed to feel a cold fluid rushing in, covering him with a chill that entered his soul. He found himself standing, trying to think of a reason why he got up. "I have to go to the bathroom."

"I'll be ready to leave when you get back. Lorraine must have forgotten us."

Dylan stepped around the partition that separated the booth from the short hall leading to the bathroom. He noticed a pay phone on the wall opposite the door.

When Dylan dropped his nickel in and dialed, he could hear the telephone ring in the bedroom of the neat cottage on Camellia Street near City Park. After ten rings a sleepy voice answered, "Hmm."

"Susan." Dylan pictured his wife, brushing the pleasant tangle of dark hair back from her face. He longed desperately to be with her, to lose himself in the fragrance and the softness and the warmth of her.

"Dylan?" she whispered hoarsely.

"Susan, I need to be with you."

Reaching over to turn the lamp on, Susan sat up in bed, positioning her pillow against the headboard. Still drugged by sleep, she tried to clear her thinking. "What's wrong?"

"I'm cold." Dylan realized his words sounded inane, childish even, but he could think of no other way to express the sudden, cold emptiness he felt.

"You're not making any sense."

"My heart, my life—everything's cold."

Susan glanced at the clock radio next to the lamp. "You're drinking, aren't you?"

"No. I just needed to talk to you."

"Dylan, don't do this! I can't take it anymore."

"I'm sorry. I just *had* to hear your voice."

Susan sighed deeply. "I don't know what to say. Nothing helps."

"Just talk to me."

"Please don't do this."

Dylan felt overwhelmed by an unnameable dread, an unbearable sadness. "I don't know what to do."

Susan made no reply. A single tear ran down her cheek, glistening like a soft, clear pearl in the amber glow of the lamp.

Dylan couldn't see the tear or the grief in Susan's eyes. He only felt that her silence had opened a great chasm between them, darkness rising from it in waves. Reaching beneath his jacket, he touched the cold steel of the .38 tucked inside his waistband. *That final rush . . .*

"I still love you, Dylan."

A sense of relief washed over him as though he had received a last-second pardon—from what? "I want to be with you, Susan."

"No. Not now."

"When?"

"I don't know. I don't know when! I wish the whole thing were over."

"Don't say that!"

"I can't help it."

"It won't ever be over! Not for us."

"You'll have to give me more time."

"I will." Dylan knew he would never understand how a few words from Susan could make such a difference in his life. Just the thought that there was hope for them . . .

"How do you feel?" Her voice sounded gentle, tender.

"Better," Dylan almost grinned. "I'm all right."

"I have to go now. We're taking the children to the State Capitol tomorrow."

"Thanks. I just needed to hear your voice."

"I know."

"I can go now."

"Dylan . . ."

"Yes."

"Be careful."

"I will."

The hum on the line made the sound of all goodbyes after they are spoken—the sound of all words left unsaid.

"I love you, Susan."

Replacing the receiver, Dylan noticed a man in his mid-forties, wearing a well-tailored but wrinkled business suit. He was shaky and used the bathroom wall for support. Across the six feet of air separating them, his breath told the story of his night better than words.

"She must be a nice girl. I hope you two can make it work. I never could." The man slid slowly down the wall until he hit the floor, sitting against it with his knees pulled up. "Maybe I just didn't try."

11

BLOOD AND BACON GREASE

Leaving the restaurant's dimly lit hall, something struck Dylan's peripheral vision. He glanced through the serving window back into the kitchen area. Wearing a white T-shirt and apron, a large man with skin the color and texture of biscuit dough stood at the grill, breaking eggs into hot grease. The six-inch scar on his neck stamped him like a birth certificate.

Dylan leaned over the back of the booth close to Dave's head. "Ridgley Triplett."

Dave glanced up. "What about him?"

"He's cooking back there in the kitchen." Dylan slid back into the booth.

"I didn't hear that, Dylan. Too noisy." Dave glanced at the register. "I'll go pay our ticket, and we'll get out of here."

"We really ought to take him in," Dylan insisted. "He could have an episode any time."

"Episode? You sound like one of those nutty psychiatrists we have to deal with." Dave's eyes grew wide as he spoke. "*Homicidal rages* is what he has—not *episodes!*"

"There's a warrant out on him."

"Let the cops get him," Dave insisted. You're starting to sound a lot like Wes. I'd worry about that, if I were you."

"There's only *one* Wes." Dylan glanced back into the kitchen area. "Ridgley looks pretty calm now. Besides, he always disliked me less than he did most people."

Dave shook his head in disgust. "I've got to find another riding partner."

"I really don't think he'll be much of a problem."

"You got your mind made up, Dylan. We might as well get this thing over with."

Dave followed a step behind Dylan as they pushed through the swinging doors into the kitchen.

"Hey, you cain't go back there." Lorraine stood three tables away, hands on her ample hips.

"We're going to talk to your cook a minute," Dylan called back over his shoulder. "He's a friend of ours."

Ridgley, the top of his white chef's cap almost two feet above Dylan's head, had a dozen eggs frying as Dylan stepped behind him and to his right. Dave stood two paces back on the left.

Leaning forward slightly, Dylan remarked offhandedly, "I'll have mine over easy, Ridg."

There was always some kind of warning—a twitch of facial muscles, rapid eye movement—something to telegraph the strike. Not only was Ridgley's face hidden from Dylan, but his reactions had a primitive quality about them, as though his muscles responded independently of the brain.

Years of psychotropic drugs, rather than slowing down response time, had served only to promote this independence from the central nervous system. Ridgley wasn't very quick, but his reactions weren't hampered by thought.

Dylan had hoped he wouldn't be much of a problem.

The first three feet of stainless steel spatula created a flashing silver curve. Dylan watched it as he would have a meteorite arcing across the night sky. During the next five feet of flight his survival instinct kicked in. He jerked his head back and down just enough to keep the heavy blade of the spatula from slicing through his left eye.

A sudden fire burned above Dylan's brow; then he felt a gushing warmth over his eye and cheek.

Spinning quickly around, Ridgley hit Dave in full stride, sending him reeling backward, tripping over a mop bucket, but he lost two seconds opening the back door. He had cleared the porch and made it down to the gravel parking lot when Dylan leaped from the top step onto the big man's back, snapping his right arm around Ridgley's thick neck in a headlock.

Ridgley didn't go down. He was spinning around like a crazed Brahma bull when Dave burst through the back door onto the porch, grabbed a mop from the rail, leaped down to the parking lot, and rammed the handle between Ridgley's legs. He went down hard and heavy, hitting on his ponderous belly with a whooshing outrush of breath.

Dylan still held on tightly, but Ridgley shook him like a terrier in the paws of a bear. Dave grabbed Ridgley's right arm, got a cuff on it, and was suddenly bowled over by a roundhouse left to the side of his head. He rolled over twice, shook it off, and headed back into the fray.

The exertion and the constant pressure of Dylan's arm against Ridgley's windpipe had begun to take their toll. With Dave's help, Dylan forced him onto his stomach and cuffed his hands behind his back. He lay there in the gravel red-faced and blowing, while Dylan sat down next to Dave, feeling the relief of Christians getting the news that the lions were all sick.

"I'm asking for a raise first thing in the morning," Dave gasped, trying to catch his breath. Then he glanced at the blood on Dylan's face. "You're gonna need stitches."

Dylan stood up uncertainly, touching the sticky warmth covering the left side of his face.

"You all right?"

"Yeah. I'll be right back." Dylan turned toward the café, its light blurred and distant looking. "Make sure Ridgley doesn't wander off with your handcuffs."

On the back porch, Lorraine stood wide-eyed, a dishrag clutched to her breast with both hands. Two other waitresses huddled behind her.

"Just a difference of opinion, Lorraine," Dylan explained, walking up the steps. "Go tell your customers somebody knocked over some pots and pans. We don't need a bunch of people rubber-necking around back here."

Dylan opened the screen door and flicked on the light in the small washroom just inside the kitchen. Staring into the water-speckled mirror, he saw that the skin above his eye was laid back in a three-inch gash, blood pumping softly from it, measuring out his fragile grasp on mortality.

After washing the blood and bacon grease from his face and cleaning what he could from his clothes, Dylan grabbed a handful of paper towels and headed back out to the parking lot. Ridgley sat cross-legged in the gravel, staring at something only he could see. Dave sat directly across from him. They looked like two Indians at a powwow.

Dylan folded two of the paper towels together, pressed them against his cut, and joined the two men. "Ridgley, we're gonna take you downtown now. They'll probably transfer you up to forensic in a day or two."

"I'd druther stay in jail," Ridgley mumbled.

"It won't be so bad."

"I ain't crazy, Dylan."

"You sure could'a fooled me ten minutes ago," Dylan shot back. "Why'd you try to hurt me that way? We always got along, didn't we?"

Ridgley hung his head. "Didn't know it was you 'til after. I just knew it was a *police* kinda voice, and I swang at it."

"A *police* kinda voice?"

"You know what I mean." Ridgley glanced up. "I just didn't thank about it. I got nothin' aginst you."

Dylan felt sorry for the man sitting in the gravel. He reminded him of a great bear caught in a trap. "How long you been workin' at Mae's, Ridg?"

Dave stood up, hands on his hips. "We're wasting time here, Dylan."

"Take it easy," Dylan snapped, still staring down at Ridgley. "We're finished for tonight, anyway."

"I been here three weeks," Ridgley replied, staring up, a mild hope beginning to glimmer in his eyes. "I ain't *never* had a job that long."

Dylan let the big man talk while Dave paced, gravel crunching under his feet.

"I like it real good here. Lorraine helps me a lot. That's how come I done so good. She even took me to church with her last Sunday. First time I went since I was jist a boy."

"I'm going inside. Don't be too long." Dave trudged off through the gravel.

"Okay. Ask Lorraine to come out here for a minute," Dylan called out over his shoulder, then turned back to Ridgley. "How come nobody's picked you up? You never stayed on the loose this long before."

"Don't mess around no more. I work from eight at night 'til six in the mornin', six days a week. Ain't had a drank since I started cookin' here."

"Where you livin'?"

"That government building over by the Capitol Lake. I pay my rent ever Friday—eighteen dollars. It's real nice too." Ridgley began sobbing softly, mucus running from his nose onto his lips.

"Take it easy, Ridg."

"Please don't lock me up no more. I get cold in them places. I won't be no more trouble."

Lorraine walked over and knelt down beside Ridgley. Dylan handed her a paper towel. She wiped his nose and mouth. Then she kissed him on the cheek and told Dylan the same story he had just heard from Ridgley.

Lorraine and Ridgley gazed at each other with the first-love wonder of two fourteen-year-olds shining in their eyes.

Dylan dug in his pockets, finding his handcuff key, and unlocked the cuffs. Ridgley stood up, a little shaky on his feet, rubbing his thick wrists. Then Dylan motioned for Lorraine to follow him a few steps away while Ridgley stared at them with another kind of wonder on his face.

"You've got to keep a tight rein on him, Lorraine," Dylan instructed.

"I shore will."

"No one's gonna be looking very hard for him, anyway, but he's always gotten picked up for getting in one kind of ruckus or another. If he can stay straight for six months or so, they just may let the whole thing slide."

"You can count on me, Dylan." Lorraine's face glowed with unexpected joy. "He ain't goin' nowhere but work, his room, and the church house."

They walked back over to Ridgley who had remembered,

probably from childhood, how to smile.

"Dylan, I'm shore sorry for what I done to yo' eye. I just didn't thank."

"Forget it, Ridg. Just don't let me down."

Leaving the two of them holding hands and grinning at each other, Dylan went back inside the café. Dave sat in the same booth, drinking more coffee. Dylan told him the Ridgley-Lorraine story, then what he had done.

"You know you're breaking the law: aiding and abetting, malfeasance."

"You gonna turn me in, Dave?"

Dave hesitated. "No. But how can you crusade against other people who don't follow the letter of the law—and then do this yourself?"

"This is about *people*, Dave," Dylan said solemnly. "Lorraine's done more to help Ridgley in three weeks than a battery of psychiatrists and social workers and a boxcar full of drugs have done in fifteen years. The worst thing he's ever done is what he did to me tonight—if I let it go, so can the law. Let's give him a chance at life. It may be his last one."

"Okay. I'll let it pass." Dave touched the swelling on the right side of his head. "But you're gonna *listen* to me. The only law you care about is your personal moral code and anybody that breaks it is the enemy. You've pretty well ruined your own career, and if you don't change, you're gonna lose a lot more. You ask too much of friendship, of everyone—except maybe yourself."

"I didn't mean to put you in a bind, Dave." Dylan's lips tightened as he stared at Ridgley, who had taken his place back in front of the grill. "You think I enjoy being under the gun all the time? Every morning I tell myself, 'Just do your job and forget the rest.'"

"You need to take that advice."

Dylan continued as though he hadn't heard Dave's comment. "Then I run up against something like Ridgley's predicament—or Remy's."

"And you go nuts."

"I just have to make decisions I can live with."

Dave swallowed the last of his coffee. "You can live with 'em, Dylan. Can Susan?"

Giving Ridgley and Lorraine some chance for happiness in the night-long labors of their lives should have made Dylan feel good. It didn't. There was a *knowing* of happiness for them, but the *feeling* didn't accompany it. His brief conversation with Susan, the slight hope that she revealed made him happy.

But there was something else down deep inside Dylan—that lake of cold that had sprung from nothing in Mae's Café just before he called Susan. Down where the light barely reached, he could almost see its surface giving back a malignant glint.

While Dave drove them toward the hospital, with the mutt asleep in the backseat, Dylan thumbed through the card catalog in the back of his mind. Looking under "Good Days," he happened to find one a year-and-a-half old: May, the merry month, sun-drenched, fat green leaves and flowers, warmth like that of an old friend—just enough, Saturday, five minutes after ten in the morning.

Susan sat on the front row of the five-tiered bleacher, her feet in white sandals primly together, hands resting on bare legs and a smile on her face that didn't quite conceal her anxiety. Her hair, worn in a ponytail, was tied with a bright blue ribbon. A few dark wisps strayed about her face and along the clean, pale line of her neck. Dylan's number-one fan in a contingent of two.

"I just know you're going to win today, darling," Susan had told Dylan as he slipped his racquet out of its cover, tapping the strings against the heel of his hand to test the tension. "Look how nervous Ralph looks."

"Will you still love me if I don't?"

For an answer, Susan had taken his face in her hands, kissing him warmly on the lips.

Glancing at the bleachers, his face coloring slightly, Dylan had walked out onto the court.

Dylan's other fan was Emile, who had shunned his khaki-colored uniform and .357 Smith and Wesson in favor of a white knit shirt and faded jeans.

The rest of the gathering of hard-core tennis fans, Ike among them, belonged to Ralph.

Donice had strongly suggested that Dylan enter the tournament for the governor's favorite charity to represent their department. "Good PR," he had said.

Dylan had worked on his endurance by running daily on the City Park Golf Course, and he had raised his game almost to the level he had played in college. Still, he felt that he was not playing well enough to beat Ralph in the final.

Ralph had grown up with the best of instruction on the courts at the Baton Rouge Country Club. At Tulane, he had played number-two singles during his senior year. There was no way, he had told Dylan after the warm-up, that he was going to be beaten by a "redneck hacker."

But as the rednecks say, "Ever' dawg has his day—even the curs."

One service break separated them in the third set. During the crossover, Dylan sat in a deck chair sipping a Coke, trying to put everything from his mind but the flight and spin of a fuzzy white ball. When he stood up, Ralph was taking the court, glaring at him as he walked past, the expression on his face one of intensity poised on the front steps of rage.

Dylan put on a fresh sweatband and walked to the base line to serve. Staring across the net at Ralph, he could feel the animus across the seventy-eight feet that separated them.

Holding two balls in his left hand, Dylan rocked back and lofted one from his fingertips, imparting no spin on it and leaving the left arm extended as his shoulders turned, his knees bent and the racquet dropped behind his back. As the ball reached its apex, he pushed up and forward with his legs, shoulders rotating, and whipped the racquet head forward and through the ball, his wrist snapping just before contact.

The serve was hard, flat, and down the center stripe. Ralph thrust his body to the left, but the ball zipped past his outstretched racquet. His face a blank mask, he walked doggedly over to the ad court, bearing no attitude of defeat.

Dylan spun a three-quarter speed serve directly at Ralph's body, jamming the forehand return which floated lazily over the net for an easy backhand volley into the far corner. Ralph reached the ball, hitting a vicious top-spin forehand crosscourt, but his momentum had taken him outside the doubles sideline. Dylan bent low from the knees and punched his forehand volley into the open court before Ralph could recover.

Dylan's chest felt as if it were on fire as he drew air deeply into his lungs. *Two more points and the tournament is yours, but Ralph's in better shape than you are. If you don't hold serve now, he's got you. His money and politics can't help him out here, though. There's only blood and breath and heart. No excuses. Time to see what you're made of.*

Ralph moved to his left, setting up for another spin serve down the middle, took the return on his forehand and drove it straight down the line for a clean winner. Shouting and pumping his arm, he clearly believed that the match was within reach. And it was—until the next point.

During the course of a match, Dylan knew just one point could completely change its direction. Sometimes there would be several, but that day there was only one and it came after two sets and nine games. It came late, but it came nonetheless.

On most any other day Ralph would have taken Dylan in straight sets. Dylan would have won a few games, only delaying the inevitable. But not that day. On that day, Dylan found himself playing in the "Zone."

The pros say the ball looks as big as a basketball when this happens. For Dylan the ball changed not at all, but the court had grown to the size of a football field. He felt it seemingly impossible to hit any shot out of bounds.

At thirty-fifteen, Dylan served wide to the backhand, and Ralph sliced a low crosscourt return. Dylan stretched for the volley. It popped up weakly, landing inside the service line. Ralph had time to hit it anywhere on the court, and he chose to drill a flat forehand, from twelve feet away, directly at Dylan's right hip.

In a reflex action, Dylan's right elbow jerked out and up as he flicked the racquet head across his body, blocking the ball to Ralph's left. Disbelief on his face, Ralph recovered quickly and moved to the ball, taking the racquet back and planting his right foot as he stopped. Dylan drifted to the right, expecting a down-the-line backhand, but Ralph whipped the racquet up and over the ball, hitting a textbook top-spin lob.

Ralph and everyone watching the match knew it was a clean winner. No such knowledge existed in the "Zone."

Dylan spun to his right, sprinted four steps obliquely, and leaped off his left foot, turning in the air back toward the net with his left arm held out for balance and his right pointing the racquet head down behind his back.

The ball was spinning beautifully, descending in a perfect parabola from the soft blue dome of the sky. The racquet head whipped up and forward, slicing the white curve out of the air and sending a streak across the net. Hitting six inches inside the base line, the ball stopped dead three feet above the court in an opening in the chain-link backstop.

After surprise had faded, Ralph's face held the look of defeat and the knowledge of what had happened. He had played in the "Zone" himself. He moved toward deuce court with a gait he would not use again for years. The score was forty-fifteen, but the match was over.

Dylan sliced his next serve wide and, in a final and futile effort, Ralph blasted a forehand that caromed off the net post into the trees. After a brief silence, a smattering of applause rose from the bleachers. Susan hugged Emile, and in the top row a large white smile spread across a coffee-colored face.

Dylan and Ralph, having the appearance of gladiators with invisible wounds, closed at the net. Ralph's sweaty handshake was firm and steady, but something in his eyes had changed. It was not respect, nor friendship, but more of an affirmation; of what, Dylan was never to find out.

———

"I'm so proud of you!" Susan sat on the front seat of Emile's big Buick, between him and Dylan. She kissed Dylan on the cheek, squeezing his hand tightly. "I could tell you were about to cave in out there, but you beat him anyway."

"I was real fortunate today, Susan," Dylan replied, weighing the truth of his words. "I hit shots I haven't made since I played in college."

Humming down the Airline Highway south of LaPlace, Emile

gazed out at the sugarcane fields lying fallow in the spring sunshine. "I don't think Ralph likes you very much, Dylan."

"You're a master of understatement, Emile."

"You better not turn your back on that boy. He's got the look in his eyes of a cottonmouth."

Susan put her arms around both men, her smile as bright as the wildflowers along the roadside. "That's enough of that kind of talk. We're out to have a good time."

They celebrated by driving to the lakefront in New Orleans, plunging into an orgy of seafood at Fitzgerald's Restaurant. Then they drove to the Quarter, visited the antique and art shops on Royal, and strolled the narrow streets, winding down the day with café au lait and beignets at Café Du Monde across from Jackson Square. Constructed in the 1810s and 20s, the café was housed in the oldest of seven colonnaded buildings comprising the Old French Market—once home to the largest slave auctions in the world.

The street entertainers and tourists were out in force as Susan and Dylan went for a walk, leaving Emile in the crowded patio to people-watch. They found a grassy place down the levee away from the lights and discovered there were still stars in the sky over New Orleans.

Lying on the darkened slope of the levee, Susan's breath warm and soft against his neck, Dylan watched the Algiers Ferry slip away from its landing in an amber mantle of light. He could almost hear the spoken words as clearly as that first time in an end-of-August classroom, "Nothing gold can stay."

12

PERFECT

"Here we are." Dave pulled into a parking space marked *Dr. J. Palemo*. "Dave's Ambulance Service—cheaper than most and not nearly as noisy."

Our Lady of the Lake Hospital stood on a low hill rising from the north end of Capitol Lake. Four hundred feet in the air across the lake, a cross glowed against the stone facade of the Capitol and the dark firmament of night. Created by workers who leave their office lights on one month each year, it celebrated a birth. In the very heart of man's power there was still room for the heart of faith.

On the opposite side of the building, a twin cross looked out upon the city, but it was pale and lost in the glitter, the merchants' big grab for the Christmas dollar that Dylan vowed each year he would not get caught up in but always did. Who had the jolliest, friendliest Santa Claus, the most serene and humble Nativity, the clothes and toys and tools, jewelry, guns and gadgets that would make you the apple of your family's and friends' collective eyes?

Dylan stared at the cross on the dark side of the Capitol. Each year he came to this quiet parking lot near the aging building for the sick and dying to feel the spirit of Christmas. This was the first year he had come because for a need of the body.

"Well, let's go see if you're going to live or not." Dave headed around to the side entrance.

The neon glare of the emergency room was painful, coming in from the dark. Dylan felt his cut throbbing as though it were

163

soaking up the brilliance. Glancing around at the surroundings, he thought of the Earl K. Long charity hospital across town where controlled bedlam was the norm.

The hospital reminded Dylan of his school days at Holy Name of Mary. Any moment he expected to see a knuckle-rapping nun making her rounds with a heavy ruler enforcing quiet decorum.

As Dylan approached the glassed-in reception area, the sturdy, middle-aged nurse glanced at him as though he were on the wrong side of the tracks.

"I'd like to see a doctor, please."

"Do you have insurance?" The nurse frowned down over her reading glasses.

"I'm like the Boy Scouts, 'always prepared,' " Dylan replied, holding out his ID card. "State Employees Insurance."

"I can see that. What seems to be the problem?"

Dylan took the bloody paper towels away from the cut, gazed at them, and pressed them back against his forehead. "I'm going to have a baby."

The nurse's lips grew thin. "That kind of attitude isn't going to do you any good in here, young man."

"It hasn't helped a whole lot anywhere *else*, either," Dylan mumbled.

"What did you say?"

"Nothing."

"Here, fill these out." The nurse handed him several forms and a yellow Bic ball-point pen.

"Let me give you a hand. I've done this before." Dave mercifully took the forms and began wading through them at the counter.

Dylan felt the throbbing in his head growing worse. He gazed up at the nurse, a pleading look on his face. "May I have a couple of aspirin, please?"

She smiled down benignly. "Sorry, no medication without a doctor's approval."

From an open door that led into a holding area, Dylan heard a moaning sound. "What's that?"

"You scared, little boy?"

"Curious."

The nurse went back to her newspaper, speaking with professional indifference. "Some older guy dressed up like a kid trying to buy drugs. They beat him up and took his money."

Dylan sat down on a leather sofa with chrome armrests. Through the open door he watched an orderly in hospital greens roll a gurney over next to a wall and leave it. The man lying on it wore zip-up leather boots, bell-bottom jeans, and a tie-dye shirt with a leather vest. Beneath his long blond hair, his face bore dark smudges, giving him the appearance of a hippie coal miner. Blood coagulated below his nose and around his mouth.

Suddenly, the man began groaning and writhing about on the gurney. The blond wig fell to the floor, revealing dark hair combed straight back and streaked with the exact amount of gray that women call distinguished.

Dylan remembered Donaldson's elegant office and the even more elegant voice. "I guess he's not *perfect* after all."

————————

The stitches had tightened the skin around Dylan's eye so that he felt as though he was leering instead of looking. As he and Dave walked across the parking lot toward the car, the slow lightening of the east was casting a red glow over the lake. Across its surface, the thin clear light of the cross reached out toward them.

Glancing to his left, Dylan gazed at the antebellum-style governor's mansion, sitting on a low hill above the lake. "Think the governor's still entertaining. They say his parties go on all night sometimes."

"Could be." Something seemed to click in Dave's expression. "You know who I saw over there a couple of months ago? You won't believe it."

"I didn't know you and the governor were that close. What are you doing in this crummy job?"

"I wasn't at his house, dimwit." Dave pointed at the six-story structure standing next to I–110 beyond the mansion. "I was at the Highway Department, trying to find a guy who hadn't reported in for three months."

"This is a fascinating story, Dave."

"Ike."

"What about him?"

"Your buddy was visiting the governor. I saw him in that Corvette of his, driving right around to the back of the mansion like he went there all the time."

"You sure it was Ike?"

"Yep. Watched him get out and go inside." Dave turned from the lake toward his car. "I didn't know he ran in those kinds of circles."

Something's wrong here. This is the kind of thing Ike usually couldn't wait to tell me. Dylan felt as if he had just gotten a quick glimpse behind somebody's Mardi Gras mask. "Neither did I."

"Think you can handle the Kringle's crowd this morning?" Dave pulled clear of the lot and headed south along the west shore of the lake.

"Might as well." Dylan lightly touched the swelling around his eye. "That Doctor Payne took all the sleep out of me with that curved needle he used."

Dave frowned as though remembering the needle piercing the tender skin above Dylan's eye.

"Did you see that thing?" Dylan glanced one last time at the lake. "It looked medieval. Needles oughta be straight."

"Why does it bother you? I imagine you saw a lot worse than that in Vietnam."

A sudden image of one of the men in Dylan's rifle company, his right leg blown off by a booby trap, flashed in Dylan's mind like a slide show. He could almost hear the deafening clatter of the chopper as the man was loaded aboard. "That was a long time ago."

"Yeah, I guess so."

Remembering how he learned to block such scenes out of his mind, Dylan pictured his balding, burly first sergeant standing in front of their headquarters tent on his first morning in Vietnam. *You men got two choices over here. Get hard—or go home in a plastic bag.*

"How does it feel?"

Dave's words pulled Dylan away from the steaming jungles half a world away. "Like your average spatula-hacking, I guess, when you're stitched up by a sadist using a scimitar instead of a needle."

"That bad, huh?"

"Nah. I'm just trying to get sympathy." As they drove into the shadow of the capitol building, Dylan gazed upward at the towering limestone facade, faintly light-rimmed. He took two pink pills from a small envelope and popped them into his mouth.

"What's that stuff?"

"Darvon." Dylan stuffed the envelope back into his pocket. "Doctor Payne said it might make me kinda goofy."

"You got a big head start on that already."

Ignoring the remark, Dylan thought about the run-down bar they were heading for. "Why do we always end up at Kringle's? The place is filthy and the service is terrible. Pop is more interested in swapping war stories with his old buddies than he is waiting on anybody."

"Is this a philosophical question? You know, like, 'What does it all mean?' "

"No. It just occurred to me. Why do we pick a dirty place in a dangerous area?"

"Maybe you just answered your own question." Dave turned left on Capitol, heading into the Spanish Town neighborhood.

"You mean because it's dirty?"

"No—dangerous. But not too dangerous. Why do we do this work? There's no money in it."

Dylan gazed out at the old frame houses with their wide front porches, tall roofs, and gabled fronts. "Is this a philosophical question, Dave?"

"Because once in a while there's a little excitement, a little danger, but not too much," Dave went on, ignoring Dylan's question. "We get to pick where we want to go and when. The cops get most of the rough stuff; they have to take whatever comes at them, whenever it comes."

"They also get some decent training," Dylan added. "The closest thing to training I ever had was my first day on the job when Donice told me, 'Go buy yourself a gun and some cuffs and put somebody in jail.' "

"B. J. took you out with him a few times, didn't he?"

"I rest my case."

Leaving Spanish Town, they crossed over the interstate. Ahead of them stood the wooden railroad trestle. Dylan remembered the day he had climbed it chasing Odell Jackson. He glanced to his right where Redbone's little cluster of shacks lay sleeping in the sunrise hour like a hobo dreading the dawn.

Dylan took a last look at Redbone, wondering if Odell's father still kept his clothes neatly pressed for him. "You wanna know why I think we're in this work?"

"Not particularly."

"We got no gumption. We come in thinking it's temporary, 'til we get something better, 'til we go to graduate school—most of us on the way to something else."

"That's so insightful. You ought to fill in for 'Dear Abby.' "

"Then we get to liking the freedom, nobody telling us what to do or when. It just gets too comfortable to leave." Dylan began to realize why Susan wasn't fond of his job. "It's not something you start out to do—it's something you just end up doing."

"Not me, Dylan. It's what I've always dreamed of." Dave eased down on the brakes, watching a black-and-white cat lead her litter of three across the street on an early morning stroll. "When I was a kid, everybody played cowboys and Indians—not me. I played parole officer."

"Why do I find that easy to believe?"

"You figured out yet why we always go to Kringle's?"

Dylan watched the last kitten hop lightly up on the curb. "I think so. The beer's cheap and we don't have to bathe."

———

Parked next to the side door of Kringle's, Wes's van angled several feet out into the street. Dave pulled in behind it. A streetlight behind them cast a weak and forgiving eye upon the old tin-roofed block building.

The cold front had passed through, the wind subsiding and changing direction as the warm flow moved up from the Gulf. The Deep South had relegated cold weather to Gypsy status, even in the dead of winter. In a parting outburst, the wind blew leaves and scraps of paper along the street and the broken sidewalk as Dylan got out of the car.

An abrupt clanging near the side door disturbed the early morning quiet. A shadow-cat leaped from a garbage can to the sidewalk. The terrier sprang from the car like a mongoose, but the shadow slipped free and disappeared down the alley two cat-lengths ahead of him.

"This looks like our night for animals," Dave observed. "We ought to work for the S.P.C.A."

As Dylan entered the building, he picked up part of the never-ending dialogue that defined the two tables reserved for the regulars where the bar L-ed across the room to form the counter for the package store up front. They drank, smoked, and talked in shifts: day shift, night shift, and the floaters who, according to Kris, didn't have the discipline to keep regular hours.

"You couldn't hit a bobwhite if it was strapped to the end of your shotgun barrel. You gotta have reflexes to hit one of them thangs."

"Yeah, and you couldn't get close enough to a whitetail to hit him with a Howitzer. It takes a real woodsman to sneak up on them. They'd hear them big feet of yours coming a mile off."

Dave led the way over to the bar and slid onto a wooden stool. "Sounds like they're slaughtering deer and quail this morning instead of Japs and Krauts."

On the wall behind the zinc-topped bar, dozens of black-and-white prints hung in disarray: men holding M–1's or carbines, standing amid bombed-out buildings; men in flight suits or coveralls perched on the wings of B–17's or P–51's; men holding strings of fish; men squatting in front of deer whose swollen tongues lolled from their dead faces; men sitting on the tailgates of pickups holding cans of beer and shotguns or .30-.30's; men wearing the garb and gear of football and baseball and basketball—and one calendar from C. J.'s Auto Parts sporting a blonde pinup hanging wash on the line in a high wind.

Pop Kringle had been in business for eight years and said he could count the number of women customers on one hand. Nothing in the bar was even remotely soft or feminine or fragrant. It was a world for men. It was the only world left for the 'regulars,' men who had come to either hate or love their women so much that their company had become intolerable.

Dave glanced toward the rear of the room. Two pinball machines and a jukebox stood against the wall. "Hey, Wes, where's Eddie?"

Wes sat on a stool in front of the jukebox, studying the selections. "In the bathroom cleaning the vomit off."

"What vomit?"

"His!"

Wes seemed disinclined to discuss the matter further. Dave left it alone, then tried another tack. "We got Henry again. Ya'll get anybody tonight?"

"No!"

"Nobody?"

"Nobody!"

Drinking tan coffee from a black-and-gold "Saints" mug, Pop stepped behind the bar from the small kitchen area in back. His face was puffy from sleep and his iron gray hair was combed close to his skull. He drew two twenty-ounce "fishbowls" of draught beer and set them on the bar. "Hope you boys had a better night than Wes. He come in with a good case of the reds and that new feller was white as a sheet."

Dave dropped a dollar next to the beer. "First time out for him. Maybe Wes broke him in too quick."

His face a grayish cast, Eddie walked out of the door of the men's room, putting on his suit coat, one sleeve ripped at the shoulder. He had tried to clean the mud from his clothes and shoes with little success. Mud clung to the back of his head. Vomit stained the front of his shirt and the side of his neck below his ear.

"What in the world happened to you?" Dave turned around on his stool.

Eddie glanced around, not over, his shoulder at Wes who was punching buttons on the jukebox. "He threw me in . . ." Unable to finish, he took two deep breaths for control.

"Where's your trench coat, Eddie?"

Eddie stared in surprise at his arm where his coat should have been hanging. "I don't know, Dylan. Lost, I guess."

"What happened?"

"He wouldn't—" Hearing a noise behind him, Eddie glanced around his shoulder again at Wes who had gotten off his stool and headed toward the bar. "I have to call home for a ride."

"Dave'll take you home," Dylan offered.

"That's okay; I'll call my wife," Eddie muttered.

His head down, Eddie shuffled over to the pay phone on the wall near the side door.

Wes walked past him as though he wasn't there.

Dylan listened to Merle Haggard begin to tell him from the jukebox about the night his bottle let him down. "What happened, Wes?"

Wes took the stool next to Dylan, slid his beer over and drank half of it before banging it down on the bar. "He almost got me killed!"

"That doesn't tell me a whole lot."

"*Almost killed* oughta be enough, Dylan."

Dave leaned forward, staring at Wes. "Don't be so rough on him."

"Yeah," Dylan added, "we all had a first arrest."

"Rough?" Wes glanced around at Eddie fishing coins out of his pocket. "I got him promoted."

"Maybe you oughta explain that one, Wes."

"Mark my words. Inside of two weeks, he'll be working at headquarters. I did him a big favor tonight." Wes took a red handkerchief out of his back pocket and wiped his forehead. "The rest of us too."

Behind them, Eddie was talking on the phone, staring at the lighted area in the front of the bar. He had the look of a man trying to come to terms with an amputation. In that alley where he lost his coat, he lost a part of himself, and the chances of recovery were about the same for both. He'd have to replace that part of himself soon with something else or decay would set in.

Wes finished Dylan's beer and looked around for Pop, who was seated at a table in front with his regulars. Laying a five on the bar, Wes walked around behind it, and started filling a glass from the tap. "Everybody ready?"

Dylan felt a dull fuzzy warmth in his head from the pills. It began spreading through his body. He recognized the false sense of well-being that accompanied the warmth. "No. These pain pills are doing it for me."

Surprised, Wes glanced over at Dylan, noticing the flesh-colored tape above his eye. His expression asked the question for him as he drew another beer.

"Ridgley Triplett," Dylan answered the unspoken question.

"You're slowing down, Dylan," Wes grinned. "A year ago he never would have touched you."

"Yeah, well I broke training a time or two."

"Dylan said ol' Ridgley wouldn't be much of a problem," Dave added.

"Maybe your brain's going too, Dylan." Wes walked back around to his stool.

"I think that *is* his problem," Dave chimed in. "Take this business with the Batiste kid. He's going to end up making trouble for all of us. What do you think?"

Wes glanced at Dylan with a puzzled expression on his face, then he turned to Dave. "I think Dylan's gonna do something stupid and self-destructive like he always does. What makes you think anything we say's going to make a difference?"

Dave swallowed the last of his beer while he watched Eddie leave through the side door to wait outside for his wife. "Nothing. I guess you're right."

"How 'bout a game, Dylan?" Wes sighted down a cue stick he had taken from the rack on the wall.

"This doctor dope's got me a little cloudy. Dave'll be glad to take your money."

Dave shoved a quarter into the side slot. The balls made a muted bowling-alley sound as they rolled in their channels to the open end of the table.

Dylan poured coffee from a pot at the end of the bar into a chipped blue mug with "Sportsman's Paradise" written on its side and a picture of two men bass fishing. Warming his hands on the coffee mug, he followed the sharp clacking and soft thudding progress of the game. Wes, shooting hard and straight, never planned his next shot, while Dave softly and surely cut him to pieces by controlling the cue ball.

Dylan could hear the regulars up front. Their conversation had taken a political bent and was holding true to an established Kringle's maxim: *An inverse relationship exists between knowledge of a subject and the volume at which it is discussed.* The first subject was being discussed softly.

"Did you read the other day where them students used machine guns to take over a building at Cornell?"

"Yep. And I read this morning that they *negotiated* with the folks in charge and that was the end of it."

"You mean nobody went to jail?"

"That's what I said. Seems like the law of the land don't mean nothing on college campuses."

"Or at one of them rock festivals like Woodstock."

"Well, what can you do with a half-million dopeheads?"

Then the volume of their conversation took a dramatic upward surge.

"Yeah, 'specially since the Communists buy all their dope for them."

"I heard the same thing last week . . ."

Dylan tuned the political strategists out. Darvon warmth was floating him to the house of lethargy just around the bend from stupor. An image returned—sharper than life: Eddie on the phone with his wife only minutes before, staring at something awful, something that had stepped into the light for the first time.

The first arrest is the one that counts. If you make it through that one you're usually all right for whatever else comes. Eddie didn't know that. I never should have sent him with Wes. He didn't get a fair trial.

Wes can smell fear like an animal, and he has only contempt for it and for the man who carries it. With me or Dave, Eddie may have been all right. With his new wife and new clothes and Wes, he didn't get a fair trial.

Pass the guilt, please. Here you are, Dylan. Take a big helping. There's plenty more where that came from.

Dylan found himself floating in warm darkness, the clacking of the pool balls and the drone of conversation coming at him from far away.

"Wake up, St. John!" Jenkins plopped down on the stool next to Dylan.

Slowly opening his eyes, Dylan stared at Jenkins, a rictus, posing as a smile, on his face.

Snowden sat next to him, making it rictus to the second power. "Yeah, St. John, we got news."

"I've never seen you two so happy," Dylan mumbled. "You see a nursing home burning down on the way over here?"

"It'll take more than your stupid cracks to make us mad this morning," Snowden smirked.

"Yeah." Jenkins picked up his part like the second member of a vaudeville team. "After we left ya'll, we caught 'Two Frost.' You and Dave been lookin' for him all year, but we caught him."

"I'm real happy for you, Larry. What'd you catch him with— shiners or crickets?"

Eugene "Two Frost" Byrd was a gambler who loved to work the big cities up north, but hated cold weather. The first frost sent him south. The last one called him back north.

"Sour grapes, St. John." Snowden refused to be thrown off track. "He's your case, and we had to find him for you. This is gonna look pretty bad for you at headquarters."

"Dylan picked up three or four of your guys, Mack." The game over, Dave walked over and joined in. "You know all headquarters cares about is getting them off the streets—not who makes the arrest. How're they gonna find out about it, anyway?"

Snowden's rictus became a chuckle. His eyes didn't change, but it was as close to fun as he ever got. Looking away, he began to work on the full glass Pop had set in front of him.

Pop crawled onto his own stool behind the bar and began his third-favorite pastime, reading the newspaper aloud. "Listen to this! They think Pete Maravich is gonna be the best player LSU ever had."

"Who?" Wes sat down on the other side of Dylan.

"If it ain't played in Tiger Stadium, Wes don't know about it," Pop said as he continued to peruse the newspaper. 'Pistol Pete'— basketball. His daddy's the coach."

"Yeah, I remember," Wes grinned. "That's the game where grown men wear little shorts and undershirts, and rub their sweaty bodies all over each other."

Pop peered over the top of his paper. "I guess you want to

talk about Terry Bradshaw being first draft choice again."

"No," Wes replied, giving Dylan a conspiratorial glance. "I don't want to hear any more stories about sports. I wanna hear 'Peter Rabbit.'"

"Uh-uh. It's my turn," Dave joined in, glancing at Snowden and Jenkins. " 'Cinderella'—that's the only story for Kringle's, with all the Prince Charmings we've got in here."

Dylan felt a silly, pill-induced grin spreading across his face. Using his coffee cup for a gavel, he rapped on the bar. "Why don't we have a round table discussion of T. Harry Williams' biography of Huey Long? It won the Pulitzer this year. We took one of his courses out at LSU, Dave."

Dave and everyone else greeted Dylan's suggestion with a cold silence.

Dylan's giddiness left him unperturbed. "No? Well, how about *Keepers of the House* by Shirley Ann Grau? A Pulitzer in '65, and she's from New Orleans."

More silence, this time accompanied by scowls of impatient disbelief from everyone but Jenkins, who was too busy stuffing pickled eggs into his mouth to notice.

Dylan glanced around at their expressions. "Or maybe not."

Pop glanced at Wes. "After that, your 'Peter Rabbit' idea sounds pretty good. Maybe we'll compromise and talk football instead."

"Why don't we *play* some football?" Dylan found himself saying, then wondering why he said it. "We haven't done that since last year."

"Where's Eddie?" Jenkins had swallowed his last egg. "We need him to make the sides even."

"He had to get home to his new bride," Wes volunteered. "Can you think of anybody, Dylan?"

"I'll call Ike. He said to let him know any time we wanted to play, and he doesn't have to be at work 'til nine." As Dylan walked over to the pay phone, the fog in his mind seemed to lift slightly and he realized why he had suggested playing football. *I want to have a talk with Ike—if I can make it through the game.*

After talking with Ike for thirty seconds, Dylan turned back toward the bar, his hand over the mouthpiece. "Hey, he says he can't make it today. How about tomorrow?"

After a brief mumbling conference, they all agreed.

"Okay. We'll play after tomorrow night's arrest run. I'll call you when we leave here." After hanging the phone up, Dylan stepped outside beneath a sky the color of old bone.

A sudden clanging in the alley as a garbage can lid struck the concrete sent Dylan down into a crouch, pointing his .38 at the dark entrance before his knee hit the sidewalk. *Guess I've still got a little of the Corps' training left in me.* Holding the pistol at arm's length, he peered around the corner of Kringle's in time to see a cardboard box fall from a stack where the alley turned behind another building. *Must have been the cat.*

Dylan slipped the .38 into his waistband behind his back and stepped back to the front of the bar. Beyond a filigree of naked mimosa limbs, a pale moon was vanishing in the west. *Funny—I don't even remember seeing it all night—only now, just before it disappears. I bet it was real pretty.*

13

THE HIDDEN COUNTRY

Dylan pulled his Volkswagen over to the curb on State Capitol Avenue, dry magnolia leaves crunching beneath the tires. With the morning chill vanishing, Dylan shucked off Wes's heavy field jacket and tossed it into the backseat. He felt his head beginning to throb, shook two pills into the palm of his hand, and popped them into his mouth.

Getting out of the car, Dylan ambled past the cedars and pines, then out among the formal rose gardens, bedded down for the season. He gazed upward at the square and austere tower, cut away to an octagon at the twenty-second floor. Five stories farther up, an observation deck sat like a limestone eyrie three hundred and fifty feet above the city. Several children peeped over the edge with two larger figures in attendance.

A sudden urge hit Dylan to visit the tower. Stopping in front of the main entrance of the capitol, he glanced at the imposing statue of Huey Long, standing before the four-hundred-and-fifty-foot monument he built to himself. He was buried beneath that statue, but there was a much less conspicuous memorial to him inside; three bullet holes in the marble wall, marking the spot where Dr. Carl Austin Weiss shot him on September 8, 1935, as he left a special session of the legislature he had called to have the doctor's father-in-law, Judge Benjamin Pavy, removed from office.

Two days later, the man who had offered to make "every man a king" in Louisiana died at Our Lady of the Lake Hospital. It

177

occurred to Dylan that Dr. Payne's father could well have been the attending physician.

Dylan felt as if Huey watched him from behind as he started up the grand staircase toward the fifty-foot-high main entrance. Carved into the first thirteen steps were the names of the original thirteen colonies from Connecticut to Virginia. The next thirty-five started with Vermont, 1791, and ended with Arizona, 1912.

The words etched into the limestone, to the right of the main entrance, read: "The instruments which we have just signed will cause no tears to be shed. They prepare ages of happiness for innumerable generations of human creatures." *Ol' Huey always did have a good sense of humor—for a politician.*

Dylan entered the building and took the two sets of elevators that brought him out onto the observation deck. Walking around to the south side, he watched Susan extolling the wonders of the city to her first graders.

Feeling as if he were floating slightly above the stone floor, Dylan jumped around the corner into his best Al Jolson posture, down on one knee, arms outstretched. "TaDaaaa. . . ." He couldn't bring himself to say, "Mammy."

Susan clutched her throat, taking two quick steps back.

No scream. Good for her. Dylan felt unable to do anything about the insipid grin on his face. He merely gazed at his wife, beaming widely. Wearing a tailored lavender blouse and gray skirt, she looked morning-fresh and lovely.

Susan stared at him for a full three seconds, then turned to her aide. "Miss Clark, will you please take the children around to the other side of the building and show them the chemical plants? Thank you."

Dylan watched the children, beautiful as all six-year-olds are, as they shuffled and hopped and skipped past him, some giggling, some waving shyly. In their burgundy and gray plaid uniforms, they looked like cherubs who had defected. As they rounded the corner, Miss Clark had already begun her lecture on the blessings of the Louisiana Chemical Corridor.

Susan took a deep breath and walked to the stone wall of the deck, looking out on the city.

At that moment, it seemed to Dylan that Susan was *always*

looking away from him at something beyond them both. He watched the wind whip through her hair as the morning light caught it shimmering about her head.

Dylan started to speak, but without warning, the long night finally took its toll. A wave of weakness and nausea swept over him as he slid down the wall into a sitting position. Pulling one leg up, resting his arms on his knee, he tried to look casually heroic with the bandage over his left eye.

Susan turned around to face him. "Dylan, you look awful . . . like a gutter–sleeping wino."

Gutter-sleeping wino? I guess the bandage isn't working.

"I perceive you're not pleased with my presence." Dylan's lips seemed to move of their own volition. He felt he had little control over his thoughts or the words that came spilling out of his mouth.

"This is no time for your nonsense, Dylan!" Susan turned a barrage of accusations against him. "How could you come here like this? Do you have to embarrass me in front of my class? Are you drunk?"

Dylan found himself bordering on maniacal laughter and fought against it. The pink pills had spawned a reddish haze. He felt as though he was looking through a thin covering of blood on a pane of glass.

"Drunk only on the wine of love, my precious. 'Mere alcohol doesn't thrill me at all.' Your presence is more intoxicating than any nectar."

"It won't work, Dylan." Susan crossed her arms as though defending herself against anything Dylan might throw at her. "You said you'd give me some time, give *us* some time and, as usual, you show up just . . . " Susan started at the bandage. "What happened to your head?"

Ah, she's seen the noble wound. Pity, that'll bring her around. Dylan felt his mind fraying at the edges, buffeted by an unseen, unknown force. He grabbed for his train of thought like a hobo for the final boxcar. "Disagreement with an old friend . . . it ended well, though. He's actually better off for having seen me . . . strangely enough."

Susan's face clouded with concern. "Wait here. I'll be right back."

Dylan watched her turn the corner, then closed his eyes and almost immediately dropped into the soft darkness. A faint roar filled his head.

"Dylan, wake up." Susan knelt on one knee next to him, a bottle of Coke in her extended hand.

Taking the Coke, Dylan sipped it carefully. He hadn't realized until then how parched his throat felt.

Susan rested her right hand on his shoulder, the left tracing the area around his cut.

Dylan closed his eyes, taking comfort in the tingling path of warmth left by her fingertips.

"This doesn't look good. Did you see a doctor?"

"More or less." Clearing his throat, Dylan sat up a little straighter but kept his eyes closed. "I think he got his degree at the Black Hole of Calcutta Medical School."

Susan inspected the bandage, lifting it slightly to see the stitches. "I have to get the children back to school now. Promise me something."

"Name it, my heart."

Leaning close to him, Susan rested her cheek against his. "Go home. Take a shower. Go to bed."

Dylan felt her hair, soft and smelling of summer, blowing across his face.

"Will you do that for me?"

"Sure."

"And Dylan . . ."

"Yes."

"Burn that shirt. It smells awful."

Dylan smiled, opening his eyes slightly.

Susan leaned back, gazing at him thoughtfully.

Turning up the bottle of Coke, Dylan gulped it all. It burned like corn liquor going down.

"I'll come by and check on you later . . . if that's all right."

"I'll just check my social calendar and see if I can pencil you in," Dylan grinned broadly.

Susan's eyes seemed to emit a serene light as she spoke.

"There's something I've been wanting to tell you."

The Coke and brief rest had begun to restore Dylan. His vision cleared as the haze seemed blown away like smoke. "I hope it's not something drastic."

"What do you mean?"

"You know, like you signed up for folk dancing lessons or started to believe that Lyndon Johnson's telling the truth about Vietnam."

In reply, Susan ran her fingers though Dylan's hair, brushing it back from his forehead.

Dylan stood up, braced himself against the wall, and reached down for Susan. As she rose, her arms went around his waist, her head beneath his chin. He felt her pressing against him, becoming a part of him. Standing between flesh and stone, he breathed her fragrance.

Susan relaxed, her arms pulling free as she moved back. Her hands on Dylan's waist, she gazed up at him. "There's nothing I need to worry about, is there?"

Dylan stared down into her eyes, light and clear in her shadowed face. "No. Everything's fine."

Standing on tiptoe, Susan kissed his cheek, turned, and walked away. At the corner of the building, she glanced back. "Dylan, for once . . . take the easy way out." Then she disappeared behind the stone wall.

The wind seemed to pick up a chill in Susan's absence. Dylan rested his arms on the wall at the edge of the deck, gazing out over the city. The sun on the river glittered like ice on a muddy road. *Susan, for once there may not be an easy way out.*

———————

At the back entrance of the building, the smell of cooking hit Dylan. His stomach began sending out distress signals. Hunger turned to amazement when he opened his door at the top of the stairs and realized it was coming from *his* apartment.

Susan, barefoot, wearing jeans and a black T-shirt, stepped through the kitchen door. Tied loosely at the back with a red ribbon, her hair gleamed in the sunlight streaming through the kitchen window. She placed her hand on her hip, tilting her head to one side and cooed, "Hello, sailor. Wanna have some fun?"

Dylan stared at his wife's face. It seemed to glow as though it had been touched with a brush dipped in light. He knew it was visible only in *his* eyes, but he saw her that way all the same. "You're a constant wonder, Susan. What brought this on?"

"Some sort of primal cooking instinct, I suppose," she smiled, crossing the room.

"I remember now. I used to think it had something to do with the phases of the moon, but it never seemed to happen quite that often."

Susan placed her arms around his waist, leaning toward him. "Ah, but wasn't it worth waiting for?" Then she kissed him wetly on the mouth.

Dylan's arms tightened around her.

Pushing away with her hands on his chest, Susan admonished mildly, "No, no! Time for that later."

Dylan watched the light flashing off her bare feet as she returned to the kitchen. Taking off his jacket, he threw it on the couch, slipped out of his boots, and dropped them next to it, then took the .38 from his belt and lay it on the end table.

Walking over to the kitchen, he leaned on the doorframe and watched Susan as she rattled and clinked and chopped and stirred about the kitchen. She was the noisiest, messiest cook he had ever seen, but her red beans and rice were the best this side of New Orleans.

"Is Teacher playing hookey today?"

Susan blew an errant wisp of hair back from her face. "I handed the little darlings over to Miss Clark for the afternoon. The domestic urge was too strong upon me."

"I didn't know if you'd come or not."

"Silly boy. I said I would, didn't I? Here, slice this and put some garlic butter on it." She placed a loaf of freshly baked French bread on the table. "But I'm leaving early in the morning for a few days in New Orleans."

Dylan no longer bothered to tell Susan to give his regards to her parents since he found out they were pleased that she had left him. Twice he had called for her at their home, and her mother had hung up at the sound of his voice. He sat down at the table, sawing at the crusty bread and listening to the plop-plopping of the beans as they simmered in the pot.

Susan stirred the beans, tasted them, and made an *Ummm* sound of approval. "I thought of asking you the details of your latest wound, but decided better of it."

"Just as well," Dylan replied, touching the bandage above his eyes. "It's a short, boring story."

"Maybe you should try a new line of work," Susan suggested, reaching up into the cabinet for a bottle of Louisiana Hot Sauce. "You're beginning to look more like a boxer than a probation and parole officer."

Dylan knew that as bad as the work sometimes got, it was the nights alone in this apartment that were siphoning off his will to get up each morning. It seemed to him at times that a sleek-bodied presence inhabited the place, its red eyes staring with supreme patience. He suddenly felt himself slipping, losing touch. "Yes, but as you can see, I've maintained the same number of orifices that I was born with."

Susan glanced around, a shadow of anxiety flicking across her brow.

"That's the ultimate secret in this line of work—if you want to survive, that is," Dylan continued.

"What in the world are you talking about?" Susan stepped over to the table.

"Negation of additional orifices," Dylan explained, unable to control the bizarre sequence of his words. It was as though he stood to the side and watched himself make a fool of himself. "That's all you have to do. Don't get shot."

A look of concern, about to mushroom into fear, crossed Susan's face. "Are you all right?"

Dylan forced his mind back into an area of relative logic and sanity. "Of course. I think the all-nighters are making me a little dopier than usual. I've got one more tonight, then I'm going to lay off them for awhile."

Susan relaxed and returned to her work. "I wish you didn't have to go again tonight. If you were in a different line of work . . ." her words trailed off.

Dylan avoided a discussion of the dangers of the midnight arrest runs. "Ironic that you should mention a different job. I got another offer. I may take it."

"Are you serious?"

"As serious as I get about jobs."

"Well, what is it?"

"I'll let you know when I'm a little bit more certain what I'm going to do."

"I hope it's something a little safer."

Dylan finished the bread, went to the refrigerator, and took out a Coke and a bottle of Barq's Root Beer. Pouring the Coke into a glass of ice for Susan, he took the root beer to the table, sipping it absently as he watched her move about in the delicious aroma and progressive clutter of the kitchen.

Twenty minutes later, Susan set a plate of light, fluffy rice down on the counter next to the stove, then spooned the creamy beans on top of it. Adding a generous portion of lean, pickled pork to the side of the plate, she put it down in front of Dylan. After taking the pan of garlic bread from the oven and fixing her own plate, she joined him.

"May we have the wisdom of old people and the peace of children." Dylan lifted a full bottle of root beer.

Susan smiled and joined him in the toast, then gazed directly into his eyes. "The peace of a child. It's wonderful."

Puzzled, Dylan didn't ask Susan to explain, knowing that she would come to it in her own time. Before they ate, he drew her into the game they had played for years. " 'A perfect woman, nobly planned.' "

"Robert Browning?" Susan asked, handing Dylan a slice of garlic bread.

" 'To warm, to comfort, and command,' " Dylan continued, shaking his head.

"Byron?"

" 'And yet a spirit still, and bright.' "

"I give up." She reached across the table, taking Dylan by the hand.

" 'With something of angelic light.' "

The light had softened to a pale gold and the children from the school below Dylan's bedroom window had long since made their ways home. Dylan gazed at his wife, her hair spread like a dark cloud on the pillow as she stretched and moaned, like a child luxuriating in dreams of Christmas and carousels.

"Enjoy your nap?"

"Ummm." Susan stretched again, opening her eyes slowly. "Did you sleep?"

"No." Dylan was still thinking of her face as she slept and of the hidden country of her dreams and of how he wanted to be on that journey with her. Staring at her now, he felt there was an inexplicable and imposing serenity about her that he had never seen before. Remorse and regret tormented him like twin demons for all the times he had taken her for granted.

A whisper of drowsiness still lingered in Susan's voice as she spoke. "I'm so happy, Dylan."

Even as she said the words, Dylan knew without an explanation that they had nothing to do with him. *She must have found somebody else. This was probably my farewell party from her.* A terrible yearning surged through him for all the years since their wedding to somehow vanish so they could start over again. "Who is it?"

"What? What are you talking about?" Susan pulled the pillow under her arm, propped on one elbow as she brushed her hair back with her left hand.

Maybe it isn't another man. Dylan felt relief flooding through him.

Susan reached out, cradling Dylan's cheek softly with the palm of her hand. "I'm a Christian now. And it's so wonderful!"

"But you've always—"

"Gone to church," Susan interrupted. "And I knew *about* Jesus. Now I *know* Him. It's so marvelous!"

"You sound like my grandmother."

"Funny you should mention that." Susan sat up cross-legged like a teenager, pulling the sheet about her. "I remembered how you told me your grandmother always read her Bible every night. I was so unhappy, Dylan, with us not being together, and everything seemed to be going wrong, so I figured, 'What have I got to lose?' "

Dylan stared with fascination as Susan poured out her good news to him.

"I started reading the Book of John—"

"Because that's your daddy's name."

Susan smiled and nodded. " 'For God so loved the world, that He gave His only begotten Son, that whosoever believeth in Him should not perish, but have everlasting life.' That's the first thing I read, Dylan. I'd heard about that verse all my life, but it's the first time I ever read it for myself."

While the shadows lengthened outside and the room glowed with a rose-colored light, Dylan listened to Susan's voice, full of the rapture of her story.

". . . and then I came to the part where Jesus said, 'I have called you friends.' " Susan's eyes glistened with tears. "I finally realized *who He is* . . . and how very much He loves us. He knows all about the hard times we go through. And in spite of the awful things we do to each other . . . and to ourselves, there's nothing we can do to make Him stop loving us.

"I let go of all the worry and the doubts and being afraid and . . . and trying to do everything my own way." Susan brushed the tears away, clearing her throat. "I just let go . . . and I fell into the arms of Jesus. That sounds silly, I guess, but that's just what it was like, and I don't know any other way to say it. I felt like—like a child again."

Dylan could see the happiness shining in her eyes. He remembered the same inexpressible joy in his father's eyes on that last Saturday morning before he died. "I'm glad for you, Susan. I could tell there was something different about you."

Susan lay down next to him, resting her head in the hollow of his shoulder. "We're going to be all right, Dylan. I don't know how, but we will."

Dylan saw a sudden image of the half-empty bottle and the faint gleam of his pistol on that July morning four months ago when Susan had left him. He forced it from his mind, losing himself in the silky warmth of having her next to him, savoring the scent of her hair as it caressed his chest and shoulder. "I'm always all right as long as I'm with you."

"I won't leave you again, Dylan, but there's so much more for us than that." Susan's voice began filling with weariness. "Now I'm exhausted and it's so good to rest. Besides, we've got *all* the time in the world."

Dylan felt a sudden chill and pulled the quilt over them.

Susan's words grew heavier. "You want me to tell you a secret?"

"Sure."

"I never told any other man that I loved him—only you."

"I didn't know that."

"Told you it was a secret."

Dylan kissed her on the top of her head, letting his face linger against her hair.

Susan's words finally trailed off into sleep. "I love you, Dylan."

"I love you too, Susan."

Dylan lay for a long time, fighting the sleep that would rob him of Susan's presence. She sighed, curling herself closer against him, and he finally let himself drift down into the soft darkness.

From somewhere out in the city's quiet streets the sound of a siren drifted through the window. The long white curtains flowed into the room. Dylan rose from the smokey depths of sleep, opening his eyes slowly to the thin, webbed light. He lay perfectly still, listening to Susan's slow, metronomic breathing, feeling her warmth against him.

Summoning his reserves, he swung his legs over the side of the bed and sat up, rubbing his face, trying to rid himself of dark, unremembered dreams. Walking barefoot down the dim hall to the bathroom, he washed the last of sleep away with cold water. In the kitchen, he found that a two-ounce Community jar held enough crusty instant coffee for one cup. While the water boiled, he returned to the bedroom and put on jeans, boots, and a khaki shirt with two flap pockets.

Five minutes later, he stood next to the bedroom window, sipping coffee and watching the moving patterns of shadows beneath the oaks in the schoolyard as the dull autumn thunder rolled up from the south. The wind through the window carried a Gulf warmth and smelled of the city and distant rain.

Dylan could almost smell the early-morning coffee twenty years before in the soft glow of the pickup cab with the sound of Ray Price singing "Crazy Arms" coming from the little radio in the dashboard. He remembered the fear of the unknown and, worse, of failing in front of his father, who sat relaxed at the wheel in his heavy work jacket singing along:

" 'This ain't no crazy dream, I know that it's real.' You're gonna love this, Dylan. I never got to hunt much when I was growing up, with the Depression and all. Everybody had to work most of the time."

Dylan gazed at his father's pale blond hair gleaming in the soft light and wished his was that color instead of dark like his mother's. Since reading "King Arthur and the Knights of the Round Table," he had pictured his father many times in shining armor, riding a white steed.

"Daddy even farmed me out to another family for a while when I was thirteen. Preachers were starving back then." A slight grimace twisted Noah St. John's face as though he had been struck by a sharp memory. "It was tough though, being young and away from home. I had a time forgiving him for that."

"Do you think we'll really see some squirrels, Daddy?" Dylan tried to talk away the cold knot of fear in his stomach.

"See some? Why, we're liable to fill this ol' pickup plumb full of 'em," Noah smiled warmly. "You reckon your grandmother can cook that many?"

Soon they were walking through the misty November woods with the cold, damp smell of leaf mold and the soft ticking sound of dripping trees.

Dylan stood on a rise next to a giant beech, holding the single-barrel twenty-gauge at port arms. The land dropped off sharply to a slough, the surface covered with gray-brown scum and dark leaves. A cedar, fallen years before, lifted its gnarled and twisted limbs from the water like some primordial animal frozen in its death throes.

A sudden twitching of burnt red color to his left and Dylan spotted a fox squirrel flattened against the side of an oak on a low ridge across the slough. He pulled the hammer back until it clicked, slowly lifting the shotgun to his shoulder as the little animal began his graceful, erratic tracking through the trees.

Dylan seemed to enter into a dreamlike state, with the shotgun barrel reaching out across the water toward the squirrel, diminishing it to the size of the bead sight, the roar of the twenty-gauge sounding as though from a great distance, echoing through the forest with the seemingly enigmatic, slow-motion tumbling of the squirrel to the leaves.

Then he found himself running through the grab and slap of vines and limbs, watching the last convulsive jerks of the animal's right hind leg, standing above the deep red stillness of death.

Ten minutes later, Noah found Dylan, shaking with cold, squatting there next to the squirrel. He built a fire and they sat together, wrapped in a blanket, drinking coffee and talking until Dylan's fear and exhilaration and sadness became a drowsy, comfortable warmth.

It was to be their only hunt together. The trips from New Orleans to the hills of Feliciana became fewer and fewer until finally there remained only the Christmas visit and a few days during the summer.

Dylan hunted again but never with that same excitement or joy or fear.

Placing the half-empty cup on his desk, he took the .38 from the top drawer, slipped it inside his belt at the small of his back, and grabbed a denim jacket from the chair. Standing next to his sleeping wife, Dylan thought of the night that lay ahead: ramshackle houses on forgotten streets and sad, empty men, living on the raw edge of desperation.

Kneeling next to the bed, Dylan took Susan's hand and placed it against his cheek. Then softly brushing back her hair, he gazed at her face and suddenly felt a comforting warmth fall like summer rain on the shadows of his heart.

PART FOUR

—

MAN OF SORROWS

14

THE SCENT OF ROSES

A tug moaned far out on the river, feeling its way downstream through the heavy mist hanging like wet cotton above the muddy surface of the river. The chimes in the cathedral tower knelled out the hour of three.

Turning in her sleep, Susan half-awakened and smiled, remembering that she had shared her husband's bed for the first time in months. Floating in that downy-soft region this side of dreams, she thought of how she would tell her mother later in the day that she and Dylan were together once more.

Susan pictured the two of them, drinking iced tea as they sat on the patio behind their little cottage, with Dylan clacking away at the battered old Underwood typewriter, a treasured legacy from his grandfather. She could almost feel the soft April breeze carrying the scent of roses and the sound of children playing in the park. Sighing with pleasure, she slid over to Dylan's side of the bed, pulling her own pillow over her head as she drifted back down into a warm, enfolding sleep.

Behind the building, a small man in fatigue pants, black jacket, and dark green baseball cap walked down the alley strewn with dry leaves, dead limbs, and the assorted castoffs of passersby. With a furtive glance behind him, he darted through the back entrance, climbed the stairs to Dylan's apartment, and slipped the lock on the hall door.

Inside the apartment, he paused, listening for any sound and allowing his eyes to become accustomed to the thick darkness. Then, crossing the living room, he felt his way silently along the hall and entered the bedroom. Standing just inside the door, he took in everything at a glance, then slipped the pistol out of his inside jacket pocket. With eyes rheumy and swollen from drink, he stared at the dim figure bundled beneath quilt and pillow, then flicked the safety off.

The man's lips curled back, baring narrow teeth as he crept over to the bed, held the pistol in both hands, and squeezed the trigger three times. The muffled coughs and the slight jarring of the silenced .22 against his palm brought a thin smile to his stubbled face. Holding one hand against his mouth to stifle his laughter, he jerked back the covers. Shrieking a curse at the darkness, he retraced his steps and vanished down the alley.

———————

The Old Arsenal, built in 1835, stood east of the capitol on its landscaped grounds. Original graffiti from the earliest soldiers barracked there remained on the interior of its heavy masonry walls. In the American Revolution, the only battle outside the thirteen colonies was fought on this site.

Down the slope from the eastern wall, an expanse of lawn stretched almost to the bridge that crossed the lake over to the governor's mansion. A thirty-by-seventy-yard area of clipped grass, bordered by crepe myrtles and surrounded by curving walkways and flower beds, made an ideal playing field for over-the-hill athletes.

As Dylan walked into that bucolic setting, a solitary swan, graceful as a Phoenician galley silhouetted against the rising sun, glided by on the lake.

Beyond the line of crepe myrtles, Ike, wearing gray sweat pants and a Brusley High School football jersey, did stretching exercises in the center of the field. After a few quick push-ups, he ran half-speed to the opposite end and followed his shadow back in an easy sprint, his feet turning slightly inward for balance.

"Mack, Ike, and me against ya'll," Jenkins declared quickly, tossing a soft pass over to Ike.

Ike caught it and nodded his head.

That simple toss of the ball decided the outcome of the game. Speed, sure hands, and decent passing would always win in touch football. Ike possessed two of the three, and Snowden's wobbly passes were accurate enough.

Unable to launch his bone-jarring tackles, Wes's power proved nothing but a source of frustration for him, and his bad knee didn't give him enough lateral movement to run a decent pass pattern. Using his height to advantage, he batted down some of Snowden's slow passes.

Jenkins, surprisingly quick for all his bulk, caught a few passes in Dave's zone. He always reminded Dylan of the hippo ballerinas in Disney's *Fantasia*, but he moved in the game with the deceptive cadence that some heavy men have.

Dylan tried only once to play Ike tight, and Ike caught the bomb for a touchdown, which is what Snowden called every pass he threw more than thirty yards. After that, Dylan played Ike five yards deep, giving him the short ones.

Thirty minutes into the game the score was eighteen-six. Divots speckled the spongy ground. Puffing and blowing like water buffalo, everyone but Ike sprawled along the edge of the crepe myrtles. He had barely broken a sweat, sitting cross-legged and looking out over the lake toward the morning rush-hour traffic on the interstate.

"Did you see that last pass I hit Ike with?" Snowden leaned back on his elbows. "It was perfect."

"You're another Johnny Unitas," Dave sneered. "That one looked more like a bad punt than a pass."

"How 'bout that touchdown I caught on you, Dave?" Jenkins wheezed, his chest heaving. "You wudn't nowhere close to stopping me."

Not being able to use his explosive power had frustrated Wes, stretching his taut nerves even further. He hoped to remedy the situation on Jenkins. "You're a whole lot better than these other boys, Larry—about my weight, too. Let's you and me play some real football, a little one-on-one in the dirt."

"Naw. I got to get on home." Jenkins gave Snowden a nervous

glance. "Brenda'll be worried about me."

As happens when people have been together too long, a time limit seemed to have expired on the conversation. With grunts and groans and protesting muscles, the men made their way toward the cars.

Dylan walked stiffly over the torn ground toward a rough semicircle of seven pines at the end of the field near the lake, where Jenkins had dropped the ball after the last play.

"Wanna go for a quick one?" Dave called out.

Dylan turned around, glancing over at Ike. "Maybe next time. I think I'll stay around and visit with Ike if he's got a few minutes to spare."

Ike nodded and lay back on the soft grass.

At the end of the field, Dylan gazed out across the lake toward the governor's mansion. Ralph's silver Porsche swung around into the back lot. Listening to the high, strange tongue of the morning wind through the pines, he bent to pick up the football. A vicious humming past his head ended abruptly with a soft *thunk*.

Dylan stared at the perfectly round hole, smaller than a pencil, that had appeared in the rough gray bark of the tree next to him. The cold surface of the lake cast a malicious glint as his spirit seemed to rush from him into that small, dark opening.

With no conscious thought, Dylan suddenly flung himself down, lying flat on the ground on the opposite side of the tree, his face pressed against the carpet of pine needles. He glanced around the base of the tree, his head exposed for a split second. At the far end of the field, Ike still lay on his back, eyes closed. A small man in fatigue pants and a black jacket flitted through the shadowed shrubs and tree trunks, disappearing like windblown smoke beyond the line of crepe myrtles.

Dylan listened to the measured hammering of his own heart, his face pressed into the pine needles. It seemed that only flesh and blood remained, that his soul had followed his spirit into some bright, empyreal distance. He reached his left hand out carefully, touching the rough bark with his fingertips. Turning over, he watched a speck of a jet blasting its vapor trail across the hard blue sky.

A sudden darkness blotted out the sky.

"You all right?"

Ike's voice pulled him back, the parts coming together. "No."

After the police left, Dylan and Ike sat under the pines, listening to the morning hum of the city all around them.

"You mean you don't have any idea who tried to kill you?" Ike shook his head in disbelief.

"I got a few threats over the years. Never worried much about 'em." Dylan ran down a quick list of his enemies, but felt he hadn't offended anyone badly enough to warrant something like this. "The police are going to check out a few leads, but I doubt they'll amount to much. Could be somebody from a long time ago deciding he could blame me for his rotten life."

"What are you gonna *do*?" Ike's voice rose with emotion. "You can't just ignore this like it was another idle threat! Whoever *this* is means business!"

"I don't know. You tell *me*. Quit the job; leave town; wear a bulletproof vest?" Dylan felt he had been involuntarily thrust into a movie role and given no script. "This ain't the CIA I'm working for. Besides, whoever it was got his message through. That might be enough to satisfy him."

Ike shrugged and stood up, staring at the sap oozing from the pine where the police had cut the slug out. "Let's get out of here. This place is giving me the willies."

They began ambling along the curving walkway through the trees toward the Old Arsenal, avoiding the open field.

Dylan felt something working around at the back of his mind like an animal preparing to come out of its lair. "You know something, Ike? That was just an ordinary .22 slug they dug out of that tree."

"That's what the police said. So what?"

Dylan thought about the path of the bullet in a direct line with his right temple until he bent down for the ball.

"That was *not* an ordinary shot."

"You mean using a silencer?"

"That too," Dylan agreed, "but I was thinking more of the distance."

Ike glanced back at the tree the man had been standing beside when he made the shot. "Seventy-five yards, with a pistol. He's had some practice, all right. A lot of 'good ol' boys' use the pistol ranges around here."

They climbed the gentle slope toward the arsenal, walking around the wall to the heavy iron gate on the west side facing the Capitol.

Dylan felt something like the stirring of another animal, but it decided to rest a while longer. He remembered why he wanted to talk to Ike and decided to barge right in. "How long you been hobnobbing with the governor?"

Ike's body tensed briefly, then relaxed as he chuckled, shaking his head slowly back and forth. "I have to give it to you, Dylan. You *do* stay on top of things."

Dylan thought of the perfect little hole in the pine tree. *Not quite everything*.

"How in the *world* did you find out about that?" The laughter played out, Ike continued to smile.

"One of my high-level contacts. I figured you wouldn't let your shirttail touch you until you could tell me some news like that . . ." Dylan braced himself for Ike's reaction. ". . . unless it's something you're *ashamed* of."

The smile vanished. Ike took a quick step toward him, his face like a breaking storm. "You're a friend, Dylan. But I don't take that kind of talk from anybody!"

"Maybe I ought to rephrase it, then," Dylan offered cordially, but he flexed his knees slightly and leaned his weight forward toward the balls of his feet, ready to defend himself. "As one friend to another, tell me—what's a dirt-poor, shotgun-shack cane-cutter like you doing at the governor's house?"

Ike's anger faded into a weak smile and a soft laugh. "You *do* have a certain charm about you, Dylan. I guess that in itself demands *some* kind of answer."

They passed through the gate, turning right along the brick path that ran between the ten-foot-high walls and the arsenal building. Large sections of the cement overlay had crumbled away, leaving the original rust-colored brick exposed.

"Ralph got me involved with one of the governor's pet projects—finding alternative placements for youth at risk," Ike began his explanation. "I guess you could call me the legal or political liaison between the governor's office and the families."

"Does this phantom program have a name?"

"Don't they all?" Ike continued. "Ralph named this one YOUR for Youth at Risk."

"How come nobody's ever heard of it?"

"You know how politicians are," Ike explained. "They're going to wait and see how things turn out and if it does well, they'll go public, with the governor getting all the credit. If it bombs, nobody knows. That's the reason for the secrecy."

Dylan felt a prickling sensation at the back of his neck. He knew that *this* governor and every other governor *always* had scapegoats set up to blame their failures on, whether the programs went public or remained private. "Exactly what *do* they have you doing, Ike?"

"The legal side of things—custody orders, release forms, that kind of stuff."

Dylan let Ike talk, sensing that he truly believed in what he was doing.

"All of the families are poverty level, single parent or foster care, not much education, no way to give their kids a real chance in life."

And no way to do anything about it if things go wrong for their children.

Ike stopped and did a few stretching exercises for his hamstrings. "Since I grew up the way a lot of these kids did, Ralph thought I'd be perfect to deal with the families."

"Why's Ralph interested in a program like this?" Dylan sat down and leaned back against the cool, damp stone of the arsenal. "His idea of poverty is anybody who has to drive last year's Mercedes."

"Same reason he works for the public defender's office. It's the fashionable thing for rich, young liberals to do. Plus it's a feather in his cap with the governor." Ike sat down next to Dylan. "I think ol' Ralph sees himself on the ballot in the next few years."

"That's a pretty good summary, Ike, but I think you've overlooked something."

"Yeah? What's that?"

"The children." Dylan didn't look at him. "What happens when they get accepted?"

"I'm basically out of it after YOUR gets custody." Ike shrugged, as though anything that happened to them would be better than where they were. "Ralph says they get accepted into special programs all over the country, most of them long-term so they can make a real change in their lives. Some of the lucky ones even get adopted."

"You know what strikes me most about this whole thing, Ike?" Dylan held Ike's eyes this time.

"What's that?"

"It's so full of *Ralph says*."

Without responding, Ike got up and walked off around the corner of the arsenal.

Dylan caught up to him. "One more question, Ike."

Ike stopped, his face dark with suppressed anger. "Make it quick."

"You see yourself up there on that ballot with Ralph?"

"Anything wrong with that?" Ike crossed his arms over his chest defensively. "Ernest Morial was elected to the House of Representatives last year. First black man to serve in the legislature since Reconstruction."

Dylan merely stared at Ike.

"You didn't grow up like I did, Dylan."

"I'm not judging you, Ike. I just don't want to see a friend mess his life up."

"You got it all wrong." The anger left Ike's face. "I'm just getting it *unmessed*."

Dylan had completed the circuit around the Old Arsenal and stood on the first of fifteen stone steps that led down to the formal gardens. *One step for each year of Remy's life.*

"If the interrogation's over, I have to get to work," Ike remarked, the tension drained from his voice.

"I didn't mean it to sound that way," Dylan apologized. "It's just that I've run across some strange things lately, and they all seem tied in to the juvenile system—one way or the other."

"Well, you don't have to worry about the YOUR program," Ike assured Dylan. "It's an advocacy program for the kids, and we've got the cooperation of the top people in the welfare *and* juvenile departments."

"With the governor backing it, did you expect anything else?"

"I guess not."

Dylan still felt the tingling in his spine. "Have you seen anything in writing yet?"

A question began forming in Ike's eyes, but he blinked it away. "The legal paperwork."

"What's that amount to?"

"Just the forms for the parents' or guardians' signatures. Strictly routine."

"No one else signs?"

"I do," Ike admitted, a slight shadow crossing his brow, "as representative for the state."

"That's all?"

"What's the matter with you?" Ike snapped. "I thought the interrogation was over."

"Something's wrong here, Ike. I don't know what, but I feel it in my bones."

Ike looked him up and down, the big grin returning. "Bones are about the only thing that's gonna be left of you before long. When March gets here. You'll have to put some rocks in your pockets to keep from blowing away."

"It's just part of my new Spartan lifestyle."

"You start treating Susan right, she might even cook a meal for you now and again."

"Maybe." Dylan knew Ike was back to his old self again. *As bad as he wants to make it big in this city, he'd never deliberately hurt kids that come from the same kind of tough background that he grew up in. Or do I just need to believe that?*

Ike took the steps two at a time, then ran off down the sidewalk toward State Capitol Avenue.

"Ike!"

He stopped and turned around, still running in place. "Are you ever gonna shut up?"

"Look out for yourself."

"I growed up looking out for myself, white boy."

Dylan watched Ike running effortlessly between a grove of cedars on his left and a stand of pines on his right, facing each other like two opposing armies across the walkway.

When Ike had vanished beyond the trees, Dylan sat on the top step, gazing across the Capitol grounds. A ridge, higher than the arsenal site, stood a hundred yards to his right. Two mounted cannons looked out on the lake. He felt about as useful as they were—cement-filled and dormant.

It suddenly occurred to Dylan that this was not a prudent thing to do, sitting out in the open a hundred yards and one hour away from a near-final violation of his thought processes by an efficient little hunk of lead. He also realized that he wasn't particularly alarmed about this situation which, in itself, was reason for concern.

Dylan remembered he'd heard once that a tumor inside the brain wasn't supposed to be painful. *I wonder how it would feel, after a bullet penetrated the soft tissue and the skull. Would there be pain in the brain? What could be so bad about cessation of sensation?*

I wish I had somebody to tell me what to do. I'm just not ready to face a man who's faceless and nameless. We all looked out for each other in Vietnam. It was the only way to stay alive. If I hadn't bent down to pick up that football . . .

State government certainly didn't prepare me for something like this. I've got to bring this up at the next staff meeting. "Donice, you've been a tad remiss in your training program. You left out 'Assassination Attempt—Defensive Tactics.' "

I better not take any more pain pills. Dylan suddenly felt his body draining of strength, his vision blurring. *What can I do? Maybe what I've always done—not much of anything. Maybe my own ignorance will protect me. This guy's probably ready for anything but somebody who doesn't have any idea what to do against him. If I was still in the corps . . .*

15

LIGHT IN THE SUMMER TREES

". . . the Great Gawd Budd—, 'Plucky lot she cared for idols when I kissed 'er where she stud!' " Ideal for reciting Kipling, the voice was rotund and resonant. The empty reception area rang with images of colonial India.

Dylan walked past the chairs and tables scattered with magazines and newspapers to the office door, glancing at the scene inside.

Irene Ryan sat cowed and captive in a leather chair while Judge Daniel Madewood hobbled about on his cane, eyes toward the ceiling, captured by the sound of his own recitation and the euphony of the poem.

Dylan listened quietly until the judge spotted him.

"Dylan, my boy! Come in, come *in*."

Irene, the judge's secretary for so long a time that few remembered any other, quickly excused herself. Plump and dimpled, with the face of a schoolmarm, she gave Dylan a look of gratitude on her way out.

At five-five, with small delicate features and wearing a perfectly tailored dark brown suit, Judge Madewood gave the impression of a gray-haired child playing grown-up. "Fine woman, Irene. Not appreciably enamored of the finer things in this life, however."

Dylan sat down for the duration.

"She much prefers B. J. Thomas to Dylan Thomas. 'Raindrops Keep Falling on my Head.' Is *this* the best our lyricists can come up with, a song about someone who hasn't got sense enough to come in out of the rain?"

The judge's comments on the latest social phenomenon had always amused Dylan. His burden even seemed lighter in the little man's presence.

"And this song's probably a cut above average." The judge returned to his hampered pacing of the office, punctuating phrases with his cane. "I have grave misgivings about our future, Dylan. Do you ever listen to what passes for *music* these days? It sounds like a tinker's wagon tumbling down a hillside, dragging a braying mule behind it.

"And the families that show up in my courtroom! I don't expect pillars of the community, but this latest crop shows precious little resemblance to the species I purport as my own."

Dylan thought of another articulate and intelligent man whose office he had recently sat in and of how his words made absolutely no sense at all, while Madewood's words formed sentences with the precision and elegance of German automobiles.

"The children respect *nothing*: not the law, not their parents, not even themselves. A few of the more precocious ones, through considerable labor, I would imagine, have achieved the level of functional illiteracy."

Dylan determined that he wouldn't interrupt Madewood's monologue.

"One or two of them may even *aspire* to mediocrity. Charles Manson seems to be their consensus role model."

During the course of his soliloquy, Madewood had gained his chair and sat with his tiny feet propped on his desk, legs crossed, cane resting in the "V" formed by the toes of his shoes. "And the *parents*. My Lord, the parents! Their time seems to be equally divided between the pursuit of almighty mammon and rutting like crazed weasels."

"You have a call, Judge." Irene's round face appeared around the doorframe.

"Who is it?"

"Senator Blount."

"That ol' pirate! Tell him I'm entertaining a courtesan from Persia and can't be disturbed."

"Yes sir." Irene's face remained as passive and disinterested as a portrait.

"Irene." Madewood called her back.

"Sir?"

"Tell him I'm in conference."

"Oh—all right."

"Poor Irene! Fine woman, but lacking in the subtleties of humor." Madewood spun his cane like a baton. "Now, where was I? Ah, yes, the parents! The rich give their children money, the poor give theirs beatings. I don't know which is worse."

Madewood seemed to have run out of words or the energy to produce them, and leaned his head against the back of his chair. His face emptied and the years clambered over his childlike features. In a few seconds he recovered, sighted down his cane as though it were a gun barrel, and turned toward Dylan with an expression both mischievous and wise.

Dylan held his gaze, thinking that Madewood was the only human being he'd ever known who actually had a twinkle in his eyes.

"Did I catch you at a bad time, Judge?"

"Not at all. Not at all," Madewood grinned. "Things aren't as awful as I make them out to be, of course. I do tend to ramble on though, don't I? Comes from spending too much time alone, I suppose."

Madewood glanced toward the sound of typing coming from the outer office. "Poor Irene, my reluctant and patient surrogate wife, listening to the saturnine rantings of an old bachelor. Fine woman, Irene."

Out of his deep respect for Madewood and the almost desperate need to talk that Dylan could see in him, he could not bring himself to interrupt the judge with his troubles.

"I should have married my little lovely and loyal Maurepas maiden, Dylan." Madewood sighed wearily. "Pride—that was my nemesis."

Dylan had heard rumors of Madewood's tragic love affair, but the man had never spoken to him about it before.

"Like a lot of small men, I always felt I had to prove myself. Fastest man on the track team, valedictorian, accepted at the

Point and then that fateful summer after graduation—polio!

"I couldn't stand to have her, or any woman for that matter, see me as a cripple," Madewood confessed, his eyes bright with the pain of memory. "She told me it didn't matter . . . that only our love mattered."

Madewood lifted his feet off the desk, leaning forward in his chair, staring at the floor.

"Judge, you all right?"

He continued as though Dylan hadn't spoken. "I know *now* that she meant it." He lifted his head, his jaw set tightly. "But it did matter . . . to me. 'Pride goeth before a fall and a haughty spirit before destruction.' "

Suddenly, Madewood's face lost its tension, a gentle light filling his eyes. "The Bible contains all truths, Dylan, mostly ignored by the creature they were written for."

"Judge . . ."

Madewood turned toward Irene, peering around the doorframe. "Yes."

"The senator's out here, insisting that you see him."

Madewood glanced at Dylan wearily, pointing to the side door that led out of the office. "This won't take long."

"Yes sir." Dylan rose quickly to leave the office. "Is there a phone in there?"

"Help yourself."

Dylan entered the judge's law library, dim and shadowed, its shelves lined with books and crammed with periodicals and stacks of papers. A telephone rested on a small stand next to the long conference table.

Sitting down in one of the blond wood and gray leather chairs, Dylan called Emile at his office, telling him about the incident on the Capitol grounds and briefly what he had found out regarding the YOUR program.

"Where are you?"

"In Judge Madewood's law library." Dylan glanced down through the plate glass window at the midmorning crowd strolling along the sidewalks.

"We've got to find a place where this guy can't get at you. Then we'll do something about him."

"I don't know, Emile." Dylan shook his head slightly as he spoke. "I think maybe it was a one-time shot from somebody who just went off the deep end for a little while."

"Maybe you're right," Emile agreed halfheartedly. "If he was a *real* pro, he'd have taken Ike out first, then made *real* sure that he got you."

"Yeah." Dylan fought against the fear that was building in him, now that the shock brought on by the attempt on his life had begun to wear off. He knew the man *could* strike again at any time. Every stranger became suspect.

"But if you're not, you might end up *dead*." Emile's voice hardened. "Where's your car?"

"At the state parking garage."

"Walk down to the ferry, and I'll pick you up over in Port Allen. That'll make it harder for anybody to follow you."

The fear had become heavy and difficult to deal with, an inconstant companion, but Dylan forced himself to do what was necessary. "I need to see Judge Madewood first. The quicker Remy gets back to Evangeline, the better."

A four-second silence followed.

"Emile?"

"You're worse than a snapping turtle. When you bite down on something, you just can't let go," Emile growled into the receiver. "I'll pick you up in two hours. No more delays."

"See you then."

"Dylan . . ."

"*You're* delaying me now, Emile."

"What about Susan?"

"What about her? She's got no part in this and no enemies that I know of."

"Can you think of anyone who'd want to hurt both of you?"

"Quit worrying. I just left her a few hours ago." Dylan pictured Susan and her mother having coffee on the high front porch that overlooked St. Charles Avenue. "She left at five this morning to spend a few days with her parents."

—————

"Glad that didn't take long. Now on to more important matters. What are you writing these days, young St. John? I miss our literary diversions before court since you spurned us in favor of the adult system."

"So have I, Judge." Dylan thought back to the times when he and Madewood had discussed Yeats or Faulkner or James Dickey while a packed courtroom restlessly awaited the arrival of the man in the black robe. "My muse seems to have deserted me."

"Balderdash! You're just lazy." Madewood cut right through Dylan's excuses. "Writing's nothing more than hard work. You just have to sit down and grind it out. Discipline and tenacity—that's what it takes to be a writer . . . along with a modicum of talent."

Sensing the impending lecture on misspent youth, Dylan tried to avoid it by walking over to the span of windows in the south wall of the office.

Undeterred, Madewood forged ahead. "Show me at least one good short story the next time we meet or I just may put a warrant out for your arrest."

Dylan gazed out at a line of clouds stacked like mounds of ash on the horizon. "Judge, I need your help."

Madewood's voice dropped out of its lecture tone. "What can I do for you?"

Making it as brief as possible, Dylan told him what had happened on the State Capitol grounds.

"You'll just have to keep out of his way until the local constabulary has him shackled and under guard." Even when deadly serious, Madewood sounded as though he was teaching a medieval law course. "I can think of a hundred secluded spots in the Atchafalaya Basin where Sherlock Holmes and a kennel of bloodhounds couldn't find you."

"I'm on my way there now."

"Splendid." Madewood picked up a thick section of willow limb from his desk. Gnawed in the form of a cone on one end, the other had been sawed flat so it would rest upright. "Beaver . . . nature's structural engineers. Now, what else is on your mind?"

Dylan told him about the problem with Remy.

"We'll transfer jurisdiction to the parish of residence. Normal procedure."

"I know what the procedure is, but *normal* doesn't seem to apply in this case."

"If the boy is there, I'll *see* to it that he gets home," Madewood assured him. "Now what's next?"

Dylan could never figure out how Madewood knew when an agenda was unfinished. "The YOUR program. Do you know anything about it?"

"Only what Ike's told me, but it seems credible, even in this incipient phase. Juveniles in the custody of the state can be placed with any person or facility deemed suitable for indefinite periods. They don't need my authorization, so I haven't had any direct input yet." Madewood, his eyes narrowed, gave Dylan an oblique glance. "You haven't run afoul of yet another authority figure, have you?"

"No sir. I kinda blundered onto the program and got interested. It's—unique, I guess you'd call it. No bureaucratic superstructure at all."

"Maybe the state inadvertently did something efficacious. Best to leave it alone." Madewood tapped his cane softly on the floor next to his chair. "Something else troubling you, Dylan? You want to talk about it?"

Sunlight slanting through the darkened glass of the windows picked up a green cast. Dylan felt as though he were in a giant aquarium, breathing water. "Nothing important. My life's unraveling a little at the edges. I think it's going to get better though."

"I perceive that you are again at odds with the grand Republic of Louisiana." Laying his cane on the desk, Madewood placed his hands together in an attitude of prayer, rubbing his fingertips back and forth on his chin. "Just humor an old man's importunate ways and listen for a moment. Maybe I can save you some heartache.

"Politics is power and power is more addictive than any drug. Just as an addict will do *anything* for his fix, a politician will do *anything* to stay in power. And his network of minions, personal staff, appointees, and upper-level managers are placed there exclusively to protect him, or them, as the case may be.

"Sometimes a little work gets accomplished, but only as a by-product. The actual work is done by the serfs with the four-figure salaries and the K–Mart suits. Some of the names change at election time, but the system always remains intact."

Madewood spoke like a father to an errant and naive son. "You're an offense to the system, Dylan, and in your own guileless ignorance, you don't even know it."

"I always suspected there was *something* I couldn't quite figure out! Guess that's why I never got any promotions, huh?"

"You have no political sensitivity whatsoever," Madewood almost smiled, "consequently you don't feel threatened by the power brokers."

Dylan lifted himself up on the window ledge, sitting with his legs dangling.

"Because you understand very little of what they're capable of, you don't show fear or even a little pedestrian deference. This, of course, infuriates them."

"I thought I was supposed to watch out for the criminals I have to put in jail, not the people I work for."

Madewood gave him a sad smile. "Dylan, if you plan to remain in government work, and for your sake I sincerely hope you don't, you need to assimilate one essential canon and all that it portends. 'Politics is the province of verbal athletes and moral cripples.'"

"Judge, you're a politician yourself—an elected official!"

With both hands on the handle of his cane, Madewood lifted himself out of his chair and made his way painfully over to the windows. He stood there gazing out on the city, the green light shining on his close-cropped gray hair.

"Judge?"

"I'm well aware of what you just said, Dylan, and I like to think that politics hasn't entirely abraded my principles over the years, but I also realize that no one escapes unscathed."

"I've always known you to be a man of conscience, Judge. In fact, I don't even *think* of you as a politician."

"I consider that the highest compliment," Madewood smiled. "But the favors granted, the facts overlooked that I tried to convince myself were only minor indiscretions, compromises to achieve necessary ends—they simply won't go away."

"Judging yourself is one option that's not open to you, even if you are a judge."

"You're right, of course. That's someone else's purview, in due time. '. . . forgetting those things which are behind . . . I press toward the mark.' A very wise man once said that, and it's still sound advice two thousand years later."

Madewood leaned on the chest-high window sill. "It's strange. I've forgotten so much of the catechism. Only remnants of the Apostle's Creed, the Rosary, and some others are left, but the Scriptures never desert me."

Turning back around, Madewood glanced up at Dylan. "Ah well, you're not here to listen to the ramblings of a unctous old man, are you?"

"They make a lot of sense—for ramblings, that is."

"You're kind, young St. John. But let me apologize for my political oracle anyway. You know my penchant for overstatement, so accept it in that context."

Easing his way back to his chair, the judge sat down heavily. "Politicians aren't all trolls and ogres committed to necromancy and other dark endeavors. It's quite possible there are several who may even see beyond their own reflection in the mirror."

"I don't know what your part is in all this," Madewood admitted, propping his feet back on the desk. "I don't think I *want* to know."

"Only doing a favor for Emile."

"And the Titanic *only* hit a piece of ice." Madewood held Dylan's eyes with a somber gaze. "Remember, Dylan, anyone standing between the junkie and his fix is in peril."

Dylan stared down into the city. He thought of the thousands of people in offices and stores, and of those who wandered aimlessly along the late-morning sidewalks. In a few hours, traffic would build toward the evening rush: to grocery stores and bars, to home-cooked meals and warmth and the reaching up of tiny arms, to furnished rooms with torn shades and paper bags bloated from their diet of empty bottles.

"Judge, what do you know about Jim Donaldson?"

Madewood began tapping the cane on the toes of his shoes.

"I can tell by the way you ask the question that you already know the answer."

"Is there anything you don't know about the people in this town?"

"Precious little and it's becoming a tiresome burden," Madewood remarked offhandedly. "Donaldson's been in two drug rehab programs, and I can tell you he's doing his best to beat the addiction."

"What about all the kids in state custody? What's he doing for them?"

"Giving them the best break he can, as far as I can tell. He's not going to deliberately hurt any of them, if that's what you mean," Madewood insisted.

Dylan realized he hadn't formulated much of an opinion about Donaldson except that the ex-addict was evasive, which was apparently ingrained in every administration appointee.

"I'm afraid that his problem makes him vulnerable for anything that happens to go wrong in his department, though. I'm sure that he realizes this too."

Dylan thought back to his visit to Donaldson's office and of how uneasy the man had seemed. *Maybe he's so afraid of being the scapegoat he'd do something drastic to prevent it.*

"Donaldson doesn't just show up for ribbon-cutting ceremonies. He actually gets involved with the day-to-day work of his department, even when there aren't any cameras or microphones around. Most people don't know about it." Madewood rested the cane between his shoes. "Maybe he's trying to make up for the shortcomings in his personal life."

Seeing the look of concern on the judge's face, Dylan explained, "I'm just trying to make some sense out of all this, Judge. I don't intend to hurt anybody."

"I know you don't, but I think it's time you tempered your impulsive behavior with a little patience, though, and you most certainly need more discernment about human nature."

"You're probably right about that."

Madewood shifted in his chair, his lips going white with pain as he held Dylan's eyes in a steady gaze. "We are—all of us, young St. John—cripples in one way or another."

Madewood turned toward the window, but his vision reached out somewhere beyond the farthest city streets and the immutable flow of time. He saw himself breaking the tape at the finish line, speaking before his black-robed classmates in a cathedral of live oaks, sitting on the banks of Lafourche with the dark-eyed love of his youth as the afternoon light softened in the summer trees.

16

Zɪᴘ-ᴀ-Dᴇᴇ-Dᴏᴏ-Dᴀʜ

"I can appreciate your wanting to look out for a friend, Dylan, but nobody took a shot at Ike." Heading north out of Port Allen, Emile drove his white Blazer through the bedlam of Poplar Grove's grinding season. "You can try to talk some sense into him later."

"It's not just Ike, Emile. It's Remy, it's . . . I don't know who or how many."

"Well, what good is it going to do anybody for you to talk to Ike's granddaddy?"

"It always comes back to this YOUR program. Maybe Ike told him something about it."

Emile threaded his way through the maze of tractors and trucks and cane buggies bouncing over chunks of mud from the fields. "I think it's a waste of time."

"Won't take but a minute." Dylan slammed both hands against the dashboard, bracing himself as Emile stomped the brakes to avoid a tractor veering out of a dirt road onto the blacktop. "You might want to keep your eyes on the road along here."

"I'll do the driving," Emile muttered, swerving hard to miss a huge clump of mud in the middle of his lane.

Enjoying the damp breeze through the truck window, Dylan thought back to his first job after graduation and the first time he had seen Chauvin Jacobs.

After his three-week purging of any independent thought called "Orientation" by the welfare department, he found himself bumping along Scale House Road in a 1959 white Ford sedan with the Seal of the Great State of Louisiana emblazoned on both doors. Grinding season was over and the windswept January fields were as cold and empty as a miser's heart.

Dylan pulled the car over in front of one of the hundred-year-old tenant homes and reread the directions he had scribbled on a legal pad in his efforts to locate an eighty-two-year-old client named Mandy Paul.

Hearing the clattering of a diesel engine, he glanced out to see a short, sturdy black man in overalls and brand new brogans pulling up next to him on a tractor. As Dylan rolled down the window, he half expected the man to break into a rousing chorus of "Zip-a-Dee-Doo-Dah."

"Well now, ain't you lookin' fine in dat new suit?" Chauvin grinned, his arms resting on the steering wheel of the tractor. "Mandy gon' be plumb tickled to see you. She worried to death wudn't nobody gon' take over her pension."

"You know Mrs. Paul?"

Without answering the unnecessary question, Chauvin leaped down from the tractor with surprising agility, walked over to the car, and leaned on the door with both hands. "Look at you now. You hardly mo' den a boy yo'self. How you gon' look out for all deese ol' folks?"

"Just do the best I can," Dylan shrugged.

"Dat's good enough for me." Chauvin pointed to a lane that led into Scale House Road. "Come on up to de house, and I'll make us some coffee and tell you where dey all stays."

Dylan turned the Ford around, following Chauvin's tractor to his house for the first of many visits and countless cups of French drip coffee and a beginning of knowledge not found in workshops or conferences or textbooks. Smiling at the memory, Dylan directed Emile left, away from the levee onto Scale House Road, then right down the dirt lane bordered by a narrow coulee overgrown with water hyacinth and the last duckweed of the long season.

"That's it, all the way to the end."

Pulling off the lane, Emile parked beneath a chinaberry tree, leaving the truck's engine idling.

The tiny cabin, constructed of rough-cut heart cypress weathered to a silver-gray by more than a hundred years of sun and wind and rain, stood in the shadow of the giant sugar factory. A tin-roofed gallery ran the brief southern span of the cabin, its yard crowded with azaleas, gardenias, and wisteria vines climbing up unpainted trellises.

The overpowering fragrance of boiling cane juice filled the air along with the clanking, clattering, hissing sound of the factory machinery.

Chauvin sat on the front porch in a cane-backed rocker, reading his Bible, laying it as well as his reading glasses down on a homemade table when he heard the truck door slam.

"You coming?" Dylan glanced back in the truck window.

"I believe I'll sit this one out."

"Suit yourself." Walking over toward the gallery, Dylan felt somehow restored at the sight of Chauvin's brogans and overalls and his Zip-a-Dee-Doo-Dah smile.

Chauvin stepped off the gallery and crossed the yard to meet Dylan. "Well now—ain't you a sight?"

For the first time, Dylan became aware of Chauvin's carrying the weight of five years since they had met. In the dozens of intervening visits, he had never noticed their effect: the stooping of back and shoulders, slowed gait, and slight tilting of the old man's head to the right.

"I thought you'd plumb forgot about me." Chauvin reached out a work-hardened hand.

"How could I forget the man who makes the best crawfish bisque in south Louisiana?" Dylan gazed down fondly as they shook hands.

Chauvin glanced at Emile, almost obscured by the light refracting off the truck's windshield. "I kin see dis ain't a sociable visit. De high sheriff ain't even turnt his motor off."

"It's about Ike."

"Come on." Chauvin turned around and headed back toward his rocking chair. "He in trouble?"

"Why would you think that?"

"Dat rich boy, Ralph. Ike brung him out here one time."

Chauvin sat wearily down in his rocker. "Don't take but *one* time wid de likes of him."

"One time for what?" Dylan sat on the edge of the porch, leaning back against a post.

"To see he jes' *using* Ike. I seen de same kine on TV. Dey uses black folks to git votes or go to jail in dey place when de law ketch up to 'em."

"Does Ike ever talk to you about his work?"

"Don't talk about *nuttin'* now. Ain't seed him in weeks. Last time he here, he tole me he workin' for de gov'ner now, goin' to de mansion."

Dylan could see the pain of memory in the old man's cloudy brown eyes.

"I axe him if dey make him go roun' to de back do' like dey made him do at de City Club. He tole me a ignernt ol' cane cutter like me don't know nuttin'."

"You know he didn't mean that, Chauvin," Dylan said earnestly. "He was always telling me how you had to be mama and daddy to him after his *own* mama died."

Only a rumor of the old man's smile was left as he put his glasses on and let his Bible rest in his lap, holding onto it with both hands as he stared out across the yard at the dark purple and gray clouds tumbling up the southern sky toward them.

Dylan could almost see the memories flickering behind Chauvin's eyes.

"Ike was always a mineful chile. Hardest worker on dis here ol' sugar farm. When grinding season over, he help wid de plantin', sack groceries down to de A&P, whatever he could. We went to de Baptist Chapel ever' time de do' open. Now it look like his pocketbook done pushed all de good plumb outta his life."

"Don't give up on him yet."

"I don't *never* give up," Chauvin replied as though the idea was a foreign concept to him. "Jes' ain't nuttin' I kin do but pray for my boy."

"Ike's working with a program that's supposed to get kids on the right track. You raised him. He'll be all right."

"I done turnt it over to de good Lawd." Chauvin stared down

at his Bible, holding it tighter. "But I still got dis feelin' dat dey 'bout to use my boy up."

At that moment the wind hit, rustling the withered banana trees at the far corner of the house. Seconds later, the rain came clattering across the tin roof like a shower of stones.

Dylan got up and quickly stepped back out of the rain. "I got to get going, Chauvin, but I'll be back to see you soon, and we'll have us a *real* visit."

"We sho' will," Chauvin agreed. He glanced up and the smile had returned to his face.

Dylan shook hands and turned to leave, but the steady pressure of Chauvin's calloused hand held him. Puzzled, he turned back around.

"Help my boy, Dylan."

Dylan answered "yes" with a nod of his head, jumped from the porch, and splashed through the yard to the truck.

Emile and Dylan sat in silence for a few moments with the truck's motor running and the wipers rubbing twin arcs on the wet windshield. All around them, the failing light was taking on a deep silver cast as it gathered in the rippling sheen of the trees.

"What are you wrestling with now, Dylan? I thought we were finished here."

"I can't quite fit all the pieces together. Maybe I don't *have* all of them yet. The truest picture I get of this whole mess is what Chauvin told me. People are being used up." Dylan gazed at the distant and blurred image of the old man sitting on his porch, his Bible open in his lap. "I don't know how it's happening or why or who's doing what, but I can't get rid of this feeling that the bad guys are wearing the white hats."

"Why don't we keep things simple for right now," Emile offered, trying to cut through the confusion. "One—we get you in a safe place. Two—we get Remy back home. Then we take the rest of it as it comes."

"That won't help me tie it all together: that business on the Capitol grounds, Remy, his little brother, the YOUR program, Ralph, Ike, Donaldson, the governor—and no telling what or who else is involved."

"No, but it might keep you alive."

"Good point."

"I've noticed you need a little help establishing priorities now and then."

"You may be right about that, but I hate to go and just *sit* somewhere. I've got this gut feeling that the whole deal—whatever it is—is going down soon."

"Nothing you can do tonight anyway. We might as well get on down to the houseboat."

"I guess that makes sense."

"You make arrangements at work?"

"Donice made them for me. Told me to stay out of sight for a while. I think he was happy about it."

Emile backed the truck out of the yard, driving carefully down the muddy lane. The fields were emptying of drivers heading to the sheds on their tractors and cutters, riding on the buggies or walking to their homes.

During grinding season, the people on the sugarcane plantations worked far into the night, but the rain had given them respite and they had the elation of men and women who give a hard, honest day. There was plenty of time for a hot bath, a good meal, and a long rest.

───────

Dylan stood next to the Blazer in Emile's shed on the bayou, listening to the din of the rain on the tin roof and breathing in the musty smell of earth and old timbers. "I'd feel a whole lot better if I had my M–16 with me right now."

"Let's see what you brought."

Dylan took the snub-nosed Smith and Wesson from his belt, handing it to Emile.

"You shoot this much?"

"Once or twice."

"You couldn't climb up in a tree and hit the ground with this thing."

Dylan took his pistol and slipped it inside his belt. "Maybe I'll just *throw* it at him."

"It's all right for your work, but right now you need some firepower." Emile reached into the backseat, coming up with a

Remington twelve-gauge pump. "If you miss him with this, at least the *sound* might scare him to death."

Dylan took the shotgun, hefting it for balance. "Some guys in Nam liked this better than the sixteens."

"You ain't got to be Buffalo Bill to hit with it, that's for sure." Emile tossed Dylan a box of double-aughts.

Opening the box, Dylan slipped seven shells into the magazine, jacked one into the chamber, and inserted the eighth shell for a full load.

"You think you can find the houseboat?" Emile rubbed the dark stubble on his chin with thumb and forefinger.

Dylan heard the wind gusting, felt a fine cold spray blowing through the opening to the road. Glancing out the door that led to the bayou, he saw the pirogue resting upside down on the dock. The rain made a flat drumming sound on its narrow pointed hull. "I have to use that?"

"Yeah. Somebody *borrowed* my bateaus."

"I go straight across and through the willow."

Emile nodded. "I have to take care of some business for the sheriff, and I told Rachel Batiste I'd drop by and give her the latest on Remy."

Dylan stared at the pirogue, thinking of the short trip he would make in it in the storm.

"I'll bring you some breakfast in the morning. You might find some peanuts or potato chips on the boat, and there's water in the storage tank."

Opening one of the school lockers, Emile took out a yellow slicker with MPSO in large black letters on the back and handed it to Dylan. Then he took the shotgun, tied a length of rope to the stock and the barrel. "This'll keep your hands free."

Dylan slung the shotgun across his shoulder, barrel down, putting the slicker on over it. "That ought to keep it dry 'til I get to the houseboat."

"If you don't fall out of the pirogue."

"You *had* to say that, didn't you."

Emile grabbed a blue baseball cap with an outline map of the state of Louisiana embroidered above the bill and jammed it down on Dylan's head. "I guess you'll do 'til morning."

"I haven't worn a hat since I left the corps." Dylan hung the cap back on its nail.

"I don't think anybody can find you down here, but I'd stay awake, all the same, if I were you." Emile climbed into the Blazer, its dashboard lights shadowing the hollows of his face.

Dylan listened to the steady sound of the engine, knowing it would bring Emile back at the end of the night.

"Want me to get you anything?"

Dylan shook his head.

"Look in the top of that locker and get a flashlight. It's going to be mighty dark when I leave."

Emile was right. When the taillights' red glow winked out in the rainy distance, the darkness felt as thick and heavy as an underground cavern.

Inside the shed, the storm sounded like the metallic roar of an aircraft engine. Dylan switched the flashlight on, making his way over to the door that opened out onto the dock. In the bright beam of light, the rain pounded the dark surface of the bayou with a dancing whiteness. The dock and the pirogue had the blurred appearance of objects seen through a waterfall.

No trip in that toy boat just now, thank you. Dylan took a metal folding chair from a nail on the wall and set it on the dirt floor near the bayou entrance. His fear of a stalking shadow-man with a silenced .22 seemed diminished in the howling darkness of the storm.

———

Nodding off in the chair, Dylan jerked his head up, realizing that the howling of the storm had become a slow, steady drumming sound on the roof. He got up wearily and walked to the door, feeling the breeze, steadying now from the south. Mixed in the cool breath of the rain was a warmth from thousands of miles of sunlit Gulf water.

Suddenly, a sound rose out in the night above the heavy drone of the rain. Yet it could not be considered merely sound, but more of a tearing agony becoming audible, guttural and keening at the same time, a scream of mortal terror giving way to a black and final despair.

In the humid warmth of the coat, Dylan felt a chill rip through him like a current of ice. He backed away from the door, stumbling over the chair. Regaining his balance, he threw off the heavy slicker, loosed the shotgun from his shoulder, and punched the safety off. Then he backed slowly next to the lockers where he could enfilade both entrances to the shed.

Nothing but the sound of the rain and the dying wind remained out in the night.

In a few minutes, determined to meet whatever was out there head on, Dylan slipped the heavy coat on, leaving it unsnapped, and pulled the hood over his head. Holding the shotgun underneath the coat, its barrel in front of his right shoulder, he walked out of the shed onto the edge of the road.

Dylan could hear nothing but the sound of the rain: in the trees, on the bayou, and on the hood of his coat. He headed north where the scream had come from, keeping to his course by feeling the edge of the shell road with his right boot.

After a few yards, he eased down on one knee, held the flashlight extended out at arm's length to the side of his body, and flicked it on, sweeping the beam along the edge of the bayou.

An armadillo meandered along next to the bordering reeds and cattails, its mulelike ears erect, light glinting off its armor plating. Farther along, out of the light, something rustled quickly through the reeds and splashed heavily into the bayou.

Enough of this! Dylan flicked the light off and returned to the shed. The rain beat flatly on the dock as he eased the pirogue into the water. Trying to imitate Emile, he paddled directly across the bayou with long, slow strokes.

When something hard grated against the bow of the pirogue, Dylan switched the light on just long enough to see a cypress knee directly in front of him and a willow five yards to his right. Pushing into the soft bottom with the paddle, he reached the willow and entered the channel.

The sound of murmuring and whispering drifted down to him from high in the canopy of tupelo gum and cypress like the mournful call of disembodied souls exiled in the fastness of the swamp.

Reaching the lake, he used the light for the last time to plot his course over to the houseboat. In less than a minute the pirogue thudded softly against a tire bumper.

After climbing aboard, Dylan found the water in the tank tepid. Taking a pan from the kitchen cabinet, he set it on the deck of the houseboat where it filled with rainwater as he checked things out inside. Then, climbing onto the top bunk, he sat with his glass of water in the tiny sleeping area, the shotgun across his lap, and waited for the morning.

17

DEEP BLUE SHADOWS

The sawmill-hardened hands of Dylan's grandfather lifted him high above the congregation in the midsummer heat of the old tabernacle. Through the wooden shutters, propped open to keep the place as cool as outdoors, the grounds shimmered in the white glare of the sun.

The preacher, his dark hair shot with silver, lowered the child in his arms and poured warm oil from the horn over his head. Rising from the back of the rostrum, a mural showed Jesus weeping on the Mount of Olives as he gazed down on the city. With tiny hands, Dylan reached toward Him as He prayed on that mountain overlooking Jerusalem in the deep blue shadows of the night.

"Wake up!"

The voice sounded far away, vaguely familiar. Caught between waking and the dream, Dylan slowly opened his eyes to Emile's scowling face.

"I can tell you're really worried about this guy trying to kill you." Emile lifted the shotgun that lay on the bunk next to Dylan. "You think this thing's a teddy bear for you to sleep with?"

Dylan pushed himself up on his elbows, squinting in the early light.

"You're lucky to be alive. I made enough noise to wake up every gator in the swamp, coming aboard, and you didn't even budge."

Swinging his legs over the edge of the bunk, Dylan took a deep breath and combed his hair back from his eyes with the spread fingers of his left hand.

227

Emile poured steaming coffee from a thermos into a red plastic cup. "Here, drink this. It'll get your heart pumping again."

Dylan pulled his boots on, took the coffee, and followed Emile through the kitchen area onto the deck of the houseboat. Clouds, low and heavy, sealed the sky. The pale light that seeped through them made for a world in shades of gray. From the top of a dead cypress at the far end of the lake, the harsh cries of a single crow came ringing across the water.

"Let's go," Emile remarked, stepping into the bateau tied off next to the pirogue.

"I thought somebody 'borrowed' this." Dylan nodded toward the aluminum boat.

"Somebody must have told them who it belonged to," Emile answered, then pointed to a grease-stained paper bag. "Have some breakfast."

Settling himself onto the seat, Dylan opened the bag and took out two biscuits soaked in butter and stuffed with thick sections of smoked sausage.

Emile pulled the starter rope on the little Evinrude. It sputtered, coughed up a cloud of blue smoke, and settled down to a steady puttering.

Dylan ate ravenously, feeling strength and warmth returning to his body as they chugged across the smooth surface of the lake toward the channel.

Passing through the willow into the main bayou, Emile pointed upstream. "I've got a little chore for you. Wanted to make sure you had your breakfast first."

Dylan stared at the activity on the far shoreline. Several men, one in a business suit, the rest in uniform, busied themselves at the edge of the water next to a large cypress. Two marked sheriff's units, their bright blue lights flashing against the green-gray morning, were parked on the road Dylan had walked along the night before.

Glancing at Emile's stoic expression, Dylan could almost hear that cry in the storm returning with a terrible clarity.

After climbing out at the dock, they walked up to the road and headed north toward the cars. Reaching them, they followed the paths of the others through the rain-drenched weeds down to the bayou.

Gazing between the legs of the deputies standing on the bank, Dylan saw a hand, as pale and cold-appearing as marble, resting against the black mud. The arm and the rest of the body was blocked from his view.

"Take a look at him," Emile said hoarsely. "Brace yourself though. I got here in time to run a gator off, but the turtles got to him during the night."

The deputies stepped back and the hollow-eyed coroner, his trousers tucked inside rubber boots, straightened up and glanced at Dylan. "You must be living right," he mumbled through the cigarette dangling from his lips.

Dylan glanced at the reeds, beaten down by a struggle. The man lay on his back, submerged from the waist down. He wore fatigue pants and a black nylon jacket. His head, twisted at an awkward angle toward the bayou with the right side of the face and neck exposed, rested in the hollow of a cypress root. A giant cottonmouth had embedded his fangs deeply into the man's neck just below the angle of the jawbone where it curved upward toward the ear. The snake's spade-shaped head was almost severed and its thick slate-colored body had been stabbed completely through several times.

Dylan felt the food turning over in his stomach and looked away toward the towering trees across the bayou.

"I'd like you to identify him if you can, Dylan," Emile insisted, stepping next to Dylan.

Taking a deep breath, Dylan stared down at what was left of his would-be assassin. The man's mouth gaped wide in a silent scream. A leather headband held his long black hair in place as though neatness still mattered.

"I don't know him. Not like this anyway." Dylan turned away and headed back up toward the road.

The coroner sat in one of the cars, cleaning his hands with brown paper towels. Two men in white coats were taking a stretcher out of the back door of a hearse that sat idling behind the coroner's car. Emile stopped to talk to them as Dylan continued on toward the shed.

"What happened back there?" Dylan gazed out the Blazer's window at the dark water as they spun along the shell road toward Evangeline.

Emile pinched the bridge of his nose between thumb and forefinger, blinking his eyes several times before he spoke. "He must have been crawling through the reeds toward the shed after I left. That way he couldn't be seen from the road in that storm, even with a flashlight."

Dylan shuddered inwardly as he imagined the sudden deadly fangs sinking into the man's neck.

"The snake hit him, and he slipped off the bank," Emile went on. "When a six-foot cottonmouth nails you in the carotid artery, you don't get very far—especially if you're bogged down in that soft mud like he was."

"You know him, don't you?"

"Too well. I was hoping that you did. Name's Haskell Dupont, from down the bayou," Emile nodded. "Comes from a long line of trappers and fishermen, good people most of 'em, but he never did take to hard work."

"That name, Dupont, sounds familiar."

"He started with a few thefts, dabbled in drugs for a while . . . gradually working his way up." Emile continued without seeming to notice Dylan's comment. "One year in parish for burglary, then four in Angola for manslaughter. I think it was murder, but the DA plea-bargained."

"You think he's our man from the capitol?"

"You tell me." Emile took an evidence bag from under his seat and handed it to Dylan.

Through the clear plastic, Dylan saw a Colt Woodsman, a cheap hunting knife, and a thick roll of bills. "That silencer looks homemade."

"Yeah. I'll have somebody run the pistol up to Baton Rouge and get a ballistics test done when we get back to the office. Not much doubt it'll match the slug they dug out of the tree at the capitol though." Emile glanced at the bag. "The money's just short of five thousand dollars. Dupont's never had that much money at one time in his life."

"Anything else?"

"He's the best pistol shot in this part of the country. Always took a lot of pride in it."

"Guess that settles it, then."

"Not quite," Emile continued. "His truck is at his house, so somebody dropped him off last night. He might have been waiting when we got there."

"Looks like *somebody* knows a lot about me."

Emile gazed at the road, his jaw muscles working beneath his tan skin.

"Did you see Rachel Batiste last night?"

"I went by but her lights were out. She doesn't have a car so somebody must have picked her up. Ramah's not much out of our way."

Dylan felt a sick feeling in the pit of his stomach. "I don't think she'll be there."

"Why?"

"Can't explain it. I hope I'm wrong."

Ten minutes later they pulled into Rachel Batiste's front yard beneath a massive live oak. The tree dwarfed the clapboard shack that backed up to the bayou.

Banging on the front door, Emile waited a few seconds, then walked around to the back, following Dylan's lead.

A tricycle with both pedals missing, a plastic baseball bat, and a few other odds and ends were scattered in the yard between the house and the bayou. A rusted dishpan and two aluminum lawn chairs, their webbing in tatters, sat on the porch. The door stood slightly ajar.

"Rachel! Rachel, you home?" Emile pushed the door open with his foot. Easing his .357 from its holster, he stepped carefully into the kitchen.

Dylan, sensing now that they would find no one inside, followed after him.

A pot on the stove contained some oil, flour, and chopped onions and garlic that were just starting to brown when someone turned the fire off. A half-peeled pile of shrimp decorated the newspaper's sports section resting on the counter.

The bathroom articles were intact. A few pieces of discarded clothing remained in the open drawers and closets of the two bedrooms.

Dylan stood in the boys' room, staring at a small neat stack of comics on a nightstand. "When's the last time you saw her?"

"Right after you called me from your office." Emile glanced over at the window where the light floated like a thin gray mist. "I stopped by to tell her you thought Remy would be transferred back here pretty soon."

"How was she?"

"Happiest I'd seen her in a long time." Emile relaxed at the memory. "She made coffee and we talked about the cane harvest, the fishing, nothing special. She certainly didn't act like somebody planning to skip town."

Dylan glanced at Emile and knew that they had both just had the same thought.

"Elaine, call the jail up in Baton Rouge and see if Remy's still there." Emile spoke loudly into the handset of his radio. "Tell them you're calling for his mother if they give you any trouble. I'm on my way in from Ramah now."

Dylan listened to the shells thunking off the bottom of the Blazer. "I think it's too late."

"Don't say that! There's always a chance."

"I figure last night that whoever dropped Dupont off gave him a half hour or so after you left to finish the job on me." Dylan thought again of the man with no face lying in the mud and weeds and water of the bayou.

"And . . ."

"When he didn't come back, they knew something had gone wrong so they decided to go with another plan. I think it started before you ever stopped by Rachel's."

"That could be," Emile agreed reluctantly, his jaw muscles working. "I had to stop at the office first. It was late before I got there."

"And I think it's already finished." Dylan glanced over at the

Blazer's speedometer, rocking on ninety.

Elaine Lebeau, wearing her deputy's uniform complete with trousers and black boots, sat at her desk outside Emile's office. In her early thirties, she had a scattering of freckles across her face and wore her deep red hair pulled back in a French braid.

"What'd you find out about Remy?"

"He's gone, Emile. According to their log book, a Maurepas deputy picked him up at seven-o-two P.M. to transport him back to his parish of residence. The DA's office had sent the authorization over earlier."

"No deputy of ours picked him up. Who was it?"

"They didn't want to tell me that at first." Elaine jammed a slip of paper onto the slim spike of her message holder. "The deputy on duty thought the uniform was enough and didn't bother to ask for I.D. Whoever it was signed the log book *Barney Fife*."

A black anger formed on Emile's face as he walked over to a table in the corner and poured coffee into two thick white mugs. "Call that place in New Orleans where Russel is and check on him, will you, Elaine?"

Elaine pulled her Rolodex over in front of her and began looking up the number.

It's too late now, Emile. It's too late! Dylan remembered his last sight of Remy in the isolation cell in Baton Rouge, his brown eyes filled with too much sorrow for a boy of fifteen. Russel was a blurred image from another time. "I'll call Fred Nelson. He's a counselor down there."

"Why don't you go to the top?"

"Because I don't trust anybody in administration to give me a straight answer."

"They're playing us for fools!" Emile slammed both mugs back down on the table, coffee sloshing out. "Treating these children like they're no more than a litter of kittens. God help me to find just one of these stinkin', no good—"

"Take it easy! It just happened too fast."

"I have them on the line." Elaine held her hand over the receiver.

Dylan took the phone from her. "Let me speak to Fred Nelson, please."

"You sure you can trust this guy?"

Dylan nodded. "Fred's not the type to be intimidated. That's why he's worked there ten years without a promotion."

"Figures." Emile wiped up the spilled coffee with a paper towel, tossing it into a green trash can next to the table.

"Fred, Dylan. Okay, and you? Give me the status on Russel Batiste, will you?" Dylan glanced at Emile. "He's checking with the duty personnel."

Emile began pacing slowly back and forth, his hands clasped behind his back.

"Yeah, Fred." Dylan listened for three minutes, punctuating Fred's discourse with a few terse questions. "Thanks a lot, Fred. I owe you one."

Emile sat on the edge of the table, holding the coffee service, his expectant face trained on Dylan.

"Fred called the security guard on the gate last night and the cottage parent for Russel's dorm. Got the same story from both of them." Dylan sat down in a heavy oak chair next to Elaine's desk. "Two men in deputy's uniforms brought Rachel there in a sedan with MPSO decals on it. Arrived at the main gate at seven-thirty-seven, picked up Russel and left at seven-fifty-three."

"They had it planned this way whether Dupont got you or not, Dylan. Whoever dropped him off never intended to pick him up again." The pewter-colored light from the window behind Emile threw his face into shadow. "This was supposed to look like Dupont was settling an old score with you."

Dylan still couldn't place Dupont's face in the hundreds he had seen in the past few years.

"Get Dupont's file, Elaine."

Elaine got up and went into a small room to the right of Emile's office, returning with a battered manila folder.

Dylan took it from her and opened it, staring at the black-and-white photograph on the first page. He remembered the man then, his face burning with a cold anger in a courtroom several years back. He had no mustache then and wore a crew cut. His black pupil-less eyes stared out from a fleshy face.

"Remember him now?"

Dylan glanced over at Emile. "He threatened me a couple of times in court during his older brother's trial. The last time was when I recommended the maximum prison time in my pre-sentence to the judge."

"Elaine, call Lonnie and A. J. Tell them to drop whatever they're doing and meet me here in an hour. We're going to hit this thing hard for the first forty-eight hours. I'm going to take Dylan home first."

"Just drop me off at the ferry, Emile. I'm not in a hurry to get anywhere today." Dylan got up to leave with Emile just as the telephone rang.

"It's for you, Dylan." Elaine held out the receiver to him.

"Yeah." Dylan listened for a few seconds. "I'll be there in about an hour."

"Who was that?" Emile turned, noticing the look of resignation on Dylan's face.

"Ike. They've got him in the downtown jail." Dylan stared at the telephone in his hand as if it were responsible for the bad news. "Chauvin's got more sense than any of us."

Later, driving north on Highway 1 through the cane harvest, Dylan's silence matched Emile's. They both knew it was over now. But how many children were lost?

"YOUR—leave off the 'Y' and it sums up politics down here. They *own* the state." Dylan stared at the stalks of cane littering the side of the road.

"Maybe it's like that everywhere," Emile muttered disconsolately.

"What would anyone want these kids for?"

Emile stared blankly through the windshield. "Children are kidnapped every day. You'd have to get inside the twisted minds of the people who do it if you want to find out the reasons."

Dylan thought of an old picture that hung in his grandmother's room when he was a boy. Two small children crossed a narrow bridge over a deep crevasse at night. Above them an angel, serene and radiant, his arms outstretched, kept watch. He saw Remy again in his cell, shoulders bowed by the weight of his youth as surely as Chauvin's were by old age. What did he find out about Russel that made him a victim?

———————

Elijah stood at his post when Dylan left the ferry and began the walk up the gravel drive that led over the levee into the city. It was the only name Dylan had ever heard for the old black man. The "prophet" looked like Odell Jackson's father, but was much taller and wore a long white robe instead of khakis. An imposing figure, carrying a Bible in one hand and a wooden staff in the other, he had preached at the ferry landing for years.

The preacher was ignored for the most part by those who passed him by in their cars. A few pointed and smiled; some called him names. But his voice rose above the tires-on-gravel accompaniment of his transient congregation.

Dylan stopped and looked back at the old man, thinking him an unlikely prophet—as unlikely as the Elijah of the Old Testament hiding in a cave from Jezebel after he had called down fire from heaven and slain the prophets of Baal.

As unlikely, Dylan thought, as the Son of God being born in a stable and angels announcing His birth to shepherds rather than the rulers of Israel. *Who would the angels appear to if He were born now rather than two thousand years ago?*

In the predawn darkness the only sounds are the clanking of trash cans, the grunts of two men and the recurrent growl of the engine. The houses are all dark. Both men pause at the back of the dump truck in the act of emptying their cans.

In a few moments the driver calls out to them, but there is no response. With a mumbled curse about their laziness, he climbs out of the cab and walks to the back of the truck to be overwhelmed by fear and wonder. A tall man bathed in pure light stands before him. In a voice that sounds like rushing water, he tells the three men not to be afraid.

Suddenly the air begins trembling as the night sky bursts apart with radiance and the sound of thousands of voices, ". . . and on earth peace, good will toward men."

Moments later, the cans lie in the street, garbage spilling out of them. Three men, their faces still shining from closeness to the light, sit together in the cab of the truck, racing toward a shotgun shack on the back side of town.

Dylan looked toward the north, away from the preacher. Light was breaking on the limestone walls of the Capitol, its shadow reaching out across the river toward the cabin where Chauvin was having his morning coffee and Scripture. *We could use you now, Elijah.*

Reaching the top of the levee, Dylan glanced back down at the white-robed prophet, sitting now on an upside-down syrup bucket beneath a willow tree while he ate his morning biscuit. *Maybe the ravens brought it to him.*

18

BRIGHT RIVER

Detached and controlled, the Muslims were holding their morning formation, flooding the room with the clamor of their silence. Jerry paced catlike behind the counter, finishing the paperwork on them.

"You got a real talent for coming in here at the wrong time, Dylan." Jerry shuffled his papers up and down the counter. "Your timing's near 'bout perfect."

"Don't rush on my account." Dylan glanced over at the row of tall, silent men.

"I ain't," Jerry replied under his breath, "I just want to get 'em out of here."

When the room had cleared, Jerry motioned for Dylan to follow him down a narrow hall away from the main cellblock. "I know who you come to see, and the sheriff's already put the word out not to let nobody back to see him." Jerry gave Dylan a quick smile. "But he didn't say nothing about bringing him out here."

"I can't let you lay your job on the line for me. You've put in too many years."

"I ain't studyin' about that. They don't like the way I run the desk, let'm get somebody else." Jerry unlocked the heavy steel door. "You might tell him that Judge Madewood sent a check over for his bail money."

Dylan nodded his thanks and pulled the door open.

"You got ten minutes."

Dressed in an orange jumpsuit and white tennis shoes with

239

holes in the toes, Ike sat in a glare of neon tubes. He smoked a cigarette awkwardly. Empty and drawn, his face had the appearance of a convalescent's.

"You look like a cub bear playing with a stick."

Ike glanced down at the cigarette, stubbing it out in the metal ashtray. "Something to pass the time. Good to see you. I feel better already."

"Anything for a friend."

"Yes sir. I was kinda worried about my appearance, then you come along and I see I ain't got no problems at all." Ike managed a weak smile, leaning forward with his elbows on the table and running his fingers through his hair.

"What time did you check into this place?"

"About midnight, I guess. Things are kind of fuzzy."

"Anybody come to see you?"

"Couple of F.B.I. agents, somewhere around three o'clock," Ike mumbled toward the tabletop.

"Somebody sure had this deal set up right. How'd it go with the Feds?"

"Quick. Easy," Ike shrugged. "They knew I couldn't tell them anything. That was pretty obvious from the way they acted. Just doing it for the record."

"What'd the cops charge you with?"

"Malfeasance, so far."

"They'll drop it. This is all smoke and mirrors. Just a show for the public."

Ike's face showed his relief at Dylan's words.

Dylan sat down in the metal chair across from Ike. "Couldn't you see something like this coming? Especially with somebody like *Ralph*."

Ike stood up and began pacing the length of the ten-foot room. "What *I* could see was all that power and my picture on a forty-foot-high billboard."

Dylan shook his head in a sympathetic gesture.

"I thought I was using Ralph. All the time, he was setting me up to take a fall if something went wrong," Ike laughed bitterly. "I even convinced myself that the program would help a few poor kids to get a real start in life."

"What happened to them, Ike?" Dylan decided to ask the question he hoped his friend couldn't answer.

"I don't know." Ike shook his head slowly back and forth. "I took the referrals and dealt with foster parents and a few mothers. None of them even had a daddy in the home."

Dylan felt a rage building in him that he knew he could not find a target for.

"These were kids that nobody really cared about, most of 'em." Ike's eyes flashed as though in sudden realization. "Nobody to cause any trouble if something happened to them."

"Anything else?"

Ike stopped pacing and leaned on the table, staring into Dylan's eyes. "Yeah. I want you to nail Ralph. At least we can stop something like this from happening again."

Dylan rubbed his left temple with the tips of his fingers. "Ralph probably doesn't know much more than you do, Ike. He might have had a bigger part, but somebody else wrote the script and directed this thing. What chance would I have against that kind of power?"

"What chance did you have in that tennis match against Ralph?"

"I wouldn't even know where to start." An image of Remy shooting basketball in his backyard flashed through Dylan's mind. He could almost hear the boy's laughter.

The brief flow of energy drained from Ike's face. He had made his plea for justice and vindication. Something more pressing replaced it. "Dylan?"

"Yeah?"

"Would you do me a favor? Call Chauvin."

"I think you should talk to him yourself. He's got nothing but a heart full of love for you."

"I can't even make my own bail. How am I going to talk to anybody?"

Dylan had almost forgotten. "The money's already out front. Judge Madewood sent it over."

Ike's face reflected the sudden and incredulous knowledge behind it. "Why would he do *that?* I don't even *know* him all that well."

"I stopped trying to figure out the judge years ago," Dylan admitted. "Guess he felt it was for a just cause. He did tell me once that his family left him more money than he could spend in a lifetime."

Ike sat down in the scarred wooden chair. "I think I'll move back in with Chauvin."

"I think you're making more sense than I've heard from you in a long time."

Ike fixed his eyes on a memory. "He's been going downhill since they made him retire. I could never repay him for what he's done for me, but it's time I started trying."

Dylan stood up. "I'll see if Jerry can get things going on your bail."

Ike nodded.

Dylan turned and knocked on the reinforced square of glass set into the door.

"Dylan?"

"Yeah."

Ike stared up at him, palms down on the table. His dark eyes were cloudy and held a foreknowledge of loss that weighed heavily on him.

For an instant, Dylan saw Ike as an old man and it sent a ray of hope through him. He looked exactly like Chauvin.

The door opened behind Dylan.

Ike merely shook his head and stared back at the table as Dylan left the room.

Judge Madewood handed the morning newspaper to Dylan across his desk. Ike's law school graduation picture stared out from the front page. He looked dignified, reserved. Next to it, in the harsh glare of a flash, Jim Donaldson, hands cuffed behind his back, was being escorted into the courthouse by two city police officers.

"There's no way it could have gotten into the newspaper that fast unless—" Dylan knew at that moment none of the children would ever be seen again. "If they can even control—"

"What are you mumbling about?"

"How could all this happen so fast?"

"I only know what I read in the newspapers." Madewood sipped coffee from a delicate china cup that made a chinking sound when he replaced it in the saucer. "Who can refute their integrity? We get our ink in bottles—they get theirs in boxcars."

Dylan scanned the article.

"Be assured, however, that this was covertly sanctioned by the powers that be," Madewood continued. "The governor's called a press conference. We'll *surely* get the truth of the matter from the royal tongue."

According to the *Morning Advocate* reporter, three children in the custody of the Welfare Department and five in the custody of the Juvenile Department were unaccounted for. All had authorizations in their files releasing them to various relatives and facilities, but could not be physically located. Donaldson had been charged with possession of controlled, dangerous substances, as well as malfeasance. The reporter stated that his information came from an unimpeachable source close to the governor. The investigation was said to be ongoing.

Dylan laid the newspaper on the judge's desk and dropped into a polished mahogany chair.

Madewood leaned back, feet propped on his desk, tapping the toes of his shoes softly with his cane. "I fear I become more sardonic of my fellowman each time another blood sacrifice like this is performed, young St. John. As one of my esteemed ancestors used to say, 'Anybody with one eye and half-sense can see 'taint true.' "

"There's nothing we can do, is there?"

"Donaldson's ruined. The evidence against Ike is circumstantial. He's tough. He'll bounce back." Madewood seemed not to notice Dylan's question.

"How can somebody just take children like this and get away with it?"

Madewood, his face almost like that of a child's with an old man's eyes, turned toward Dylan. "It's a realm of moral darkness, of powers and principalities."

For once Dylan took no pleasure in the judge's oratory and wished he'd get to the point.

"Let's take Remy's situation," Madewood explained. "I sent an order to the DA's office transferring jurisdiction to the boy's home parish, and they cut an order for the jail to release him to the proper authorities from Maurepas Parish. This kind of information is readily available to anybody in the justice system. It was easy after that. The rest of the children were merely variations on the same theme.

"The people responsible for these kinds of affairs are vapors and shadows," Madewood's voice seemed to lose its power, "in all this darkness."

As Madewood spoke, he seemed to enter a shadowland of the mind, pointing out its various landmarks with his cane. He came back abruptly and glanced at his watch. "Turn on the television. Let's see if the governor has collected himself sufficiently to speak. He's habitually encumbered by a kind of matutinal frowsiness."

Dylan clicked the knob of the television. As the picture came on, the governor, clothed in a burgundy smoking jacket, sat in the study of his mansion, the artifacts of a lifetime in politics decorated it.

The governor's statement was, for Dylan, reminiscent of his visit to Donaldson's office, but the governor's speech was more polished, containing prettier words that said even less. Beyond the drone of his voice and his affected visage, there was a flash of color. As the camera closed in, Dylan stared over the burgundy shoulder at a credenza directly behind him. Among all the political memorabilia lay a single comic book.

After the brief statement, Dylan flicked the television off. "Does the governor have any grandchildren?"

"No. He has one daughter who lives in France. She never married." Madewood's eyebrows raised almost imperceptibly. "Why do you ask?"

"Dylan—"

Jerking his head around, Dylan stared at Emile, standing in the doorway.

Emile's face carried a terrible grief. "Could I see you out here for a minute?"

Dylan could feel the sorrow reflected in Emile's face as though it were his own. He wanted to run from the room before it could touch him. Forcing himself under control, he stood up. "Excuse me, Judge."

Dylan walked into the empty reception area, unable to take his eyes from Emile's face, from whatever it was that was about to become a part of his life.

"I wish you'd sit down, Dylan."

"I'm all right." Dylan folded his arms across his chest as though to soften the impact.

Emile sat down on the edge of Elaine's desk. "They found Susan last night. She's been hurt. The police couldn't run you down and finally got ahold of me."

Dylan felt the room going out of focus. The light grew fuzzy, then cloudy. A slight ringing began in his ears. "What do mean 'hurt'?" He knew the word *hurt* held more meaning than Emile was willing to give him all at once. The sound of his own words rang hollow and empty deep inside him.

"She's—she's been shot—but she's holding her own. She's in ICU now."

Carrying a pail and mop, a janitor entered a door across from the office. Dylan listened to the sound of the man's whistling echo down the stairwell.

Feeling the need to get everything out in the open now, Emile hurried on, "It was Dupont. The first thing the police did was ballistics."

Dylan shook his head to stop the ringing in his ears, but it didn't help. "It must be a mistake. Susan's in New Orleans with her folks."

"She was—it happened night before last, son." Seeing the shock in Dylan's eyes, Emile stood up and walked over to him. "Probably not long before he tried to get you at the capitol. He must have thought she *was* you."

"But it can't be . . . she, we were together and . . ."

"She's going to make it through this, son. You've got to hold on to that." Emile put his arm around Dylan's shoulder. "The police want a statement from you. No hurry. I told them you'd go by in a day or two."

Dylan saw Susan again plainly as he had seen her on that last

245

night, her face childlike in sleep. He could almost smell the scent of gardenias. "Where is she?"

"At the 'Lake'." Emile took a deep breath. "Her mother and daddy came up here yesterday."

Staring at the cloudy light streaming in the window, Dylan wished that things would come into clear focus. He shook his head again, but the ringing persisted.

"Why don't you come stay at the house a day or two—you know, after she's out of danger?" Emile offered. "We've got plenty of room."

"I've got to go now."

"Let me give you a lift."

Dylan shook his head slowly. He hadn't thought that far ahead. "I'd rather walk. It's not very far."

Emile took him by the arm. "I don't think you oughta be going off by yourself like this."

"I'm all right." Dylan stared at his old friend, his face slightly blurred. "And thanks. I'm glad I heard it from you."

Emile nodded, his face clouded with helplessness and loss as Dylan walked across the reception area, passing Elaine on her way in without noticing her.

———

After leaving the hospital, Dylan found himself walking along the crowded sidewalks of Third Street in the rush-hour din of traffic. He held to the doctor's words but they seemed, like quicksilver, to be slipping through his grasp. Still, he kept repeating them over and over in his mind. *Your wife's past the crisis now. She's going to be all right.*

Dylan noticed that several people gave him suspicious looks or whispered to one another as he passed them. The city seemed foreign and unfamiliar as though he had walked out into a strange country, a country slightly out of focus. He had almost grown accustomed to the faint ringing inside his head.

Drawn to the river, Dylan turned west, walked two blocks and up the gravel drive that crossed over to the ferry landing. At the top of the levee, he stopped and gazed across the river. Clouds were breaking away in the west, the pale gold light of autumn gleaming on the white ferry churning across the water toward him. Down below, Elijah sat beneath his willow tree.

His boots crunching in the gravel, Dylan walked down toward the landing, passing the line of cars waiting for the ferry. Stopping before he reached the willow, he watched the ferry thud into the landing and the deckhands tying it off, lowering the gangplank and directing the traffic off the boat.

Elijah rose from beneath his willow and walked the few yards over to the line of cars bumping down the gangplank onto the landing. Leaning on his staff, he spoke above the noise, " 'He was in the world, and the world was made by him, and the world knew him not.' "

Dylan walked over to the willow tree, sat down, and leaned back against the trunk.

The cars growled by as the old man continued to speak. " 'But as many as received him, to them gave he power to become the sons of God, even to them that believe on his name.' "

The last car cleared the ramp.

" 'I am the voice of one crying in the wilderness.' "

The people waiting in line to board put their cars in gear and began grinding down the levee and onto the ferry.

" 'For God so loved the world, that he gave his only begotten son, that whosoever believeth in him should not perish, but have everlasting life.' "

The preacher ignored the insults and name-calling that came from a few of the cars. " 'He was despised and rejected of men; a man of sorrows and acquainted with grief: and we hid our faces from him; he was despised, and we esteemed him not.' "

A man of sorrows. Dylan stared at the man in the white robe. The ringing in his head quieted, and the world came again into focus as he felt his own sorrow begin. Dylan felt a sudden warmth on the back of his hand. Staring down, he saw a single teardrop catching the light, glistening like pale amber.

" 'But he was wounded for our transgressions, he was bruised for our iniquities; the chastisement of our peace was upon him; and with his stripes we are healed.' "

The last of the cars climbed the ramp onto the ferry.

Dylan felt the tears running down his cheeks now as the terrible pain flowed out of him.

The preacher sat back down on his shiny syrup bucket beneath the willow, reached over and laid his hand on Dylan's shoulder, giving it a few pats before closing his eyes and resting his head back against the tree.

Somehow the old man's brief touch made Dylan feel better. Wiping his eyes with both hands, Dylan glanced at him. He was not a striking figure; he looked nothing like a prophet now, merely a slightly bent old black man in a tattered bedsheet. *But he looked so tall and powerful when he was out there preaching.*

Feeling the breeze off the river, Dylan heard faintly the waves lapping against the muddy bank. He had accepted the fact that his carelessness and the selfish, uncaring way he was living had almost caused Susan's death. The pain of it rested deep inside his chest, but he knew he had the strength to stand up now and walk around with it. And even more than that, he realized that he had to change his life or risk losing her forever.

Dylan remembered the touch of Susan's hand on their wedding day as he slipped the ring on her finger. He gazed again into her clear green eyes, felt the warmth of her kiss and the love that flowed through both of them—that same bright river that would never leave him.

EPILOGUE

An hour before, next to the brick patio in the backyard of the little cottage on Camelia street, bees were lifting off the new clover, green and April-tender. The sounds of children at play in the shelter of ancient oaks at City Park seemed to drift like summer memories on the jasmine-scented air.

Then the weather turned around. A wind blew out of the southwest, scattering the cotton-ball clouds before it like thistledown, then the sky turned slate gray and filled with rain that drummed on the glass-topped table where the stanzas on crumpled sheets of paper grew sodden and insubstantial as smoke—but the poem had begun.

"What a shame! It was such a lovely afternoon." Susan, in white shorts and a pale green blouse, peered out the bank of windows that looked out on the backyard. Three sparrows, their brown feathers darkened with rain, sat motionless in the lower limbs of a crepe myrtle.

Carefully printing the last word, Dylan lay the yellow pencil on top of the legal pad. " 'Nothing gold can stay.' "

Susan had come to understand something of the workings of her husband's mind. "Especially golden afternoons."

"I guess so."

"Robert Frost?" Susan's fondness for the game hadn't faded with the years. She turned to gaze at her husband, dressed in cut-off jeans and an LSU T-shirt.

"Yeah. At least I think so," Dylan muttered, glancing toward the windows where the light had changed from amber to the color of dark pearls.

"You *always* remember the poets."

"Not anymore." Dylan had rushed into the living room as soon as the first raindrops hit, the poem itself seeming to rush toward its own finish. Staring at Susan, he thought her face as soft and perfect as a child's, her skin slightly flushed from mornings spent reading on the patio as she slowly recovered from her wounds. "Parts of the poems seem to come back almost by themselves, the names of the poets—that's another story."

"Did you finish?"

Dylan nodded.

"May I see it?"

This time he smiled at Susan's formality. He handed her the legal pad holding the poem he had, after a week of gentle persuasion by his wife, agreed to write.

Susan fluffed up a pillow and settled down on the couch next to Dylan. "You haven't written a poem for me in so long . . ." She took a deep breath and began to read.

> Silence of the day-worn sky
> Settled down about the weathered,
> Curving benches of the Greek Theatre
> Abandoned in darkness. . . .

After a few more lines, Susan's clear green eyes brightened with the beginnings of tears. "I remember that night!" She leaned toward Dylan and placed her hand on his. "We had a big fight— I can't remember why now—and you came back to the dorm later and asked me to go for a walk around the campus. I can still see that big gold harvest moon."

"Tank Hammond."

"What?"

"That's what the fight was about."

"Oh, *him!*" Susan dismissed her long-ago flirtation with a flick of her slim fingers. "That big linebacker. I never even went out with him."

Dylan gave her an oblique glance.

"Well—maybe once. But I didn't have any fun." Susan squeezed Dylan's hand and returned to the poem, reading the last two lines out loud. " 'Flowing upward, to set the night ablaze with the meaning of their embrace.' How romantic! You've never written anything like *this* before."

Dylan shrugged, embarrassed that his feelings had been put on display, even for his wife, even after years of marriage.

"You really think we set the night ablaze back then?" Susan teased.

"Well . . ." Dylan mused out loud, "maybe we only warmed it up a degree or two."

Susan touched his cheek. "I think that's why I couldn't seem to get you out of my blood."

"What are you talking about?" Dylan leaned forward, having lost the path of their conversation.

"I think it was because I never knew when we were together if you were going to recite a sonnet or start a brawl," Susan smiled. "Maybe I just hung around for the uncertainty."

Dylan laughed softly. "I never could figure it out myself," he agreed, sliding over and putting his arm around her. "Let's hope those days are over."

"The brawls anyway," Susan added, laying her head on his shoulder. "We'll keep the sonnets."

Susan took Dylan's hand, snuggling closer to him. She felt a sense of comfort in their simply being together, sharing a rainy evening.

"You still want to move down to Evangeline?"

It was the second time that Susan had caught him off guard. "How did you know about that?"

"We wives have our sources."

"You've been talking to Emile."

"Maybe."

"I discounted that a while back. Remember how you hated living out in Feliciana?"

"I think I might like Evangeline. It's such a pretty little town. And we could get away from all the noise and traffic and pollution."

Dylan was content to let Susan talk.

"And everybody rushing around like crazy. Maybe down there people still take time for friends and church and family picnics—things like that."

With some reluctance, Dylan entered the conversation. "Emile offered me his little cabin out on the bayou next to the Basin, but it's so small—only one bedroom."

"That's all we'll need," Susan replied matter-of-factly. Her eyes lighted with a secret knowledge. "That is, for about seven more months."

Five seconds later the meaning of her words hit Dylan like a bucket of cold water. His eyes grew wide, followed by a grin that spread across his face, threatening to tear the corners of his mouth. "You mean—"

Susan nodded.

"But how did—where—why didn't you tell me?"

"I just did."

Dylan leaped off the couch, took Susan by the hands and pulled her up, embracing her tightly. Then he released her quickly and stepped back. "I'm sorry—I didn't mean. . . ?"

"Don't be so silly. I'm just going to have a baby," Susan assured him. "It happens all the time, you know."

"Not to *us*, it doesn't."

Susan smiled her agreement.

"But you're not well yet. Are you sure you can do it?"

Susan's face already held a glow of expectancy. "We're certainly going to find out, aren't we?"

Feeling the portent of his wife's words, Dylan envisioned himself in a hospital waiting room staring at a wall clock with hands that seemed to have petrified since his arrival.

Susan sat back down, patting the cushion next to her. "Let's not talk anymore."

Dylan sat down, staring with concern into Susan's face. "You feel okay, don't you?"

Nodding, Susan lifted her bare feet up on the couch and lay her head in Dylan's lap. "I'm just enjoying being a woman. One who's in love with her husband and simply ecstatic about having their first child—that's all."

Taking his wife's hand, Dylan closed his eyes and let the joy of the moment settle over him.

Susan sighed deeply, knowing these hours together were something to be treasured—they could never come again. As Susan felt herself drifting off to sleep, she smiled in the certainty of their timeless covenant.

Out in the gathering darkness, the rain murmured on the roof and whispered in the trees beyond the windows.